Love Lost

Book 1 of the Love Lost Series

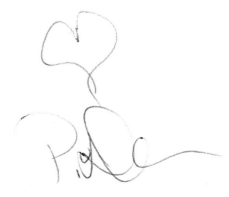

Books by Porsha Deun

The Love Lost Series
Love Lost
Love Lost Forever
Love Lost Revenge

The Addict Series
Addict – A Fatal Attraction Story
Addict 2.0 – Andre's Story
Addict 3.0—DeAngelo's Story
Addict—DeMario's Story

Flash Fiction Collection
Eyes of the BeholdHer

Standalones
Intoxic (Oct 2021)

Children's Book
Princesses Can Do Anything! (March 2021)

LOVE LOST

By

Porsha Deun

ISBN (paperback): 978-1-7364778-0-9

Cover art by Rebecca Brown @beckysketchbook (Twitter); @beckyssketchbook (Instagram)

To Jay,
Thanks for the typewriter.
Your big sis.

CHAPTER I

The alarm on my phone goes off. I sigh. Another lonely morning. More specifically, another morning without *him*. I shake my head. I really need to get over him.

"It has been nearly four years since you last saw him, Alise. Just stop," I say to myself.

I sit up on the edge of my queen-size bed, place my feet on the hardwood floor, and look around the room. The work I brought home but never took out sits on the gray leather chaise lounge against the red brick wall to the right of my bed. Sheer pale-yellow fabric hangs from the ceiling to the floor in each corner. I love that look and try to do it whenever I can. I only wish they were moving with a light breeze, but all the windows in my two-bedroom loft are in the living room. That's one of the two things I dislike about my apartment.

A large ivory dresser with an ornately decorated mirror is facing me. Checking out my reflection, I see some of my hair twists have escaped the satin bonnet in my sleep.

I hear the elevator moving—that's the second thing I don't like about my apartment. The bedrooms are to the front, sharing a wall with the floor's main hallway and again, are windowless. The side of the building facing the street is where the living areas are and therefore, the only part of the building to get natural light.

I stretch my arms up to the ceiling and slowly bring them down, caressing my oval-shaped face, neck, shoulders, full breast, and flat stomach. My short, black teddy is the softest sheer satin with ivory lace trim that barely billows out around my hips on the bed. I love the feel of my body and I like to be touched. Unfortunately, I haven't been touched in years. Last touched by *him*. He is the only one I want to feel my body again. I get aroused at just the thought of the man I used to submit to and touch myself more. I lay back but stop midway.

"No, Alise." I sit back up and sigh. I have less than an hour to get ready to go. I don't have time to pleasure myself right now.

I walk out of the bedroom, into the hallway, pass by the living room, and into the kitchen. I pop a green tea K-cup into my Keurig machine and walk by the black granite top island that is big enough to seat five, and across the living room towards the floor to ceiling windows facing the street. My hand caresses the soft leather of the tan half circle sofa as I walk behind it. I open the purple taffeta and soft pink sheer organza curtains, gathering them together in the hooks on the bricks between each window, then open the windows. The light breeze moving into my apartment makes the ends of the curtains dance to the rhythm of nature.

I look out into waking downtown Flint, Michigan. I can see the city buses turning out of the terminal two blocks to the west. City and county workers are making their way to and from either the coffee or crepe shops just north of my building. The employees of various businesses located downtown are just getting in. Despite the poor reputation for crime, tainted water, and blight in this city, I love my hometown. I wouldn't live anywhere else.

Returning to the kitchen, I drink my tea while fixing my breakfast of scrambled egg whites with chopped baby spinach, strawberries, turkey bacon, and whole wheat toast. In the last year, I've lost nearly 100 pounds. I love my new fit and curvaceous figure. I try to keep it by eating healthy and working out most days. However, I have some early appointments with clients today, so I'll be skipping the workout this morning.

My boutique and studio are just two blocks away from the Rowe Building in which I stay. The location was a Family Dollar in my teens and a drug store years before that. I purchased it nearly three years ago, to be the store front for Timeless Elegance, both the name of my store and my fashion line. I added a floor for the design studio. Four employees work the storefront, including the manager, my best friend Charlie Evans. There are three dress makers in the work studio, including my other best friend, Joc. Timeless Elegance is my pride and joy.

After five years of driving to and from the Detroit area for classes at The Art Institute for Fashion Design and Management, headaches, tears, and being denied seven times for a business loan until finally getting a yes, I have established a well-known and highly sought-after fashion brand. The storefront sells my designs exclusively. People come from all over the world to purchase one of my ready-to-wear designs or to get a custom design from me.

It's a beautiful spring day in early May with the sun shining brightly and a light breeze. I walk to work wearing a white wide-legged pants jumpsuit, turquoise peep toe pumps, and a platinum necklace with a single teardrop cut diamond with matching earrings. I carry a cropped black blazer in one hand and a white and turquoise triangle clutch by Fannie Lucille, another fashion brand that started in Flint, in the other. My wild, black natural hair is bouncing with the wind and my walk. The smell of coffee fills the air. I cross the street and walk by the courthouse. There's a gang of smokers just outside the doors getting those stress relief puffs before they have to go before the judge for their various reasons. I've always found smoking to be a disgusting habit.

I'm standing on the corner of Saginaw Street and Third Avenue, waiting for traffic to clear so I can cross the street when I hear three loud knocks coming from my design studio. I look up, and there is my forever glamorous with way too much energy at 9:00 A.M. friend, Joc. He waves at me like I am his most favorite person ever. I shyly wave back and shake my head, hoping the fellow pedestrians on the corner with me haven't noticed him. He tries to mouth something to me, but I've always sucked at reading lips, and he knows this.

I have no clue what he is saying to me. He seems to be happier than usual, which means he must have made headway with the guy he's been crushing on. I will soon hear all about it either way.

I walk into the boutique and am greeted by Charlie. "Good morning, Alise," her soprano voice chimes. She walks across the mahogany wood floor towards me as I look around the store.

"Morning, Charlie." She's changed the setup. The mannequins throughout the store and in the display windows are all dressed in white, ivory, and soft gold wedding dresses that match the blush pink walls with champagne colored trim perfectly. We hug, and Charlie gives me an unexpected peck on the lips.

"Charlie!" I don't know why, but I always feel embarrassed when she does that. "I like the new displays. Good job." She looks around, smiling brightly, proud of her work. The mannequin bridal party in the windows have been a change from the four prom dresses and one bridal gown that had been on display for the last couple of months. "I love the color of that blouse on you," I say.

Charlie is wearing a classic black pants suit with a bright fuchsia collared top and matching fuchsia flats. Her latte color skin and hazel eyes glow against the bright top. The freckles on her nose and cheeks even seem to glow.

"Thank you," she replies.

I step back and give her a good look over. Something is different, but in a good way. "Am I missing something? You are glowing. At first, I thought it was the top, but now I'm thinking that the glow is coming from within. Are you giving me another godchild?"

"No! I told you I'm not giving you or Devon another kid. I love Amber, but that was a compromise. But since you asked, Devon had the night off and it was pleasant," she states.

Choosing to overlook the part about the compromise with her husband about having kids, I congratulate her. "I'm happy to hear that! I don't need to know what's been going on with you two, but I'm glad things are going in the right direction again."

Charlie gives me a bright smile. I'm happy for her, for them both.

"Well, I'm going to head upstairs. My first appointment should be here shortly, and I need to brief the team before that. Who is working the floor with you today?"

"Right now, Rebecca is prepping the dressing rooms for the first of our final fittings. Kitty will be in at noon. It's a full day. Matter of fact, we don't have any openings this week." Kitty is Charlie's little sister and is studying management and marketing at the University of Michigan-Flint Campus. In opening my business, I made sure to employee those I'm closest to first. Nepotism is my thing since people in my circle are qualified to fill those positions.

"I like the sound of that," I say with a smile as I head to the stairs leading to the work studio.

It has been busy at Timeless Elegance for the last few months. We operate solely by appointment. With prom season getting ready to end, things will ease up a bit. Dealing with brides and prom moms at the same time is always rough. In a couple of weeks, we'll be able to focus solely on our brides, and I can start working on designs for next year.

The stairs continue the same color scheme as the store front—mahogany wood stairs and banister with blush pink walls. I open the mahogany wood door at the top of the stairs.

"Good morning Ms. Rogers," Joc and Kim greet me. Kim is one of my three seamstresses.

"Good morning, ladies and gentleman," I smile at them both. I look at Mi Ling, my third seamstress, who has more attitude than I like to deal with, but she is too damn good for me to let go. "That included you too, Mi Ling."

She looks up from her workstation. "Mm-hmm. Good morning, Ms. Rogers," she says quickly and goes right back to work. Sometimes I really want to ask her what the hell is wrong with her. I look at Joc and Kim, and they both shrug their shoulders.

The studio has mahogany floors with lavender walls and violet purple trim. Just like the storefront, it has floor to ceiling windows. It is a spacious room. Four workstations equipped with two sewing tables, one for a serger and another for a regular sewing machine, make up the work floor. I keep my sewing station on the floor for making samples and runway pieces or when we are so busy that a fourth seamstress is needed. Adjustable mannequins to cover a wide range of sizes are scattered throughout the studio.

The two front workstations are for Joc and me, his being the one closest to the stairs. The other two are for Kim and Mi Ling. My office is at the front of the stairs, facing them and the workstations with a glass panel wall so I can keep an eye on things. Although, I don't have to step in often as Mi Ling doesn't let too much fun happen around her. She pops that balloon regularly.

Joc sits his coffee down on his workstation, picks up his work tablet (he's the only person with one other than me and Charlie), takes my clutch and blazer from me as he does every morning and escorts me into my office. Joc doubles as my personal assistant - a position he appointed himself to. However, I must say Joc is excellent at it and I need one. He doesn't know it yet, but I'm thinking of looking for another seamstress so I can make him my assistant full-time.

"Okay, Alise. You have---"

"Hold on Joc," I interrupt. "I just remembered that I need to brief the three of you before my first appointment. It'll be quick. You'll still have time to run through my schedule today." I walk back into the work studio with Joc following closely behind me.

"Everyone, I want to say thank you and a job well done for all the hard work so far this prom season. It's been the busiest season in our history. Now that it's almost over, there will be a little of a reprieve. When I say little, I mean little. Charlie informed me this morning that we are fully booked this week, plus I have about five appointments for custom designs in the same time frame."

"You have eight appointments for custom designs this week," Joc corrects.

"Joc, whatever will I do without you?" I look at him appreciatively. "Correction, eight appointments and counting! This is looking to be one of our busiest wedding seasons as well. Again, I appreciate everyone for their hard work. Lunch is on me today. Joc will go around a little later to everyone to get their order from 501. That is all."

Everyone upstairs, including Mi Ling, says "thank you." Joc and I return to my office. I gather my sketch pad and sketch and color chiseled markers as Joc begins his rundown of today's schedule.

"As you know, you have a 9:30 appointment with a Gina Marshall for a custom gown for a ball this October. You also have a one o'clock for a custom wedding dress for an October wedding and another at three o'clock for a December wedding. You have two appointments for custom designs tomorrow, as well as an afternoon meeting with the Vehicle City Fashion Week Board for designers to be featured in this year's fashion show," Joc says.

"I don't know if I'm going to do that fashion show this year. I may try to do Nolcha this September if there is still room or the Bridal Fashion Week early next year. Can you get the--"

My office phone rings. "Alise."

"Ms. Rogers, Gina Marshall is here for her appointment. She's waiting for you in the consultation room," Rebecca says.

"Thank you, Rebecca. Offer her a drink, and I will be down shortly."

"Yes, ma'am." We both hang up.

"I will send the dates and fees for both shows for you to review."

"Yes, thank you, Joc," I say. "You are great at this."

"I am at your service Madam," Joc jokes and bows. "Oh, and I have plenty of gossip for you. We can discuss during lunch."

"Get out of here and get sewing, you," I chuckle back.

Joc sashays out of my office as only he can. I was so busy with getting ready for my first appointment that until now I didn't notice his brilliant wardrobe today. His trousers are a white, lime green, electric blue, and orange plaid with an orange belt, electric blue short-sleeve dress shirt, which looks even brighter against his cocoa skin, and lime green dress shoes. It isn't until he turns around to sit in his chair that I see the lime green with blue polka-dot bow tie. I'm not sure how I missed all of this earlier. Joc could light up a stage with both his personality and outfit. He flips his long, straight black hair over his shoulders. It looks like he has a fresh relaxer.

With his thin mustache and tall willowy frame, Joc looks a lot like Verdine White of Earth, Wind, and Fire. His manicured hands pick up some fabric, and he starts to make work of it. I shake my head and laugh to myself.

Joc and I have known each other since high school. Despite being bullied relentlessly, he has always embraced who he is. Back then, he went by his given name, Jonathan Campbell. Now, after his family disowned him, he goes by Joc Bell. He's one of the strongest people I know and one of my biggest cheerleaders. I love him dearly.

* * *

The day passes in a blur. Joc keeps me on schedule as I see my clients. The only break I could get was during lunch when Joc made me go with him to pick up the food. It was nice to take a moment to catch up on all things Joc related. I was right—he did finally land a date with his crush.

I let him have his moment, not stopping him. After a few quick bites, it was back to the rest of the workday. Charlie needed some help with final fittings and then we were finished for the day. I was ready for a drink.

Charlie, Joc, and I are at The Cork, a wine and appetizer place located downtown, just up the street from work and my apartment. We are listening to Joc repeat the story he told me earlier over lunch of how he has finally wooed his crush into going out on a date with him this coming weekend. Only Joc can turn what should be a ten-minute story into a thirty-minute tale with all the emotional drama of a soap opera. I laugh all over again like I didn't hear this story earlier.

Charlie raises her hand and waves when her husband, Devon, comes through the door. He joins us in the back booth and orders a round of drinks and a basket of calamari for everyone. He's sporting a soft blue dress shirt and black slacks. His diamond crusted cufflinks sparkle as he hugs everyone even though the lights are dim.

Devon went to high school with us, but he wasn't a part of our group until he and Charlie started dating. Though not nearly as relentlessly as Joc, Devon was also teased in high school. However, it was for being from a mixed family. The bullying mainly came from the "it" boys in school, as many of the girls had a crush on Devon. With his cashew colored skin and curly long brown hair that fell over his green eyes, he was on the top of the list of both the popular and unpopular girls alike.

Now his hair is a short curly coif, and Charlie is the envy of many of the nurses at Hurley Medical Center. Clean shaven, he looks like he hasn't aged a day since high school.

"So, how was today in the fashion world?" Devon asks.

Joc throws his hands up in the air. "Oh My Gosh! You would not believe how busy we are! We're fully booked with appointments. There are fashion shows coming up, fabric shopping that needs to be done, not to mention we have to get started on next year's designs. I really think we need to extend our operating hours by an hour each day and hire another seamstress."

Everyone at the table sits there and looks at Joc with one eyebrow up. "What?" he asks with a slight trace of innocence in his voice.

I shake my head at him. "The fashion business is just fine, booming even. Thank you for asking, Devon," I say while Charlie asks Joc what is wrong with him in a whisper. Joc raises his shoulders like he did nothing wrong.

"How was your day at work, husband?" Charlie asks.

"Well, wife," Devon chuckles, "I removed a gallbladder and repaired a spleen. All of my patients are recouping nicely."

"Look at my husband saving lives," Charlie says proudly. They really must have had a breakthrough, because she didn't give him a snide remark.

"People can save their own lives if they would take better care of themselves," Devon states.

"Very true," Charlie says.

"Wouldn't that hurt you?" I ask him. "Well, the medical industry, I mean."

"No, there are always other reasons to cut. Plus, there's that beautiful thing called medical research."

"How is your research for a cure for diabetes coming?" I ask.

"It would move along further if the Chief of Surgery would allow me to give some of my operations to another general surgeon so I could spend more time in the lab. He doesn't think that curing diabetes is something achievable, so he's not giving much support for it."

"But that's something that can help many people," Joc says.

Devon shrugs his shoulders. "It doesn't help hospital and insurance provider pockets." Changing the subject, Devon then looks at me and says, "Alise, you will never believe who I ran into today?"

"Who?" I asked, puzzled.

"Jaylen Williams."

Him. That was not the name I was expecting, though I had no idea who he was going to mention. I try to hide my gasp.

Everyone at the table gauges my reaction. Charlie and Joc having a very hushed conversation, which I'm sure is about me.

"Jaylen? Where did you see him at?" I ask, trying and failing to keep the excitement out of my voice.

"Apparently, he opened his gym a couple of years ago. I know he had been talking about doing that for a while, but his divorce from Calondra took a lot out of him financially."

"I remember that," I whisper. I don't know why I'm suddenly breathless. Then again, yes, I do. My heart is racing at just the mention of Jaylen, the man that I loved with everything but never loved me back. I haven't seen him in nearly four years, and I can honestly say I still love him.

"Some guys at work were talking about playing basketball and I went with them. The gym we played at was Jaylen's. We started catching up. He remarried three years ago and is already getting a divorce."

"Oh." The news of this stings. He never loved me, so for him, there wasn't anything to move on from. "I didn't realize the two of you were out of touch. You used to be close. What happened?"

"I asked Jaylen about that because I didn't know what happened either. He said after he had ended things with you, he thought it would be best to distance himself from me, to spare you."

"Spare me," I snap. Now my emotions are all over the place.

"Alise, calm down," Devon says with his hands up. "He knew he had hurt you. He was trying to keep from hurting you any further." I take a deep breath. "Jaylen asked about you. He wanted me to tell you 'hi.'"

"Tell her 'hi,'" Charlie and Joc say in unison, snapping their necks in Devon's direction.

"Don't shoot the messenger!" Devon turns his attention back to me. "He also wanted me to give you this."

Devon passes me a business card. It is Jaylen's. "He wrote his cell phone number on the back."

I caress the card. Jaylen wants me to call him. I sit there looking at the card for what seems to be an eternity. If anyone has said anything to me, I haven't noticed. I'm feeling so many emotions right now. I'm hopeful and angry. Excited and ridiculously sad. I can't focus on one, not to mention all the questions running through my head.

Why does he want me to call? Does he really think I would come running back to him after all this time? Does he suddenly want me again because he is going through a divorce, YET AGAIN? Does he finally realize the mistake he made in not giving us a try? I can't decide if I am going to call him or not.

I lay my head on my arm on top of the table, confused about what to do. *How dare he think he can run in and out of my life like this! After all this time, I still love him. He doesn't deserve my love.* I want to cry. I want to scream. I want to call him, but I don't want to call him. I've never been so confused in my life.

"Alise?" Joc's hand is on my shoulder.

Downing the rest of the drink Devon ordered earlier, I quickly get up from the table and head for the door without a word to anyone. I hear Joc ask if he should go after me. I'm assuming they told him no because there aren't any footsteps behind me when I hit the sidewalk. This is yet another reason I'm glad I live downtown. My home, my haven, is only a block and a half away.

I get inside my building and run to the elevator, pushing the call button manically once I get to it. *Hold it together, Alise—just long enough for you to get inside your apartment.*

The elevator finally opens for me to step inside. I push the button to the third floor and wrap my arms around myself. *Why is the elevator moving so slow?*

When I get to my door, I fumble with the keys. Once inside the apartment, I go straight to my room. This is probably the first time I've appreciated the three or four steps it takes to get from my front door to my bedroom. I flop down onto the bed and grab a pillow to bury my face in all in one motion. I don't know what else to do but cry.

This man, he broke my heart. He told me we could never see each other again without giving any reason. I loved him and gave myself to him in ways I had not done with any other. Jaylen introduced me to BDSM, taught me to submit. He dominated, protected, and cared for me. The more I submitted, the more I loved him. I was his "baby girl", and he was my "Daddy Dom."

At one point, I thought he loved me back, but it was just an illusion. I cry harder at this thought. I was heavier then—much heavier. Jaylen wasn't known to have a plus size woman and as far as I'm concerned, he never wanted to be seen with a fuller woman. But it was more than okay to bang a big girl behind closed doors. I was nothing but sex to him.

"Oh, the sex!"

In my state of emotional and now horny mess, I quickly remove my jumpsuit, lay back across the bed and begin to massage and pinch my nipples. My mind goes to one of many times my former lover put clamps on them. I pinch them harder and moan. I need to cum now. My left-hand travels south as I open my legs. The wetness between my thighs turns me on even more. Jaylen would be pleased with how wet I am.

I rub on my clitoris, slowly at first. Then memories of how Jaylen would beat into my pussy like he was trying to break me in two comes to mind. I rub faster. My back arches off the bed as I get closer to what I want, what I need. I pinch and pull my right nipple like Jaylen used to.

This pushes me over the edge. I cum hard. My body's quaking and tears are rolling down my face. Even with toys, I have not orgasmed like this since I was last with Jaylen.

When I was his, he forbad me from touching myself without his permission. I put my fingers in my mouth and suck off my salty goodness. I smirk and say, "bad girl."

CHAPTER II

The end of the work week is here and I'm in my office sitting in my oversized ivory leather chair behind the desk. One more hour until I get out of here. It has been a busy week, and I've been having trouble focusing ever since Devon gave me Jaylen's number on Monday. I still don't know if I'm going to call him or not. All of this has my emotions in nots like twist bread. I'm going through my wine faster than normal and am pleasuring myself a lot more, too. *How is it that my body still yearns for him?* There's a knock on my door, waking me out of my reverie.

"Come in."

"How are you?" Charlie asks when she peeps her head into the door. That's a loaded question, and she knows it. I just look at her and shake my head. Charlie comes in, closes the door behind her, and sits in one of the two ivory leather chairs on the other side of my desk. "I love the new way you've decorated your office." It was all black and white a couple of weeks ago. Now it is ivory with an array of pastel color curtains, trays, and cabinets.

I give Charlie a half smile. "Joc did most of the work." I look around my office. "He said my space needed to tie in with the store and studio."

"It has Joc's colorful flare," Charlie laughs. I sigh. "Still haven't decided what you are going to do?"

"Nope."

"I had a long talk with Devon that night," she states.

"Oh," I say with a raised eyebrow. I don't like for my lack of a love life to get in the way of my friend's relationship.

"I don't think he should have given you Jaylen's number, let alone tell you that he even saw him."

"Hmmm," I say as I sip on tea. "What did Devon say?"

Charlie looks at me for a few moments. "It doesn't matter."

"Charlie, what did Devon say?" I ask again.

"He said Jaylen has always cared for you still does."

"And leaving me was his way of showing me that?"

Charlie stares at me for a few moments before speaking again. "Well, you know what I think."

"You want me to keep my distance from him."

"He hurt you emotionally. Honestly, I think he hurt you physically, but you won't admit it. That lifestyle isn't healthy."

I put my hand up. "Charlie, stop it. The BDSM lifestyle isn't unhealthy. Everything we did was consensual, as it should be."

"So, you wanted him to beat you? To have this ridiculous sense of power over you?" Charlie ask with both a sense of concern and sarcasm in her voice. "Why would you want that over someone who really loves you?"

I rub my temples because even though it has been a good minute, this is the millionth time that I've discussed this with her. "He didn't beat me, Charlie. He spanked me." Charlie opens her mouth, but I put my hand up again to stop her. "And before you say anything else, YES, there is a difference. There was no abuse. He had his rules, as any Dominant or Daddy Dom does. When I broke them, and sometimes... most of the time I did so intentionally, I had to be punished," I explained.

"See, that is what I don't get? How can punishment and rules be healthy in any relationship other than that of a parent and child?"

"You don't have rules in your marriage?" It comes out more curtly than I intend.

"That's different. If I didn't put limits on Devon's wants, I'd be pregnant with my eighth child right now."

"Why did you marry Devon knowing he wants kids? Multiple kids?"

"Marriage was the next thing to do, and I wasn't going to start over with someone else. I gave him a child. He's content with that." She crosses her arms to emphasize her statement.

"That man loves you and you do him so wrong." I shake my head at my best friend. Sometimes I feel bad for Devon because he is a great guy. Is it bad that I think my best friend's husband, whom is also my friend, is too good for her and deserves someone better than her?

"Stop deflecting." Being the straight shooter she was, Charlie caught on to what I was doing.

"Charlie, we have had this conversation many times," I say, exasperated.

"I know," she sighs. She wipes away a nonexistent piece of lint from her shirt. "Agree to disagree?"

"As usual, where this is concerned," I smile.

27

"I wish you had gotten over him. I hate seeing you like this. You deserve someone who knows you well enough to treat you right." Charlie says with a voice is full of concern.

"I don't think that person exists unless it is you or Joc, and neither of you are an option."

"You have an option, you just don't realize it," she responds.

"What is that supposed to mean?" I ask.

"In time, you will see."

"I still love him, Charlie. He was it for me." I look at her with my eyes full of hope.

"But you weren't it for him."

This stings. I know Charlie doesn't mean for it to. She's just honest. I love her for it, but it doesn't make it hurt any less. I look away from her as tears fill my eyes.

"Alise, don't cry," Charlie says as she gets up and walks around the desk to hug me. She turns away to grab a tissue off the desk and dabs away my tears.

"You are the best of best friends, Charlie," I whisper.

She gives me her brightest smile and says, "That is because I love you and there is nothing you can do about it."

I smile back at her. We hug again, and she doesn't resist the urge to give me a chaste kiss on the lips as we pull away. I make a face to show my irritation with it and shoo her back. "For the one hundredth million time, stop kissing me like that."

"I kiss you because I love you, so I won't stop." I roll my eyes at her. She ignores me and keeps talking. "Luckily, I am great at blotting. Your makeup is still in place for the fundraiser dinner tonight."

"Joc reminded me of that event earlier. I don't want to go."

"You are not going back to your apartment to wallow. You are going to this fundraiser, and I am going to be your plus one. My outfit is already in the upstairs bedroom of your apartment," Charlie says sternly.

I start to protest, but there is no sense in fighting with Charlie over this. Plus, she is right. Getting out just may be good for me.

* * *

I support many causes in my city. This fundraiser is for the Fashion Against Violence Movement, a project put on by the board of Vehicle City Fashion Week, which promotes the education of the fashion business to high school students through sewing and pattern making lessons, trips to the New York and L.A. Fashion weeks, and interning at local fashion houses instead of falling through the cracks and getting into trouble.

This fundraiser dinner is being held on the patio at the Brick Street Bar and Grill in Grand Blanc, a small suburban city just outside of Flint.

As the name of the restaurant says, the patio is all brick in a mix of shades of red and brown. There are round dark wood tables with red and brown umbrellas all around. I'm having meaningless conversations with people I don't care about or for. Money this… crime that… what a bore.

But it's better than just being completely alone thinking of *him*. As I make my way around the room, putting my bids in for various items in the silent auction, I'm thankful I have a friend like Charlie. It is better to be with people instead of being alone in my apartment with nothing but thoughts of Jaylen to keep me company.

As I finish yet another conversation, I look for Charlie. It doesn't take long to find her since she's in a lime green shift dress. Given her dress and Joc's outfit a few days ago, one would think lime green was the color of the week. I'm in a soft pink cotton summer dress that has a ruffle around the neck with silver sandals.

I make my way to Charlie, who's talking with some of the other local designers that take part in the program.

"Our student worked out perfectly for us this year, which is not always the case. She has a natural talent for designing she didn't realize she had. She's graduating this year and is throwing a fashion show for her graduation party to display some designs she made for our teen line," the single male in the group says.

"That is one of the great things about this program. Students may express themselves and discover talents otherwise gone untapped," I say when I reach them.

"So far, it has been so busy that we haven't had the time to take on a student this school year," Charlie says to the group of two women and one man.

"After the start of the next school year, maybe?" asks one woman.

"Yes. That is a better time for us. Wedding season will be on a decline, and we will be in full swing of finishing the designs for next season," I answer.

"Have you started on next season's designs yet?" the same woman asks.

"No," I chuckle.

"Shame. I was hoping for a preview," says the man with a wink.

"Now, you know I'd never do that," I say as a matter of fact.

We all chuckle. The three designers excuse themselves to chat with someone else.

Charlie and I go to fix our plates of the various finger foods served buffet style. Once we get our food and drinks, we are off to find a table. Only my feet can't move. My eyes are stuck on the entryway to the patio from inside the restaurant. Dark brown eyes are staring back at me. I can't breathe. I can't do anything. Charlie nudges me to move, but I am frozen where I stand.

"Alise, what is wrong with you?" she asks, puzzled. I go to open my mouth but cannot find my voice or the words to speak. Charlie looks in the direction that my eyes are stuck in. "Oh, no," she says in a hushed, almost irritated tone.

After what feels like an eternity, I inhale.

In barely a whisper, I say, "It's Jaylen. Jaylen is here."

He gives me that shy smile I've missed so much. It takes my breath away. *How can such a small thing give me so much life?*

Jaylen walks over to where we stand. His dark chocolate skin and smooth bald head glow in the now sunset sky. He wears a black button-down shirt, collar undone, black dress pants, and black leather dress shoes. With his left hand in his pocket, Jaylen has the smoothest walk, as if he's on the runway. His tall, athletic build glides across the brick floor. He looks like the sweetest, darkest, and most refreshing glass of chocolate milk ever made.

"Hello, Charlie," his deep velvet voice says, never taking his eyes off me.

"Jaylen," she says shortly. "Alise and I were just going to sit down and…"

"Alise, will you please sit and talk with me?" Jaylen asks me, rudely interrupting Charlie.

"I know you heard me talking!"

I stand there, unable to do anything. All I can think about is how much I want to fall to my knees and submit to this man all over again.

"Alise?" Jaylen asks again.

"Jaylen and I need to talk," I say to Charlie when I find my words.

She shakes her head in disapproval and walks off.

"I won't be far," she stops and says, talking directly to Jaylen.

I give Charlie a small smile to let her know that it's okay, and she is off to socialize on behalf of Timeless Elegance.

Jaylen takes my plate and drink from me and leads me to a table near the far corner. He sits my food and drink down, and I sit in the next chair, taking my food and drink with me.

Jaylen nods his head. He knows I'm trying to establish that I am no longer under his control. I catch a whiff of his cologne as he walks around to sit opposite of me. He smells good. *Delicious.*

He sits there, looking at me, leaning forward with his hands clasped together on top of the table. I can't get a read for what he is thinking or his mood. I sit here, looking at him just as blankly, trying to give away nothing. Inside, my emotions are raging. *Keep it cool, Alise.*

Our dance begins.

CHAPTER III

We continue to sit there staring at each other, saying and giving away nothing. I'm doing my best to control my breathing while my heart tries to pump out of my chest. As I stare at him, I can't decide what I want to do more: slap him or kiss him. There's such a fine line between love and hate. Well, I don't hate him, but I'm still mad as hell... and hurt. I decide to keep my hands resting in my lap. I don't want to go to jail and I'm not kissing him after the hell he put me through.

He rubs on his bottom lip. I remember how he moaned when I would bite it. My breath catches. He smiles, showing just the edges of his white teeth. He's trying to lower my guard. Sadly, it's working. *Damn.*

"That dress is gorgeous against your coffee complexion."

"You completely walked out of my life nearly four years ago and now you want to have small talk?" I ask, tilting my head to one side. *The audacity of this guy!*

"You still have a smart mouth, I see," Jaylen chuckles.

I roll my eyes at him.

"But seriously, you look sensational."

This time, he is referring to my weight loss. I was much heavier the last time he saw me. *I bet you think I look sensational now.*

"Will you just take my compliment?" He stares at me, awaiting my answer.

"No."

He sighs. "Have it your way, my dear Alise."

"I'm not yours. I haven't been for a long time. You made it that way."

He looks at me deeply, like he's trying to tell me something. What, I don't know.

"What are you doing here?" I ask. I figure it's better to just cut to the chase.

"It's a fundraiser."

"And yet, I don't see you donating any funds."

"I knew it was a fashion related event. I came here hoping to find you," Jaylen explains.

"Find me?"

"Yes."

"Why?"

"I know I hurt you," Jaylen says sorrowfully.

"You almost sound sympathetic," I say sarcastically.

"I'm sorry that I hurt you. I know you think I didn't care for you."

"I suppose you're going to tell me you did?" He gives me a single nod. "You have a mighty funny way of showing it," I laugh. I regret it instantly, as he looks as if I hurt him. Then I regret regretting it after all the hurt he's caused me.

Again, we sit in silence.

"You didn't call," Jaylen states.

"So, Devon reported back to you he gave me your number," I say rhetorically. "That's why you are here? Because I didn't call you?"

Jaylen nods his head.

"Considering that it has taken you four years to want to see me again, don't you think you should have given me more time? I mean, it's only fair since you took so long?"

Yet again, we sit in silence. He knows I'm right.

"Have you missed me?" he asks.

I don't answer.

"I've missed you and what we had," he states.

Yeah, right.

"You moved on quickly after me."

"It didn't last, as I'm sure you already know."

"Devon told me. Your second failed marriage. Pity," I retort.

"I know you're trying to hurt me."

"I could never do as much damage as you did to me."

"I said I was sorry," Jaylen says.

"And that's supposed to be enough? Do you have any idea how much of myself I had given to you? How much I lo--," I stop myself before saying that four letter word, my voice cracking with emotions. It's getting very hard to hold it together.

Jaylen rubs his head in frustration. "Alise, what do you want me to do?" he asks with his hand reached out to me.

"What do I want you to do?" I look at him, puzzled. He looks at me, pleading with his eyes.

Oh my, maybe he cares.

"Jaylen, I... I don't know," I answer.

"Look, I know I fucked up. I should never have left you. I just wasn't ready for what you wanted."

35

"You mean you didn't want a fatty for a girlfriend, but it was more than okay for you to bang one," I retort. My emotions are getting the best of me. I feel tears forming in my eyes. I don't know how long I can hold them off.

"That's not true!" Now he's angry. "Alise, I…" He stops, looking everywhere but at me as if he can't find the words, then he drops his head.

"Jaylen, you what?" He doesn't respond. "Jaylen? What were you going to say?" I demand.

"There is so much you don't know. So much you don't understand," Jaylen says with his head still down.

I pause. "That isn't what you were going to say," I respond.

Now he pauses. When he looks back up, he looks me directly in my eyes, all earlier frustration gone.

"Have lunch with me on Monday?" he asks, almost not sure of himself.

"What?" His mood swings are something I have not missed. I often used to wonder if he was bipolar.

He straightens up and sits back in his seat. "I'm taking you to lunch on Monday. I'll meet you at your store at 11:30."

"I didn't agree to have lunch with you, Jaylen." I'm becoming irritated again.

"I have something to prove to you. I will not let you mess that up because you won't forgive me," Jaylen states. He stands from his chair and comes around to my seat. "And eventually," he adds as he picks up my hand to bring it to his lips, "you will forgive me, Alise." He plants the softest kiss on my hand. My entire body responds, especially my sweet spot.

Before I can even respond—and I wouldn't know what to say if I tried—he turns and leaves. I'm left sitting at the table breathless.

Charlie rushes over and sits in the chair next to me. She looks me over, trying to get a read on my emotional state. I can do nothing but stare at the seat Jaylen has left empty.

"Alise, are you okay?" she finally asks.

"I'm having lunch on Monday."

"With him! Alise!" Charlie says exasperatedly.

I give her a look that lets her know not to push it. Charlie is my best friend, but I don't need her lecturing me right now. My mind is clouded enough. "I need a drink or two," I declare as I stand and head to the bar inside the restaurant.

* * *

It's nearly midnight. Charlie and I are heading back to my place on US-23 in my silver GL550 Mercedes. I've had four too many drinks, so Charlie is driving.

"Stop at a Taco Bell," I say. "I'm going to need something greasy to combat the alcohol."

"Okay."

I know Charlie has a lot to say about me letting Jaylen back into my life. *I'm not exactly letting him, but…* I'm very thankful she is choosing not to say anything. In fact, she hasn't said a word about it since I opted to end my night at the bar. I don't say anything either. I lean against the door and look out the window at the night sky, thinking about Jaylen's last words to me.

There is something I have to prove to you. What on earth does he think he has to prove? That he's sorry for hurting me? I shake my head to clear my thoughts, close my eyes and let the sounds of Amerie coming through the car stereo wash over me.

* * *

"Do you want me to stay?"

"No, Charlie, but thanks for asking," I answer. "You have a family to get home to."

"Are you sure? Devon is working, but Kitty will watch Amber if you need me to stay."

"Charlie, go home. I will be all right."

"Okay. I'll get my things from upstairs."

I sit down at the kitchen bar and start eating my Taco Bell hangover prevention food: Nacho Bell Grande with chicken, no beans, extra cheese and sour cream, one chicken soft shell Taco Supreme, and a Fiesta Potato. I haven't had this in a long time. It's good.

"I'm going to ask one more time," Charlie says as she is coming down the dark wood curved stairs from the loft with a small travel bag.

"Don't bother. Go home and kiss my god-daughter for me," I say when I look up, just finishing my food.

"You were hungry," Charlie says when she realizes I ate it all in the short time she was upstairs.

I shake my head. "Not that hungry, but it was okay. I haven't had that in a long time. Plus, with the alcohol, I needed it. It will be back to healthy eating tomorrow," I say as I stand and pat my stomach.

I walk Charlie to the door, and we hug. My friend is worried about me and her hug says it all. "I will be okay, Charlie."

"You'll be more than okay with someone who loves you."

"Charlie, stop it already. Call me once you've made it home." I'm ready for this night to end.

We embrace a little tighter before letting go of each other. She goes to kiss me, but I successfully dodge her this time. She shakes her head. "I love you."

"I love you too, Charlie. Go home."

She takes her leave, and I head back to the kitchen, dispose of my fast food containers, and grab a bottle of water out of the wide double door stainless steel fridge. I walk to the windows and stare out into the city. People are making their way to the various nearby bars and restaurants for what they hope to be a fun night out.

I think about my encounter with Jaylen tonight. *What could he possibly have to prove to me I could hinder him from doing? Can I forgive him for telling me he was done with me?* I lean against the brick next to the window when suddenly my phone rings, jarring me from my thoughts.

It's been less than ten minutes. No way has Charlie made it to her home in Grand Blanc that quick.

I head back to the island where the phone sits on the countertop. It's not a number I have saved on my phone, so I send it to voicemail. It's after one in the morning. Anyone who knows me knows not to call this late. I walk back to the wall of windows, tossing the phone onto the tan leather ottoman on the way. Before I get back to the windows, my phone rings again. *What the fuck!*

I pick the phone up to see it's the same number from before. *This person must want to get cursed out.*

"What?" I answer with my voice full of irritation.

"What were you thinking about?" a familiar husky voice asks.

I pause. *I'm not that damn tipsy. How in the hell did he get my number?*

"Alise, what were you thinking about when you were standing in the window?"

"You saw me in my window? Are you stalking me, Jaylen?"

He chuckles. "No, I'm not stalking you. Though I'm flattered, you think I would go to such extremes where you're concerned."

"Fuck you."

"That was supposed to be a compliment, Alise."

"How did you get my number, Jaylen?"

"Devon. I told him I wouldn't use it until you gave me permission to do so, but you looked so exquisite and lost at the same time just now that I wanted to know if I was on your mind."

"Has anyone told you that you're an arrogant bastard lately?" I snark.

"No, but I guess you would like to."

I walk back over to the window and spot Jaylen instantly. Still in the all black he had on earlier, he stands on the sidewalk across from my building, looking right at me. *Why does he have to look so damn good?*

"Jaylen," my tone is much softer than before, "what do you want from me?"

"I want many things from you, Alise. But we will discuss the bulk of those at another time. Right now, I would like to know what you were thinking about when I called," he responds.

For a second, I think about lying, but there is no point. Jaylen knows me too well. He would know.

"Trying to figure out what it is you feel you need to prove to me," I whisper.

"I already told you what I need to prove to you."

"You already told me?" My mind starts quickly running through our conversation earlier.

"I care about you, Alise. I didn't mean to hurt you, but at the time, I didn't have a choice," Jaylen explains.

"What do you mean, you didn't have a choice?" I ask.

"We'll talk about that at lunch on Monday."

"What are you doing here?"

"I don't understand your question."

"What are you doing downtown?"

"I was having drinks with some business associates at Blackstones. I looked up while walking to my car and saw you gazing out of your window."

Speaking of fellas, I need to have a talk with Devon.

"Was that all you were thinking?" he asks.

"No. I was also wondering if I could forgive you," I murmur.

He gasps and gives me a hopeful smile. "And?" He sounds wishful.

"I don't know," I shrug.

"That you're thinking about it makes me happy. It means there's a chance. And I believe you will forgive me."

"Do you " I chuckle.

"Yes, I do," he says while giving me a bright smile that takes my breath away.

We hold the phone, looking at each other through my third-story window.

"I need to get going," Jaylen finally says.

"Okay."

"Alise?"

"Yeah, Jaylen."

"Don't be hard on Devon. He supports us."

"Us?"

"Goodnight, Alise." He flashes another megawatt smile and hangs up. As far as I can see down Saginaw Street, I watch him until he disappears.

I turn off the lights in the kitchen and sit in the center of the sofa in the living room. I should go to bed, but I suddenly have a jolt of energy that I know won't let me sleep. Energy that Jaylen just gave me. *I'm such a sucker for him.* I smile. *He said he cares.* My smile grows larger. *It will take some time, but maybe I can forgive Jaylen if he cares.*

Turning on the television, I pick back up where I left off on *Dexter* before running into my bedroom to change into a teddy. When I remove my blush pink lace panties, I finally notice just how wet I am. *Damn.* I put the crotch of my panties in my mouth while pinching and rolling my nipples. I love the taste of myself.

"Jay-len," I moan, dropping the panties out of my mouth. I climb up on my bed and lay on my stomach with two fingers inside my soaking pussy. Slowly, I ride my fingers. I close my eyes as I think about how sexy Jaylen looked earlier today and imagine undressing him.

"Did I give you permission to undress me, little baby?"

"No, Daddy," I moan and pout at the same time.

He walks away from me and sits in the chaise lounge on the other side of my room.

"On all fours, now," he demands.

I instantly drop to my hands and knees. I already have one strike against me for trying to undress Jaylen without him telling me to.

"Come here," he says in a low, seductive tone.

Slowly and seductively, I crawl to him, my Dominant. My Daddy Dom. My Sir and Master. He looks at me, his eyes hooded with seduction and pleasure. Pleasing him makes me feel powerful. But I know what's coming. This will be for both our pleasure and my punishment.

"Put your knees here," he pats an area of the lounge next to his leg.

I do as I'm told.

"Cross your arms and lay them on the arm of the lounge. Rest your head on top of your arms."

Again, I do as I'm told. My ass is in the air, and my breasts are hanging down over his lap. He pinches and pulls one of my nipples and then the other, while his other hand massages my firm, round ass.

"You were a bad girl just now," he says in a menacing tone.

Before I can respond, his hand leaves my ass and comes back down with a loud smack.

"Mmm mmm." That's all that I can manage.

He continues with my punishment, making sure not to spank me in the same spot twice. The spanking is turning both of us on. I feel my wetness growing, and his massive dick is trying to burst through his pants.

His breath is ragged when he finishes.

"Undo my pants," he demands through clenched teeth.

I quickly undo his belt, pants' button and zipper. He lifts his butt just enough for me to pull his pants and Calvin Klein boxer briefs down at the same time.

"Open wide."

He hustles his Mandingo of a dick right to the back of my throat, holding my head in place. He continues to hold my head so I can't move while he fucks my face from underneath. I love it when he's this rough. This controlling. This dominating. Suddenly, he puts two fingers of his other hand in my ass.

"Aaaahhhh!"

Jaylen shoves my head down and pushes his groin up, keeping me there while he roughly fucks my ass with his fingers. It hurts and feels good. I want to scream, but that's impossible with his dick in my throat. I gag for air. He stops with the assault on my throat and ass, stands while lifting me up, and places me back down with my chest in the corner of the chaise lounge and knees right on the edge. Jaylen grabs my wrists, and with one hand, holds them behind my back. He rams his well-endowed dick into my pussy, hard.

I scream.

He fucks me ferociously. I can't move. I have no way to brace myself. All I can do is moan and take it. "Fuck!" I yell. I'm building. This is why I like to break the rules. I knew exactly what I was doing when I went to undress him. Jaylen is such an animal when he's correcting my behavior.

A growl escapes from deep within his chest. He smacks my ass and grips my hip with his free hand.

"Daddy," I moan.

"Give it to me. Cum for me, my little baby. Cum for your Daddy."

And on cue, as always, I cum hard for him. My body quakes as he thrusts into me a few more times before demanding me to turn around.

I plant my tender ass into the seat of the lounge, and he puts the fingers of one hand into my hair and strokes his dick with the other.

I pull him into my mouth, and my hand replaces his on his dick. Sucking him hard and slow, I make him cum inside my mouth in no time. I swallow his sweet cream like it's the essence that gives me life. Jaylen pulls out of my mouth and cups my chin.

"Good girl," he says, and then he kisses my forehead.

I lay on my bed, panting and spent. That daydream and my very skilled fingers made me reach orgasm over three times. I stop counting after three.

I pull the duvet over me, and I drift off to sleep.

Porsha Deun

CHAPTER IV

Another busy morning at Timeless Elegance. I've had back-to-back custom order appointments and managed to get a couple of sketches done for our next season's line. I'm in my office at my drawing table with my back to the door when there is a soft knock, and it swings open.

"Ummm, you aren't going to wait for me to say, 'come in,'" I say without turning around to see who it is.

"No," a familiar deep, but smooth as velvet voice says.

I smile and turn around. *My gosh, he is breathtaking!* In black jeans, a navy blue button-up shirt with the collar undone, and black leather casual shoes, Jaylen is just... beautiful. Again, he gives me his megawatt smile.

"Careful, Jaylen. That smile might lead me to think there's no one in the world you want to see more than me."

"There isn't anyone I want to see more than you," he responds. "Are you ready?"

I grab my purse. "Now I am."

Jaylen, always the gentleman on the outside, offers me his arm. We head to the stairs outside of the work studio. I can feel Joc's eyes on me. I know I'll hear an earful later.

"I'm surprised Charlie let you upstairs, let alone beyond the front door," I say as we go down the stairs.

"She didn't exactly let me. I kept walking after she told me to wait by the door. She was busy with a customer, so there wasn't much she could do."

"Jaylen, Charlie's my best friend. She and Joc are all the family I have left."

"And I don't have a problem with Joc."

"I know you two will never be friends, but I need you to respect her. After all, she was there to help me pick up the pieces after you dropped me like a bad habit," I explain. "You were rude to her at the Brick on Saturday, too."

"Can she stop treating me like I'm a plague?"

"You both need to work on respecting each other, especially if you want me to forgive you and expect to be back in my life."

"Oh, I expect and want," Jaylen says with a sly smile.

"Then try, please," I beg when we reach the bottom of the stairs.

I turn towards the dressing room area to find Charlie with Jaylen still by my side. She is overlooking while Kitty places a veil on a bride. Charlie looks ever the professional in a black pants suit, a white ruffle collar blouse, and black ballet flats. Interestingly enough, I now feel like watching *Purple Rain*.

"Charlie, I'm heading out to lunch now. I'll be gone for only an hour."

"Okay. See you in one hour," Charlie responds.

"Charlie, I would like to apologize for how I treated you on Saturday. It was rude of me to act like you weren't there," Jaylen says.

Not wanting to break her professional demeanor with a customer just a few feet away, she nods to accept the apology and pivots her attention back to the client. Jaylen looks at me. "I will talk to her later, but thank you."

"Let's go," he whispers into my ear as he guides me to the door with my arm still in his.

Once we are outside, he opens the door to his black Land Rover that is illegally parked in front of the store. I get in. He walks around and climbs into the driver's seat.

"You look gorgeous," he says while he looks me over in my fitted baby blue capris with a baby blue cami, soft yellow lace tee, and ivory pumps as he starts the truck.

"Thank you."

"Where are we going for lunch?"

"You'll see. It's not far. You will love it." Jaylen's grinning like a schoolboy with a pillowcase full of candy on Halloween. His smile is infectious. I can't help but smile back.

"You think so?"

"I know so," Jaylen says with all the confidence in the world.

"You know the red paint on the curb means you can't park there."

"Don't worry about it," he says as he pulls out into traffic.

As he continues to drive, I look at his profile. *Oh, how I have missed admiring this man.* He has a strong jawline, faint dimples that only appear when he smiles wide, and full lips. I can get lost looking into his dark brown eyes if I let myself. I have done so many times before.

He turns to see me staring at him. He smiles and caresses my face, then goes back to watching the light. So much promise was in his touch. He drives on and when the delicious aroma of tacos fills my nose; I know where he's going.

"La Familia," I say with a smile upon realizing we're having lunch at our favorite taco house in the city. He turns and smiles back at me. This is where Jaylen and I first met.

Inside, Jaylen escorts me to a small table in the far corner. Mexican memorabilia hang on the white walls of the small sitting area. A short, long-haired, middle-aged waitress comes over to get our drink order.

"I'll have a Coke, and the lady will have a lemonade. And we'll have twelve tacos with cheese, medium shells, and hot sauce," Jaylen orders.

She quickly heads to the kitchen.

"You remember what to order," I say, surprised.

Jaylen nods his head. "I remember we met standing in line to pick up orders right over there," he says, pointing at the front counter.

"You were getting food for your kids." I remember that day too.

"Charlie was with you. She was pregnant and didn't like me even then. The two of you were going to meet Devon for dinner in Hurley's cafeteria."

"You remember all of that?"

Jaylen nods. The waitress returns with our drinks and lets us know that our food will be up shortly and leaves.

"Why didn't you have a choice?" I ask, cutting right to the chase.

Jaylen takes a sip of his drink. "You wanted… *needed…* more than I could give you," He answers, looking right into my eyes. "The best thing I could do was let you go, to protect you from Calondra and myself."

"Protect me?"

"Calondra threatened your life," Jaylen states.

"Why didn't you tell me?" I ask. This is news to me.

"Because you would have put yourself in danger by fighting for us. I couldn't have that on my conscience."

"But you married less than a year later."

"And you see how well that went," he says, raising his left hand to show his empty ring finger. The imprint of the band is still there. "That marriage was for all the wrong reasons. I cared for Angela, but I never loved her."

"I know how that feels," I retort. My painful feelings are surfacing again.

"Dammit, Alise," he says in frustration.

Before either of us can say anything else, the waitress returns with our food - six tacos on each plate. "Thank you," we both say. She leaves quickly again.

"Alise, I more than cared for you. I loved you. I still love you. That's why I'm here now." His eyes are full of sincerity.

"How am I supposed to believe that? You told me you didn't want me anymore." I'm probably pouring the hot sauce heavier on my tacos than what I need to in order to keep from showing my emotions.

"My feelings for you were so strong, so intense. I always knew I would end up hurting you. But what I feared the most was you hurting me."

"Me hurting you? Jaylen, I would never hurt you," I say.

"You still have the power to hurt me." This stops me midway into taking a bite of my first taco.

"What is different now?" I ask before sinking my teeth into the fried corn shell.

"While I was with Angela and wondering what I was doing in that marriage, I realized I was causing more harm than good by keeping my feelings for you hidden, not only to myself, but to you, and Angela, too."

I just look at him.

"You were expecting me to say that your weight was no longer an issue?" he asks.

"Well, it isn't." My insecurities are showing again.

"Your weight was never an issue for me. You will always be the most beautiful woman in the room, no matter what size you are."

I don't know what to say, so I focus on eating my tacos. As good as I know they are, I can't taste them. *Jaylen loved me then. He still loves me now.*

"Please don't hide your thoughts and feelings from me," Jaylen pleads. "I know better than anyone how unhealthy it is."

This is too much for me to handle at the moment. I'm happy with Jaylen's confession, but I'm angry and hurt, too. *All this time. All this time we could have been together, been happy together.*

"Alise, talk to me," he says, unable to read my face.

"How are your kids?" I ask. I need to think over all he's said. Changing the subject is my only way to get to that time now.

"They are fine. Stop changing the subject. Tell me what you are thinking and feeling."

I sigh. *Fuck it.*

"You broke my heart for no reason. You're damn right. I would have fought for us and fought your crazy ex if I had to. We both know Calondra's threat was all talk because she wouldn't risk losing custody of the kids. They are all she has to hold on to. You know I would have done nothing to hurt you intentionally. But because you feared me hurting you, you hurt me instead. What kind of love is that?" Tears are forming in my eyes.

"Alise, I'm s~~~"

"You're what, Jaylen? Sorry? We could have been happy all this time. We could have been by each other's side. I go home to an empty apartment every night, all because you were scared." My voice is getting higher as it becomes full of hurt and anger, and my breathing becomes ragged.

"Please don't cry," he says.

The moment Jaylen says that the tears I've been willing to stay in my eyes start rolling down my cheeks. I try to catch my breath to get control of my feelings, but all this does is make me cry even more.

Jaylen is at my side in a nanosecond, pulling me up from my chair, wrapping his arms around me, and holding me tight.

"I could never say I'm sorry enough. I know you're hurt and angry with me and you have every right to be. I want to make things right with you and have you back in my life how you should have been a long time ago. Tell me what I have to do. Tell me and I will do it."

I pull away and look at him. "What?" I ask.

"What can I do to make this up to you and have you back in my life?" he asks while wiping away my tears.

"Jaylen," I say while shaking my head and trying to pull away from him.

"Tell me, Alise. I will do anything to get you back." He isn't letting me go.

"I need time. This is too much for me to process so soon." He searches my eyes for what I don't know. "Please, Jaylen. I need some time," I say. He lets me go, though I could tell he didn't want to.

"I'll give you all the time you need. Whatever it takes."

He steps away and sits back down in his seat. I follow suit. Something dawns on me. "How did you know where my business was?"

"Who in Flint doesn't know where your business is?"

Though this is true, I smell bullshit. I cock my head to the side to let him know.

"Okay. I've been keeping tabs on you over the years. It hasn't been that hard, since everything you do ends up in the news."

I don't have an immediate response to this.

"If I'm going to be honest, Friday wasn't my first time seeing you since things ended between us years ago."

This piques my interest, as I'm sure I've not seen him, but I also don't go out much. He continues. "I kept my distance because of circumstances, but would always snap a picture or two of you to add to the book," Jaylen explains.

"So, you became a stalker in the last few years," I chuckle. If anyone else had said that to me, I would be creeped out or feel like I was in danger. But because it's Jaylen, the thought of it is funny.

He laughs too, and the mood instantly lightens. *Thank goodness.*

"Timeless Elegance seems to have been very successful for you," Jaylen says as we go back to eating our lunch.

"Yes. Each year, we seem to be busier and busier. Tell me about your gym."

"It's more like a sports recreational and fitness center. But yes, it has a workout area with equipment, rooms for yoga, kickboxing, and martial arts, a basketball gym, a swimming pool, track, and a 50-yard arena for football and soccer training," he says.

"I remember that was a dream of yours. Congrats."

"Thank you and same to you for your success."

I nod to accept his praises. "You didn't call it Dragon House, did you?" I ask. I remember him saying he wanted to name his gym that and I would always tell him to come up with something else.

"No," he chuckles. "Even though you all never met, the kids didn't like Dragon House either and said I should name it after the family. So, Williams Fitness and Recreational Center is what it became."

"The kids are smart. I'm glad you listened to them."

The waitress brings us fresh drinks.

"Is everything okay?" she asks.

"Everything is perfect," Jaylen answers, looking at me. "Please bring the bill."

The waitress walks off.

"This was splendid. Thank you," I say, finishing my last taco.

"You're welcome, beautiful. It's nice to see that you can still eat."

"I'm stuffed. And I had a not-so-healthy meal from Taco Bell the other night. I need to hit the gym."

"I'll set you up at my place. Don't worry about the cost."

"Jaylen, I--"

"What's mine is yours. You are welcome there any time," Jaylen interrupts.

I give him a small smile. I don't want to fight.

The waitress returns with the bill and Jaylen hands her a credit card. We sit there looking at each other, not saying a word until she returns. He signs the receipt and rises from his chair.

"Let's get you back to the fashion world," he says as he holds out his hand for me.

We ride back to Timeless Elegance in silence, holding each other's hands. Jaylen caresses my knuckles gently. When he pulls up in front of my store, he pulls my hand to his lips and softly kisses it.

"Thank you for lunch," I say.

"I have plans for us to have dinner on Saturday, but if you think it's too soon…"

"Dinner on Saturday sounds great," I reassure him.

"I'll pick you up from your place at 6 pm."

"Okay."

"Whatever it takes, Alise." Jaylen kisses my hand again and hops out of the car to come around and open my door. "See you Saturday," he says as he hugs me.

"See ya." As I walk into the store, a customer is leaving out carrying her wedding dress in a garment bag. "Best of wishes to you," I say as I hold the door open for her.

"Thank you," she says.

"How was lunch?" Charlie asks when she sees me walking through the store.

"Great and informative," I say with a smile.

"The only reason I'm not rolling my eyes at that is because you're smiling."

"Thank you, Charlie." I stop by the counter where she is before heading upstairs. "Which reminds me, I need you to show Jaylen some respect."

"Respect? HIM?" Charlie snorts.

"I don't know where this is going with Jaylen, but it would be a lot easier for me if the two of you could at least be cordial to each other. I've already talked to Jaylen, and he agreed to do the same for you. Your complicity, best friend, is needed, too."

Charlie sighs. "I will try for now, but I will not make any long-term promises."

"Thank you."

"Oh, you better prepare yourself for the drama of Joc. He's hurt and feels out of the loop because you didn't tell him about Jaylen."

"Oh boy," I sigh.

Kitty comes out from the back room.

"Hey Alise," she chimes, her voice has the same soprano tone as her big sister.

"Hi, Kitty. How are classes going?" I ask.

"Great. I have one instructor that is being a pain, but it's nothing I can't handle. I have some ideas on a marketing campaign for next season if you have time to hear them out."

"Kitty," Charlie says, almost embarrassed.

"Charlie, it's okay. I encourage it. Kitty, I would love to hear. Put your proposal on a PowerPoint and have Joc put you on the schedule once you have your presentation together."

"Thank you, Alise," Kitty says, full of excitement.

There is a buzz from the front door. "Looks like the next appointment is here," Charlie says.

"I'll see you ladies later," I say before heading upstairs.

I'm halfway up the stairs when the door at the top swings open.

"You have some explaining to do, girlfriend," Joc says, with his arms folded across his chest.

"Want to discuss over wine at my place after work?" I put my hand on his arm when I reach the top of the stairs.

Raising an eyebrow, Joc asks, "What kind of wine?"

I already know he's going to say yes. He can't resist a superb wine. "I'm sure that I have some *La Crema Sonoma* and *Bogle Zinfandel* chilling in the fridge."

"Dinner?"

"Salad, spinach & artichoke dip with pita chips, and lamb from 501."

"Fine. Wine and dinner then," Joc says.

"Thanks," I say as I rub his arm and head into my office. "By the way, Joc, Kitty will come to you to put her on my calendar for a marketing presentation. Find some room for her, but not until she comes to you first."

"Alright," he says. With a flip of his long, relaxed hair, he goes back to his workstation and starts working. "I'll put the order in for dinner so that we can pick it up on the way to your place."

"Thank you, Joc."

* * *

"Mmmmm. I love their artichoke dip," I say to Joc as we sit at the island in my kitchen having dinner.

"Yeah, it's good. Spill the beans, girl," Joc says as he pours the *La Creme*.

"Jaylen showed up at the fundraiser event Saturday."

"The last I knew, he wasn't in the fashion industry."

"He was there looking for me because I hadn't called him," I respond.

"Devon?"

"Yup."

"Does Charlie know Devon has practically been setting you up with Jaylen?" Joc asks with a raised eyebrow.

"No. At least I don't think so, but I do plan on having a talk with Devon."

"So how did it go from Jaylen stalking you at the fundraiser to him taking you out to lunch today?"

"Before he left the Brick, Jaylen told me he had something to prove to me and that he was taking me to lunch today," I explain.

"He told you he was taking you to lunch?" I nod my head. "Slick bastard," Joc retorts with a grin. I chuckle. "What's happening with the two of you?"

"He wants to prove his love to me and that he intends to be with me. I told him I need time. It's just a lot to process after years of thinking otherwise."

"You still love him, don't you?" Joc asks. Again, I nod my head. "You do what is right for you," he says sincerely.

"Thank you, Joc."

I finish my lamb and wine.

"So, what is the latest on your new beau?" I ask, while pouring myself another glass.

"Girl, that is so done. We went out a few times and whenever someone gave me a compliment, he would say, 'what do you think about me?' I couldn't figure out if he was so arrogant that he couldn't let anyone else around to get a compliment without getting one himself, or if he was that damn insecure."

I burst out laughing.

"It was sad," Joc explains. "Such a fine specimen and so messed up in the head."

I laugh even harder.

"Shut up heifer. Just because you have an active love life for the first time in years doesn't mean you can laugh at other's failing love life," Joc pouts sarcastically.

I stand and wrap my arms around Joc's neck and kiss his cheek.

"Oh, I'm sorry, Joc. Your love life is not failing. You just haven't found the guy for you yet. But he's out there somewhere." I put our plates in the sink.

"You know, it's a damn shame that you never use this kitchen," Joc says. Dark wood cabinets, black granite countertops, countertop gas range, and double oven. My kitchen is beautiful.

"I use it. I just put our plates in the sink, and they will later go into the dishwasher. Both the sink and dishwasher are in the kitchen," I say while putting my hands out like a model at a car show.

Joc shakes his head. "Where are you on *Dexter*?" he asks.

I grab the bottle of wine and head into the living room and Joc follows behind me. "Season three."

"Girl, I'm almost done with season four. You need to catch up."

I turn on the flat screen, open the Netflix app and hand Joc the remote control.

"Umm, according to this, you are a couple of episodes into season four."

"I started watching the other day and fell asleep. I didn't see most of it. Go back to episode six."

CHAPTER V

It's early Saturday evening. I'm in my bathroom putting on the finishing touches to my makeup—red lipstick and sultry dark eyeshadow. I couldn't settle on what to wear. Joc came over and picked something out for me to make sure I didn't mess up my first dinner date in years with the wrong outfit. Sometimes I think he forgets I'm in the fashion industry too.

"Girl, are you still in the bathroom?" he asks as he comes back into my bedroom.

"I'm finished," I say as I walk out in a knee-length black satin robe.

"Go back in. We have to do something with that hair."

"I was just going to wear it wild like I always do."

"Not with the dress I picked out for you, you aren't," he says as he pushes me back into the bathroom.

Fifteen minutes later, Joc has made over my hair. I have several large two strand twists that are softly pulled up into a bun at the top of my head.

"Joc, my hair is beautiful. Thank you."

"Every moment that Jaylen is with you, I want him to regret ever hurting you."

"He regrets hurting me, Joc," I explain.

"Whatever. Get dressed. Your outfit is hanging on the closet door and shoes are over there," Joc says, pointing to the strappy gold stilettos near the bed. "I will be in the kitchen."

"Hands off my wine selection, you!"

"Oh, honey, I didn't just volunteer to help you get ready solely to help you get ready," Joc says walking out of my room.

I shake my head and chuckle.

I walk towards the closet. *Joc really didn't have to go through the trouble of putting the dress in a garment bag.* I unzip the bag and immediately shake my head. *Of course, he would pick this dress.*

This dress is the first item I purchased once I got down to my goal size, though I've never worn it. It's black, stops just under my ass, and is sleeveless. The collar is a gold link chain and is backless except for the six gold chains that connect from the back of the collar to the top of the butt of the dress. It's the ultimate freak'um dress. That further explains why Joc has been playing nothing but Beyoncé anthems while I get ready.

I put on the dress and the shoes. Joc even laid out a pair of gold and diamond drop earrings. I look myself over in the mirror once I'm ready. *Joc deserves some credit. I look damn good.*

Walking into the kitchen, I find Joc pouring white wine into a second glass. I clear my throat to get his attention.

"Oh, I did good, child," Joc says proudly.

"Yes, you did," I chuckle.

Joc walks over and gives me a glass of wine. "He's going to be eating out of your hands and thighs."

"Joc!" I hit him on his arm. "I told you, we are going slow. I don't want to rush into anything."

"You know I know you better than that, right? You've been involved with this man for years. Jaylen is your kryptonite. All he has to do is look at you a certain way and you're gushing."

I shake my head at him and sip the wine he gave me. I know he's telling the truth, so there's no use in arguing. The buzzer in my apartment goes off. Jaylen's here. "Now, you sit over here," Joc instructs as he escorts me to the center of my u-shaped couch.

I gulp down the rest of my wine. I'm suddenly all nerves.

"Alise's assistant," Joc answers the buzzard.

"Alise's date, Jaylen," he responds, a little confused.

"We're expecting you. Take the elevator to the third floor after I buzz you in."

Joc buzzes Jaylen in and cracks the door to listen for the elevator.

"Good evening, Jaylen," Joc says to my date.

"Good evening. Joc, right?" Jaylen asks as he enters my apartment.

"Yes." Joc closes the door. "Right this way."

I giggle to myself. Joc is something else.

I'm sitting with my legs crossed, showing a lot of thighs, when Joc escorts Jaylen into my living room. I uncross them slowly and stand to hug Jaylen. *Damn, he smells good*, like cedarwood and cotton. He hands me a double dozen bouquet of mixed sterling silver and ivory roses, my favorites.

"The flowers are lovely, Jaylen. Thank you."

Jaylen steps back to look me over. "You are… wow," he says, astonished. I smile. *Wait until you see the back.*

"You look like your classic self." Again, Jaylen sports all black except the collar, buttons, and French cuffs of his black shirt are white.

"Are you ready?" Jaylen asks, putting his elbow out.

"Yes, I am," I coo.

"I will take these," Joc says, taking the roses from me and puts them in the vase he prepared while Jaylen and I were greeting each other.

"Thank you, Joc. Are you staying the night?" I ask him as he arranges the flowers on the bar.

"Yes. Inventory needs to be done on your wine cabinet," Joc responds with a wink.

"See you later." I can't help but laugh.

"Good night, Joc. Nice to see you again," Jaylen says.

"Jaylen, this is my one time saying this. You be good to her. If you are serious about a relationship this time, love and care for her. She's more than worth it. I don't want to see her a mess because you broke her heart again," Joc says sternly.

"I have no intentions of breaking her heart again and I regret I did. Don't worry, I'll do right by her," Jaylen responds.

"Well, in that case, it's nice to see you two together again."

"We're not~~," I start.

"It's nice for us to be together again," Jaylen says to Joc, interrupting me.

Joc closes the door behind us and Jaylen hits the call button for the elevator. It hasn't moved since he came in, so the door opens immediately. Once inside the elevator, Jaylen steps away from me. I look at him to find his eyes heated with lust.

"Turn around," he demands. His voice is low, calm, and hella sexy.

I slowly spin around, giving him a good view of the back of the dress. When I face him again, he's biting his bottom lip and his eyes are hooded. Just as he goes to lunge towards me, the elevator door opens and he stops himself. I was so distracted by putting on a show for him I didn't even hear it ping.

I loop my arm through Jaylen's elbow. We get outside and I see his truck's parked illegally on the corner again.

"One of these days you're going to get a ticket, you know?"

"It's a ticket. Not the end of the world," he says.

Jaylen opens the passenger door for me. His fingertips softly caress my back as I step into the truck. Just a few seconds later, he's in the driver's seat and starting the ignition.

"I thought you wanted to take things slow?" Jaylen asks.

"I do."

"Well, that dress says otherwise."

I blush. It's the only response I can give.

We ride towards the city's north side listening to music, not saying anything to each other. Stevie Wonder is playing, one of Jaylen's favorite artists.

"You can never go wrong with Stevie," I say.

"Stevie Wonder is the best," Jaylen agrees. "This is a mix of his greatest hits."

He skips to the next song. It's *I Wish*.

"I love this song," I say as I dance in my seat and snapping my fingers.

"You are too young to know about this," he teases.

"Hey, I'm 30. Just because I'm ten years younger than you doesn't mean I don't know good music when I hear it."

Jaylen chuckles and I continue dancing. While sitting at a red light, I catch Jaylen watching me out the corner of his eyes. I pretend I don't notice and continue dancing, only a little more seductively. The glass of wine I gulped down before leaving has me letting go of any previous inhibitions. *It's been almost four years. I might just go for it tonight.*

He pulls up to a brick ranch style home with a two-car attached garage in the Mott Neighborhood on the north side of the city. Jaylen had this house when we were together before.

"You still have this house?" I ask.

"Angela and I are having an amicable divorce, which is a significant change from the divorce with Calondra," he says with a sarcastic chuckle. "I kept this place after Angela and I got married, but we lived somewhere else. She's keeping that house. I don't have any use for it."

Jaylen and I met while he was divorcing his first wife, Calondra. Talk about a woman scorned. She tried to take everything from him. Even tried to bully him into giving up his rights to their three kids, which was beyond wrong because from what I could tell, he was a great father. She dropped that idea when she realized she wouldn't get child support if her then ex-husband-to-be had no rights.

I never met his children, though. Our relationship never went that far. Well, it didn't go that far for Jaylen, at least. Even though I was very much in love with him, he kept me at a distance. I fully invited him into my life while I was an outsider wishing for a way into his life, but was never an actual part of it. That thought alone puts a damper on my mood.

"Are you going to stay in the car all night?"

I look up to see Jaylen standing inside the passenger door, waiting for me to step out. "Oh, sorry."

"Where did you just go?"

"Nowhere," I say while shaking my head. I shift in my seat to step out of his truck, but Jaylen blocks my way.

"Don't do this. Don't clam up on me." Jaylen holds my chin between his thumb and pointer finger so he can look into my eyes. "What's on your mind?"

"I wasn't a part of your life before. It was just sex and scenes," I murmur.

"It was never just sex and scenes." I look down at my lap and pick off an imaginary piece of lint. "Alise, talk to me. This will never work if you don't talk to me."

"Where do you want this to go?" I ask him while looking straight into his eyes. I want no bullshit.

Jaylen looks at me, baffled. He collects himself and steps back from the door.

"Let's discuss this in the house. Dinner is waiting for us," he says.

"Where do you want this to go?" I ask louder, desperation in my voice.

"You want to discuss this right here, in the driveway?"

"I'm not getting out of the car until you give me an answer."

Jaylen nods his head. "Okay then," he says. He leans into the car, putting his face close to mine, all business. "I told you earlier that it was a mistake letting you go. I want you back. I want you in my life and me in yours. Our life—the one we should have had, that is what I want.

"No more walls. No more keeping things with you a secret and separate from the rest of my life. I wouldn't be going through a second divorce right now if you were my wife. I will remarry again and it'll be to you. I know I hurt you, and I will

69

do whatever it takes to make up for it. You are my forever love, Alise."

I search his eyes to find any trace of lying, faking, or deception. To my surprise. I find nothing but sincerity. Jaylen steps back from the car and extends his hand to me. I take it and we walk up the red stone walkway in silence. Jaylen opens the door and waits for me to walk in.

"Stop over analyzing things," Jaylen says to me as I walk through the door.

Habit of mine. I can't help but play Jaylen's words again and again in my head. *He wants a life with me and to have me as his wife.* I feel like I'm walking in a daze.

Those words. His words.

I've been waiting to hear Jaylen say them for so long. But at the same time, I can't help but want to run. *I should not have worn this dress. This is too much, too soon. We just came back into each other's lives.*

"If you would stay in the here and now, you wouldn't have that fight-or-flight look on your face."

I look up at Jaylen as we stand in the small foyer. He looks at me in the softest, most endearing way. Here I am, finally getting everything I've ever wanted from the love of my life, and I'm the most confused I've ever been. I look towards the door. *I really should go.*

"No," Jaylen says firmly.

"Jaylen, this is…"

"Everything that I should have given you four years ago," he says just before softly kissing my forehead. He takes my hand. "Come on."

Jaylen leads me into the living room. I sit on the love seat and he excuses himself to get drinks.

His place is just as I remember it. There is a half wall to the right of the foyer with the living room just on the other side of it. The walls are dark gray with a maroon colored accent wall where the fireplace is. I smile at the memories of him having me leaning against the mantel while pounding into me. The light gray leather sofa set is new, well, new to me. Pictures of the kids and their trophies are on the walls and mounted shelving. The dark wood flooring still looks good.

He returns from the kitchen with two glasses of red wine. I take a slow sip with my eyes closed. It's refreshing and helps to calm my nerves.

Like many of the abandoned homes in Flint, the homes behind and to the side of Jaylen have been torn down. Jaylen purchased both lots to add to his property back when we were first together.

"I'm going to put the finishing touches on dinner," Jaylen says as he caresses my face. Then he's off to the kitchen again. Jaylen is a superb cook.

"Do you want some help in there?" I ask jokingly.

"No. I want to live past this dinner, thank you," Jaylen chuckles.

He knows my version of cooking is fixing a bowl of cereal or a peanut butter and jelly sandwich. Of course, I would have a glass of wine with just about anything. *I wonder how much damage Joc will do to my wine collection tonight.*

The smell coming from the kitchen is intoxicating. I don't realize how hungry I am until my stomach growls. I follow the savory aroma and enter the open concept dining room and kitchen. My heels click louder on the ivory stone tiles than they do on the hardwood in the living room and hallway. I pass by the mahogany wood rectangular dining table large enough to sit eight in the cushioned cream leather chairs.

There is a sliding patio door in the back of the dining room that leads to a fully furnished wood double deck. We have had sex on every piece of furniture out there. The memory makes me smile.

On the floor next to the patio door are cases of bottled water stacked on top of each other. This is now a normal sight in the homes of Flint residents because of the water crisis. It has been over three years and the water still isn't safe to drink. Even after they finish putting down new service lines for the entire city, most still won't trust it after how the then city and state government officials tried to cover it up and deflect responsibility to each other.

I walk into the kitchen and sit in one of the three black bar stools on the other side of the island. There are black shiny cabinets, countertops, and an island with white walls. A countertop gas range sits in the middle of the island. The doors to both the garage and basement are off to the side of the kitchen.

Jaylen's plating our meal.

"Are those salmon steaks?" I ask.

"Cooked just the way you like," Jaylen says, nodding his head. Grilled salmon steaks with lots of fresh herbs and topped with parmesan cheese and Italian breadcrumbs, sautéed asparagus, ranch mashed potatoes, and black bread. All my favorites.

He carries the plates to the dining table while I follow him with our wine glasses in hand. We sit across from each other on the short side of the table. Jaylen grabs his phone and music comes over the speakers. *In A Sentimental Mood* by Duke Ellington plays… a perfect song for both our moods.

As we eat our meal, we can't help but exchange stares at each other—both of us smiling at one another for no particular reason.

"I want to ask you something, and I need you to give me an honest answer," Jaylen says, breaking the beautiful silence.

"You can ask me anything. I won't lie to you, you know that."

He wipes his mouth with a napkin. "Why haven't you been with anyone else?"

"What makes you think that?" Then it dawns on me. "Devon," I say, shaking my head. *I really need to have that talk with my friend.*

"Well?"

"Love hurts. I didn't want to open myself up to be hurt by anyone else again." Suddenly, Jaylen looks sad. "I threw myself into school and later my business. I didn't have time for a relationship," I further explain.

"But you made time for me," he states.

"Old habits."

"Is there a chance that you still love me, or is this just an old habit for you?"

I don't answer. It's a combination of both, but I can't tell Jaylen how I feel just yet. A small smile plays across his lips. "You still love me," he answers for himself.

Again, I don't respond.

"I know you want to take things… slow. I know you still love me. You'll say it soon enough."

"Anyone ever tell you that you're an arrogant asshole?" I chuckle.

"I believe you told me that just last week," Jaylen smiles.

"The food is exquisite," I say, before taking in another mouthful of salmon and mashed potatoes. I need to get the subject off my feelings for him.

He sits there and smiles at me. We look at each other like star-crossed lovers when suddenly the front door comes open.

"Really, Dad? The divorce with Angela isn't even final yet, and you already have a greedy-looking whore in the house?"

It's Jaylen's oldest son, Jaylen Jr. Everyone just calls him J.J. I recognize him from the pictures in the living room. He is just as tall and dark as his father, but with a slightly wider athletic frame and a short high-top fade. If I remember correctly, he must be going into his senior year of high school this fall.

"Did he just call me a whore?" I asked, shocked.

"Boy, despite what your mother says, you are not too old to get your ass kicked. You will not walk into my house being disrespectful to my guest or me," Jaylen says as he rises to his feet.

Did Jaylen just refer to me as a guest? Well, I guess I am a guest.

"I remember when this was *our* house. With all of us, including mom," J.J. states.

"If the next words out of your mouth are not an apology to both of us," Jaylen gestures his hand back and forth to the two of us, "you are going to be in a world of trouble."

J.J.'s eyes go from his father and me, then back again, and in the most disrespectful tone I've ever heard, he says, "Sorry. I'm out of here. I don't want to ruin your date, Dad." Then J.J. storms out of the door, slamming it behind him.

Jaylen stands there looking at the door, rubbing his bald head.

"Go after him, Jaylen." He looks at me to see if I mean it. "Go. I'll be all right."

"I'm so sorry about this, Alise," Jaylen apologizes before jogging to the door and yelling after his son.

I finish my wine and text Joc to come get me, then I remember Joc has been welcoming himself to my wine collection. He can't rescue me right now. I schedule a ride share as I feel awkward just sitting here. I absentmindedly eat more of my dinner. Apparently, J.J. hasn't gotten over his parents' divorce.

J.J. comes back into the house a while later. He stops in front of the dining table and looks at me.

"I apologize for calling you a whore. It was wrong of me."

"Apology accepted," I say sympathetically.

"Ms. Alise, is it?" he asks.

"Yes, and you are J.J."

"Yeah." He looks down at his feet before looking back up and bidding me goodnight. I smile at him and he heads down the hallway.

I didn't notice Jaylen standing in the foyer while I was talking to his son. Jaylen walks over to me and looks deeply into my eyes. "This is not how I planned for our dinner to go," Jaylen explains.

"I know." My phone dings to let me know my ordered car is here. "That's my ride," I say.

"You're leaving?" Jaylen asks puzzled.

"Yes, you need to be with your son."

"My son is not a baby."

"But he needs you to explain this to him. He obviously is still sore about one of the two divorces, if not both. Divorce isn't a simple thing for kids to get over. I know. My parents divorced when I was a teenager. He needs you. I can imagine what this must look like to him."

"I don't want it to end like this," Jaylen says.

"The night is ending. Not our reconnecting."

"You don't know how bad I want to order you to stay."

"We haven't made it to you being my Daddy Dom again."

He cups my chin. "Oh, but you will be my baby girl again. And so much more." He bends down and plants a soft kiss on my lips.

"Goodnight, Jaylen."

"Goodnight, Alise."

* * *

I walk into my apartment. Joc is passed out on the couch with an empty bottle of wine on the floor near him and another empty bottle on the island. I grab a cover out of the linen closet, lay it over him, and kiss his forehead before heading to my bedroom.

I change into a lavender satin cami and short set, go into the kitchen, and pour myself two shots of vodka back to back. "What am I getting myself into?" I ask myself.

I lay my head on the cold countertop. Reconnecting with the love of my life will not be smooth sailing like I thought it would be. J.J. was very upset. It's only a matter of time before he tells Calondra. But maybe she won't be upset about it after all this time. Jaylen remarried. Calondra didn't cause his marriage with Angela to end... I don't think.

I stay in this position for a while, trying to think through an alcohol induced fog. It isn't working. It's still too early for bed. I walk to the DVD player in the living room and put in my favorite love story, *Titanic*. I sit near Joc's feet and pull the throw cover on the ottoman over my lap.

Earlier, Jaylen told me to stop over analyzing everything. Well, I'm making a conscious decision to do just that and get lost in this movie.

Porsha Deun

CHAPTER VI

"What in the hell are you doing here?" I lift my head to see Joc standing by my bed. I look at the alarm clock. It's five minutes before 6 a.m.

"What in the hell are you doing up?" I groan in my pillow.

"I was trying to get up in time to see your walk of shame," he says, patting his head.

"I came home last night. There was no walk of shame."

"So, that's how the cover ended up on me."

"Mm-hmm."

"And you couldn't put my hair into a ponytail? Got me looking like a troll."

"JOC, SHUT UP," I scream and laugh, while turning over in my bed. I feel the mattress shift, and I scoot over to make room for Joc as he gets under the covers with me.

"So, no walk of shame, huh?"

"Nope." *I just want to go back to sleep.* "His oldest son came home while we were having dinner. He's still very much upset over his parents' divorce."

"Wasn't that like six years ago?"

"They separated that long ago, but the divorce wasn't settled until after Jaylen and I met. But I have been there. Kids are always the innocent victims of divorce. My parents divorced when I was in high school. Granted, I was older than what Jaylen's kids were when he divorced their mother, but it was still hard. Then my mom died. It only made me wish they had reconciled even more. My dad died a few years later. The desire for your family to be together again doesn't easily go away, even when it was dysfunctional."

"Divorce isn't the only thing kids are an innocent victim of."

Joc sighs. I look up at him. He has a sullen look on his face. Talking about parents is hard for him. His parents are still alive, but they disowned him when their only child boldly told them he was happily gay. His father is a fire and brimstone strict Baptist preacher of a prominent church in Flint. His mother is a retired nurse. To them, it was the end of the world for their pride and joy to be gay.

I remember the day when Joc showed up at my old place beaten and bruised physically and emotionally, with nothing but the clothes on his back. He had received his acceptance letter to Central Michigan University's fashion program. His parents wanted him to go to medical or theology school. His father couldn't understand what he had done to be cursed with a gay son. He tried everything from praying and exorcising the gay away to beating the gay away. His mother just stood by, praying for her son's deliverance. When they realized it wasn't working, they kicked him out and wouldn't let him get any of his things.

I tried to get some of his stuff a couple of days later. His mother made it clear that as long as I was supporting Joc, I wasn't welcomed in their home. The next week I found his things out on the curb for trash. I managed to get his sewing machines and some clothes before his father came out with a baseball bat.

It still had some of Joc's blood on it. If I had a gun, I would have shot him dead at that moment.

I made it to my car safely, but he knocked out the back window of my Grand-Am. I took him to court over that. Flint is a small city, so I run into them here and there, as I'm sure Joc does too. We just go on like we don't know each other, but I know it still hurts my dear friend.

"I know. Come here, you," I say as I lift my arm up to embrace Joc. I lay my head on his chest and wrap my arm around his slim torso.

"I don't know what I would do without you, Alise," Joc says.

"And I you, Joc," I say as I kiss his chest.

We snuggle into each other's arms and drift back off to sleep.

* * *

I'm startled awake. *What the hell is going on?* I take a few seconds to realize it's just my cellphone ringing.

"Please turn that thing off," Joc grumbles.

"It's Jaylen," I say after picking up the phone.

Joc turns over and moans. I quickly rush out of my room to answer the call.

"Hello," I say with my best I didn't just wake up voice. Then I pause. *Why did I hurry out of my room to take a call?* I shake my head at myself and Joc. I sit on the ottoman in the living room. My stomach feels a little sick, but it isn't bad. *Damn vodka.*

"Good morning, beautiful," his velvet baritone voice says.

"Good morning."

"Did you just wake up?"

Shit. My acting skills need some work.

"Yeah. I need to get up anyway, so thank you for the wake-up call."

"Sorry about last night."

"Jaylen, stop apologizing for that. It was out of your control and your son needed you."

"It's the boys' weekend with Calondra, so I wasn't expecting him. Apparently, the two of them got into it over me and he left," Jaylen explains.

"Over you?"

"Calondra was bad-mouthing me to Jaleel and JaQuese when JaQuese said she wants to live with her brothers and me."

"The boys live with you?" I ask.

"J.J. has been with me since I moved back to the house. Jaleel moved in with Angela and me a couple of years ago. JaQuese wanted to come then, but she also wasn't ready to leave her mother."

"How old is she now?"

"Twelve."

"She needs her mother in those preteen years."

"Honestly, I think her mother guilted her into staying then. She'll resort to that if nothing else works. She knows the only way she can hurt me is to turn the kids against me.

Somehow, she doesn't realize she is hurting herself and turning the kids against her in the process."

"That is sad. Calondra really wants you to be as unhappy as she is."

"It would be so much easier if her life's mission were to be happy herself," Jaylen sighs.

I feel sorry for Jaylen and his kids. At least my parents didn't fight over me when they divorced and gave the appearance of being cordial. If they fought, they didn't let me see it.

"How is J.J.?" I ask.

"He's good. He remembers more of the happier times with his mother and I more than the younger two. Calondra and I were high school sweethearts. We were young, dumb, and in love. He just wants that family unity back, but he knows we aren't good for each other now. The people we grew into weren't meant to be together. We fought all the time. I was tired of her being manipulative and not supporting my dreams. She wanted to do whatever she wanted, regardless of the fact that she had a husband and kids."

There is so much that could be said about Calondra and her actions, but I choose to not say anything else on the matter… for now.

"I explained to him you and I have known each other for some time and that you were the one that I should have married instead of Angela. He understands my future is with you."

"Jaylen, we are just getting to know~~"

"Hold on a second," Jaylen interrupts.

He told his son that his future was with me. WTF! Jaylen needs to slow down here.

I hear some talking in the background, but can't make out what's being said.

"How about brunch?" Jaylen asks clearly into the phone.

"I'm sorry. Are you talking to me?" I ask.

"Yes, I'm speaking to you, Alise. Let's have brunch to make up for dinner last night."

"Jaylen, I don't know."

"Do you have anything to do today?"

"It's Sunday. No."

"Be at my place in an hour," he demands and then hangs up.

"This is not our past relationship!" I scream at my phone as if Jaylen could still hear me.

Before Jaylen would call to tell me to be at his place in an hour, and I would be there in exactly an hour to do his bidding. To have him exert his dominance over me, remind me why he was my Daddy Dom and me his baby girl.

What can I say, old habits die hard.

I head to my bedroom and am cut off by Joc running out with a lamp from one nightstand, ready to hit someone with it.

"Joc! What the hell!"

"Who is in here?" he screams back at me.

"Nobody!"

"Why in the hell were you screaming "

"I was screaming at Jaylen and my phone!"

"Why are you still screaming at me!" he yells while dropping his arms.

"Because you are fucking crazy!"

We stand there and look at each other for a few seconds before bursting into hearty laughter.

"The lamp, though", I chuckle, pointing to the pale gold lamp.

"I was going to take a sucker out," he says, still laughing. "I got your back."

"Indeed, you do. I wish I had that on camera. Charlie would pass out. You should have seen your face. Your eyes were so big that you looked deranged." We laugh some more. "Let's put the lamp back on the nightstand. I have to be at Jaylen's in an hour for brunch."

* * *

With Joc's help, I'm pulling up in front of Jaylen's in exactly one hour. I'm wearing a black sleeveless crop top with dark wash jeans, black sandals, and diamond stud earrings. The twists that Joc put in my hair yesterday are pulled up into a high ponytail, with one strand hanging down in the front. With half of a piece of toast, a couple of turkey sausage links, and some orange juice in my stomach, the light queasiness I felt earlier is gone.

As I walk up to the house, I notice a silver Ford Taurus in the driveway. It must be J.J.'s car. I go to ring the doorbell, but Jaylen opens the door before I touch it.

"Come in." Jaylen looks like a fine specimen in a white cotton V-neck tee and relaxed fit stonewashed jeans. His feet are bare. They look decent for a man's feet.

"Oh my god, is that French toast I smell?" I ask once I step inside. Its aroma is heavenly.

"And scrambled egg whites with spinach, turkey ham, fruit, and cheese and chocolate fondue."

"Please tell me it's finished." My stomach instantly growls.

"Yeah, but first things first."

"What?"

Jaylen snakes his arms around my exposed waist and he holds me close. Out of old habit, wrap my arms around his neck and hold him too. "I've wanted to hold you for so long," he says as his hug tightens, and he kisses my bare shoulder.

I bury my head in his neck. *God, I've missed being in his arms.* I inhale. *He always smells so good.*

His kisses travel slowly up my neck to my earlobe, then along my jawline to my lips. I'm so turned on and the hardening bulge in his pants tells me he is, too. It's been an excruciating amount of time since hands other than my own have explored by body. I could explode right here, right now.

Jaylen grabs my ponytail to deepen our kiss. His tongue enters my mouth and I bite it. He moans and bites my bottom lip in return. Suddenly, he pulls me back and looks at me with desire in his eyes.

"You need to eat first," he says before kissing my forehead. With his hand on the small of my back, he leads me to a chair at the island. Everything sits in its own serving dish. There are two empty white square china plates waiting for us.

"It looks and smells splendid, Jaylen," I say as I watch him take his seat beside me.

"I may teach you how to fix it someday," he says, smiling at me. I goofily smile back at him.

Our smiles say everything. I am his and he is mine. We're falling right back in step so naturally. We are together, more than before. A couple, in every sense of the word. *Finally.*

I put four pieces of French toast and a heaping of eggs with spinach on my plate. I drench the French toast in syrup, take a bite, and it's like heaven. Thinking about it, I haven't had French toast since the last time Jaylen made it for me. With my eyes close, I savor it.

Jaylen kisses my temple, calling my attention to him. He places a hot cup of green tea and a bottle of honey in front of me. I was so far in my own little world with the French toast I didn't notice him get up.

"Thank you for everything. The food is really great."

"You deserve it," he responds as he leans in towards me. I meet him halfway and we kiss gently, yet passionately.

"Umm." Jaylen and I look up to see J.J. standing near the dining table. I feel a little embarrassed. "Sorry about last night again," he says to me. "My problem wasn't with you or my dad."

"Apology accepted." I smile at him.

"I'm about to pick Jaleel and JaQuese up and take them out for lunch and then the movies. I'll be back later with Jaleel," he says to his father.

"Alright. Be safe," Jaylen says, and then his son is gone.

"He seems to be a good big brother," I say before continuing to eat.

"He is. He's a good kid and a beast on the football field. Plays wide receiver and is too tall for defenders. He's already being scouted by several schools, but I think he'll end up at MSU."

"That's awesome. You sound proud." I've always enjoyed listening to him talk about his kids.

"He's my namesake. Of course, I'm proud."

"Are your daughter and youngest son into any activities?"

"Jaleel made the junior varsity basketball team this year. He'll be a sophomore next year and hopefully will make the varsity team. Quese cheerleads and dances."

"What genre of dance?" I ask.

"Contemporary. It's all ballet to me," Jaylen chuckles.

"There is classical and contemporary. There's a difference."

"My daughter has explained this to me many times." We both laugh.

Jaylen picks up a piece of cubed turkey ham with a toothpick and dips it into the cheese fondue.

"Here," he says for me to open my mouth.

Some of the cheese drips onto my lip when he feeds it to me. He wipes it off with his thumb and puts it in my mouth. I hold his hand in place and greedily suck on his finger. I feel my wetness growing just from this little act of seduction. Jaylen's eyes are hooded, and he gasps a little when I drag my teeth on the pad of his thumb.

"That's enough," he whispers.

I let go of his hand and bite my lip in anticipation of whatever's next. He feeds me another one. It's not what I was hoping for, but the food is good and I'm enjoying this.

"Take a drink."

I take a couple of sips of my tea, never taking my eyes off him. He picks up a plump strawberry and dips it into the melted milk chocolate and feeds it to me.

He eats the half of the fruit I left. This is so sensual. Jaylen has never fed me before. Well, not like this.

"Want another one?" he asks.

"Yes."

He raises an eyebrow at me. I know what that means. It's a test to see if I will fall in line.

"Yes, Daddy," I whisper.

Jaylen gasps. Those two words give him so much power, so much satisfaction.

"Good girl," he responds.

And those two words send a shiver down my spine. They are everything I want to hear, and I only want to hear them from the man I love.

He feeds me another chocolate dipped strawberry, only this time when he pulls the leafy top away, his lips are on mine. I push some of the strawberry into his mouth. We both moan. We're all lips, strawberry, chocolate, and unfiltered passion.

In one move, he stands and lifts me up out of my seat with just one arm wrapped around my waist. His other hand tangles in my ponytail, keeping me in place and his lips on mine. I instinctively wrap my legs around his waist. His hard bulge pushes up against my clothed sex as he sits me on the countertop of the bar.

My body is screaming for this—for him. I bite his lower lip. He moans and pulls on my ponytail, hard. I gasp as he bites and nibbles on my neck. I can feel the moisture building down below. *Yes, this is what I have needed for so long.*

Jaylen pulls away and looks me in the eyes as if he's asking if I want this. I nod slightly. He snatches my top over my head and tosses it onto the floor. His lips are on mine before I can bring my arms back down.

He lifts me up again and carries me down to the end of the hallway to the white French doors of the master bedroom. He opens one with one hand and places me down on my feet once we are inside. We never take our eyes off each other as he closes the door behind him.

"Take off your jeans," he demands in a whisper.

I oblige, never taking my eyes off him. I stand before him in nothing but a black lace strapless bra and matching boyfriend cut panties. My breathing deepens as he looks me up and down, admiring what is now his again. He steps towards me and takes down my ponytail, letting my twists fall just past my shoulders. He takes a step back to admire me once again.

"You are so beautiful."

I can't give him a response. I'm lost in his eyes, in his passion for me, in his admiration of me. I'm so lost that I don't even notice he has removed his shirt until he wraps his arms around me again and I feel the heat from his dark brown skin.

Again, we are all lips and passion as he walks me backward until I bump into the side of the bed. Jaylen continues to push up against me, rubbing his still covered dick against my lower stomach. My bra falls. *When did he unhook my bra?*

He is such an expert at this sexual game, and I've been out of play for so long that he can take me by surprise. Jaylen grabs onto the back of my thighs and lifts me onto his raised king size fourposter bed. Placing me in the middle of the bed, Jaylen climbs on top of me and I wrap my legs around his waist. His jeans feel rough against my lace panties as he slowly grinds against me.

Jaylen nibbles along my jawline and down my neck. The sensation it sends through my body is beyond amazing. I angle my head to catch his ear in my teeth. He bites my neck harder, and it makes me moan.

His lips travel further south, kissing and nibbling along my collarbone and down my chest to my right nipple. He pinches and rolls my left nipple with his thumb and index finger as his tongue flicks quickly, then slowly, then quickly, then slowly, on and around my right nipple. The need to have him inside me increases ten folds with his rhythmic teasing.

"Fuck," I gasp. My body is on fire.

"Slow, my little baby. Slow."

He knows he can make me cum like this. He has many times before. I have to control my breathing and regain some control of myself to not combust in the next few seconds.

He moves his mouth over to my other nipple while his hand travels to my sweet spot.

"Oh. My. Fucking. God," Jaylen moans over my nipple when he realizes how wet I am. He removes his hand and puts two fingers into my mouth to have me taste my salty nectar.

"Mmmmm," I moan.

"Don't be stingy," Jaylen says as his mouth comes up to meet mine. We kiss deeply, savoring the taste of my juices. Suddenly, Jaylen rises off the bed and pulls me to the edge by my thighs. I love it when he manhandles me. He drops to his knees out of my view, and his tongue takes a single quick flick across my clitoris.

"Aaaahhh!"

"So ready. Don't cum until I tell you to," Jaylen instructs. Again, I'm trying to focus on my breathing. Jaylen reaches up and pinches and pulls my right nipple hard.

"Yes, Daddy! Yes. Not until you tell me to," I scream.

"Good girl."

Jaylen focuses his attention back to my magic button, alternating between fast and slow licks, sucking on it, and fucking my pussy with his tongue. My back arches off the bed as I try to push back my impending orgasm. Jaylen makes that task harder to do when he inserts two fingers inside of me and starts massaging my walls. I grip the duvet.

"Daddy, please," I ask as my thighs begin to quake.

"Please what, little baby?" he responds as he pushes his fingers deeper inside of me and gently blows on my clitoris.

"FUCK!"

"What is it, Alise?"

"Please! Can I cum, Daddy, please?"

He doesn't answer immediately. Instead, he motions his fingers inside of me to signal 'come here' as he continues to lick on my clitoris.

"Daddy," I scream. I'm about to combust whether or not he wants me to.

"Cum," he whispers lowly.

On command, I explode. I try to close my legs as my entire body quakes out of control, but Jaylen holds them open, forcing me to absorb all the pleasure he is giving me. I'm pretty sure I ripped a hole into the duvet. I haven't orgasmed like this in a very long time, and it seems to go on forever.

Before I can come back to the here and now, I feel the bed shift and my thighs rising with Jaylen's body. He slowly sinks into me.

"Thank you for waiting for me to get my shit together," he moans - my tightness confirms that no one else has been inside his special place.

I wrap my arms around his back. My knees and elbows are touching. Jaylen's strokes are deep and slow. I match him thrust for thrust. His arms wrap tightly around my shoulders, holding me in place while our faces are in each other's necks.

"I told you years ago that I was yours. I meant that," I respond.

He moans deep from within as if my words touch the core of his being. He sinks as deep as he can into me, stretching my walls. Jaylen lifts his head and kisses me with need and passion. Even though he keeps a slow pace, his thrusts are getting harder and harder.

"I love you, Alise. I'll never let you go again," Jaylen says, looking deep into my eyes.

Even so, his words and the look in his eyes take me by surprise. His desire for me is so much more than what he has ever given me before. This is everything I've always wanted from him. The feelings this evokes in me bring tears to my eyes.

"I love you too, Jaylen."

We kiss again; me expressing years of love, want, and need for him, and him showing years of apologies and love for me. It's more than enough to send us both overboard.

"Alise," Jaylen moans in reverence as he pours himself into me.

"Jaylen," I whisper as I dig my nails into his back and tears continue to fall from my eyes as I orgasm again with him.

Not moving from off or inside of me, Jaylen kisses away my tears. All I can do is wrap myself tightly around him like a koala bear holding onto a tree.

"You mean so much to me," he whispers into my ear.

"You are my everything," I whisper back.

We kiss again, gently this time, exchanging silent 'I love you's.' Then, from nowhere, Jaylen's kisses become harder, more passionate. Jaylen bites my tongue. I moan into his mouth.

"You are mine," Jaylen growls through gritted teeth.

I feel him hardening inside me. He thrusts forward as he bites my neck.

"Aaaahhh," I gasp.

He strokes hard in and out of me over and over again, each thrust coming faster and faster. Jaylen's like a jackhammer, moving quickly and strong. I feel as though he's going to break me in two. I have to stretch my arms above my head and place my hands on the headboard to brace myself.

"Fuck, Jaylen," I scream.

"Give it to me, now," he growls.

"JAAAAYYYY-LLLEEEEENNNNNNN," I scream as I cum around his mad dick.

"GOOD. FUCKING. GIRL." Jaylen says in between thrusts.

I'm cumming so hard that my legs close around his body and I accidentally push him out of me. Jaylen pushes my knees into my chest, putting my ankles near his ear.

"Keep your fucking legs open," he says as he drives into me again.

I moan at how he manhandles me. I love this shit. He puts his hand around my neck.

"Did you hear me, little baby?"

"Yes, Daddy. I will keep… oh shit… my legs… aaahhh… open."

Jaylen continues to pound into me like he's trying to reach some magical destination and he has a short amount of time to get there. I don't even get to come completely down from my last orgasm before I feel that familiar and delicious build inside me again. Jaylen is getting close, too. I can feel it. He picks up his pace, which I honestly didn't think was possible.

"Oh, baby girl," Jaylen moans.

"Daddy!"

We both cum together again, and it's delicious. Jaylen collapses on top of me. We're both panting and sweating. The scent of the room with the enchanting mixture of sweat and sex. I haven't inhaled this scent in such a long, long time. I'm sated. Beyond sated. My body feels weak, but in the best way possible. I wince when Jaylen pulls out of me and he rolls over to lie on his back.

"God, I have missed you," Jaylen says, out of breath.

"You missed sex with me," I retort, without thinking first. I instantly regret saying it.

Jaylen turns onto his side to face me. "How many times do I have to tell you--"

"I know, I know. I'm sorry. I said it without thinking about it. I know this time it's more than just sex for you," I say.

Jaylen raises an eyebrow at me. "Did you interrupt me, little baby?"

Uh-oh. I bite my bottom lip as I wonder how much this small indiscretion will cost me.

"I'm going to have to put in some work to get you back in line." Jaylen gets out of bed and walks around to the foot of it. He stands there and looks at me with a menacing look on his face. "Come."

I go to get out of the bed. "No. Stay on the bed and come here."

I get on my hands and knees and crawl slowly to the end of the bed. Jaylen's eyes go from menacing to chocolate molten lava. *Damn, he is hot. This is hot.*

When I get to him, I keep my ass up in the air and lower my chest down to the bed. Doing so puts my face directly in

95

front of his thick, dark, magical dick. I blow on it and watch it twitch. I want to put it in my mouth, but I know doing so without permission will only get me in more trouble than what I'm already in.

I've never been able to resist sucking on him when his dick is in front of me. I look up at him. He knows what I'm thinking, and he's wondering just how far I will go.

I'm already in trouble. Fuck it.

I lick the tip.

"Mmmmm." My juices have always tasted better off of him. His dick starts to get hard. I take another lick. *Oh, I have missed tasting him.* He becomes even harder. A beautiful pearl of pre-cum forms on the tip. I can't help it. I have to have it.

I take him into my mouth. He gasps. As I pull back, I swirl my tongue around the tip. I pull back completely and swallow the juices that I have sucked off. *Good.*

I reach for his cock, but Jaylen grabs my wrist and twists my arm so that I have to flip over onto my back. "Did I give you permission to suck on my dick?" he asks.

I shake my head with a devious smile on my face. Jaylen lets me go. *I want to be punished.*

"On your knees. Face the headboard." I do as I'm told. I know what's coming. My heart is racing, and my breathing becomes shallow. "Get into position," Jaylen demands.

Just like the dream I had the other night, I get into the proper spanking position, ass all the way up and face all the way down with my arms stretched straight out above my head.

I feel Jaylen shift, putting one knee on the edge of the bed so that his front is to my side. He places one hand on my back to hold me in place while his other hand rubs my ass. I'm panting with anticipation. I honestly don't remember the last time Jaylen spanked me.

"I'm sure I don't have to remind you of what your indiscretions are, Alise. I want you to count the spanks out, okay?"

"Yes, Daddy," I answer. Jaylen's hand lifts off my ass and comes down with a hard and swift smack.

"One," I moan. I dig my hands into the duvet. Jaylen massages my ass. It helps with the sting. He smacks me again.

"Two." Such sweet agony. Again.

"Three." I've missed this so much. Another slap.

"Four." The sting is delicious. Another.

"Five." My ass is tender and screaming.

"Six!" I'm getting to my threshold, but I don't want to stop him. I've needed this for so long. The sound of another hard smack cracks through the air.

"Seven!" I let out a silent "ouch."

"Eight," I whisper. I'm praying that Jaylen stops at ten. He never went past ten before. *Please stop at ten.*

"Nine," I whisper again.

When I think he is going to come down with smack number ten, he doesn't. All I know is that his dominant hand is not touching me. Either it's in the air, ready to come down on my sore ass, or it's at his side. I don't know which, but I don't dare to look. Doing so would be a reason for more punishment. I stay in my kneeling position, anxiously waiting for the last of the spanking. His breathing is ragged. It feels like an eternity is passing.

I guess he is done. I relax as I hear his breath slowing. Then suddenly my ass is burning like Jaylen placed it directly into hell itself.

"Ten!" I scream at the top of my lungs. That last smack was harder than the nine before. My ass is screaming as loud as I am.

Jaylen roughly massages my ass. This lets me know that my punishment is not over. He's in the moment right now. *I wonder how long it's been since he has let out his inner Dominant?*

While I'm in my head hating the thought of Jaylen being a Dom to anyone else since we were last together, I don't notice him shift behind me until he rams into me.

"Aaaahhh, FUCK JAYLEN," I scream.

Jaylen quickly smacks my ass three times while he plummets into me with a veracity that I haven't experienced in a very long time. Then again, I haven't experienced much of anything sexual or kinky in a long time.

"What the fuck is my name, little baby?" he yells.

"Daddy!"

"Good girl," he says as he digs his fingertips into my waist.

I thought Jaylen was going like a jackhammer during our last round. Now he's like a jackhammer being operated by the devil himself. This time I don't have anything near me to brace myself against.

Jaylen sticks his thumb into my asshole. The sensation it gives me, along with his hard and fast fucking is phenomenal. I know it means that he will shove himself up my ass soon. The thought makes me tighten up and, doing so pushes Jaylen out of me.

"Just the thumb today," he says as he puts his meat stick back inside of me.

How did he know what I was thinking about?

Jaylen continues with his relentless pace. He has to keep a hand on my hips to keep me in place. Even when he is punishment fucking me, it's hard to resist the urge to cum all over his thick dick, and he knows it. I'm ready.

"Cum!" Jaylen demands with a hard smack on my ass.

And just like that, I'm spiraling out of control and cumming all over him again. I'm even squirting some and I rarely ever do that. I call out my name for him repeatedly. With one last thrust, Jaylen explodes his warm goo into me.

When he lets go of my hips, I collapse onto the bed. Jaylen leans down and wraps one arm around my waist and pulls me with him as he climbs to the head of the bed. We lay spooning, my back to his chest. He caresses me gently while planting sweet butterfly kisses along my shoulder.

"You are so special," he whispers into my ear.

I smile. "So are you."

"How do your ass cheeks feel?"

"Screaming red, Daddy."

Jaylen leans over to grab a bottle of baby oil on the nightstand behind him. He massages some of it into my ass. His tender touch feels good right now. When he finishes, he wraps his arms around me again.

"I love you," I whisper. I feel him smile.

"I love you too, little baby." It isn't long until I drift off into a peaceful and much-needed nap.

Porsha Deun

CHAPTER VII

I wake up to the sound of a deep voice in the distance. It's Jaylen, but he is somewhere else in the house. The alarm clock on the nightstand closest to the door says it's almost 3 p.m. I have been out for a couple of hours… at least. I sit up in the raised king size poster bed and look around the room.

The décor is dark, like the rest of the house. The wall with the French doors and the wall opposite it are pewter gray, and the other two walls are the deepest eggplant color I've ever seen. There is a mahogany wood dresser with an oversized mirror across the room facing the bed, facing me. I look at myself in the mirror. Even I have to admit that I'm glowing in my sated state.

Pale gray sheets cover me, while an array of pillows mixed in shades of gray and dark purples are scattered on the floor. Ivory ceramic lamps sit atop the nightstands on either side of the bed. Though so much differs from what I remember, I imagine that bathroom and closet are still on either wall besides the dresser.

I can't help but think about how our rooms are so different and match our relationship roles perfectly. His room is dark and dominant, just like him, my Daddy Dom. My room is light and bright, just like me, his baby girl.

One thing we have in common is that we do not believe a television should be in the bedroom. The bedroom is for resting and much more interesting ways to entertain yourself other than some crap television show.

I climb out of bed and head to the bathroom. The neutral stone like tiles are cold underneath my feet. I glance at the shower and smile when I realize it is just as I remember. The shower has a dark cobblestone interior wall, which I have always loved, and a dark tile floor with a clear glass door. The steps around the separate tub give the tub a romantic feel. Like the shower, the wall behind the tub is a dark cobblestone.

Neutral granite countertop surrounds two sinks and make up a vanity. All of Jaylen's grooming products and items are around one sink while the other sink and vanity are empty. An ivory high-back chair sits at the vanity. Straight ahead of me is where my bladder is screaming I need to be.

Once done there, I head to Jaylen's closet. When we were together before, I always wore one of his shirts around the house after sex. There have been additions to his wardrobe since then, but the overall set up and how he organizes everything is the same. The closet is larger than most of the more generous bedrooms of the houses in this neighborhood, or within the city limits, for that matter. Everything has its place and is organized by color: black, gray, white, and denim.

I'm going to have to get him in some colors.

I select a black dress shirt and head out to find him.

Jaylen is sitting at the dining room table with some papers when I find him. He's changed into a pair of gray sweatpants, no shirt and barefoot. He looks up at me when he notices my presence. A wicked smile comes across his face as he assesses me.

"Schedule a meeting with the superintendent for as soon as possible and get the presentation materials together. Call me back once you have a date." He hangs up the phone.

"Don't stop taking care of your business on my account," I say.

"I'm done, anyway. Come here," Jaylen says as he scoots his chair back. I walk over to him and sit in his lap. He kisses me gently on my lips, cheeks, and nose. "If I want to stop taking care of business to admire what is mine, I will. Understand?"

"Yes, Big Daddy," I reply with a smile.

"You still look as beautiful as ever in my shirts," he says while caressing my legs and thighs.

I chuckle and bury my head in his neck. His scent is a heady mix of sweat, sex, musk. I love it.

"Do you feel rested?" I nod my head. "How does your ass feel?"

"Still a little sore," I laugh. "When was the last time that you were in Dom mode?"

"Not since you," he breathes.

I raise my head to look him in his eyes. "So, I'm still your first baby girl?" Jaylen places both of his hands on either side of my face.

"My one and only baby girl," he answers before placing a chaste kiss on my lips. Knowing this makes me smile even more. *I'm his one and only baby girl.* That's something that I'm very proud of, something only I have ever given him.

I recall him telling me about when he tried to introduce the Daddy Dom/little girl dynamic into his marriage with

Calondra. Let's just say she wasn't going for it. There's not a submissive bone in that woman's body. Then she tried to flip it so that she would be the Dominant and Jaylen the submissive. Jaylen wasn't having that either.

"What do you want to do today? I didn't plan anything past brunch," Jaylen says.

I lay my head on his chest and wrap my arms around his waist. "I just want to be in Daddy's arms," I coo.

Jaylen wraps his arms around me tightly. It feels so good to be held by him again. Right here is where I belong. His arms are my home.

"It's nice outside. Let's go out to the hammock," Jaylen suggests.

"Isn't it supposed to rain today?"

"The storm is hours away. We have time to hang out outside. Plus, I want to grill some steaks for dinner."

"Won't the kids be back soon?"

"No. They are going back to their mom's. The boys will be back later tonight. Now stop stalling and start walking," he says, just before lightly smacking my ass.

"Yes, Daddy," I giggle.

I step out of the patio door—it feels nice out. We walk across the deck hand-in-hand to the hammock in the middle of the backyard. The two trees it's tied to provide plenty of shade. I'm sure these trees marked where the property line was before Jaylen purchased the additional lots. I think it's illegal to collect rainwater in Michigan, but Jaylen has large drum barrels placed around the edges of his property line to do just that.

"We drink the bottled water, but I installed a system to use rainwater for everything else but the toilets. That's all I'm willing to pay the city for," Jaylen explains when he notices me looking at the drums.

We settle into the hammock with my head on his chest. It seems like even Mother Nature is happy with us being back together. A gentle breeze caresses us while a few birds are chirping. The neighborhood is quiet, which is good, considering there was a shooting not too far from here last week. Slowly, but surely, my city is getting better.

We are content laying on the hammock, enjoying each other's company in silence. This has truly been the perfect day. Not only are Jaylen and I back together, but we made love and rekindled our romantic and BDSM relationship. Everything is right in the world.

After about thirty minutes, the rain clouds open up without even a sign. We both jump up and forget about keeping our balance in the hammock and fall to the ground. I'm a giggling mess as Jaylen tries to get both of us up and into the house. Once he is on his feet, he stands me up and throws me over his shoulder caveman style and jogs towards the patio door. This only makes me giggle more. Once we're safely inside the house, he places me on my feet and looks at me quizzically.

"What's so funny, little baby?"

"You. Us. The rain. Everything." I can't stop laughing.

"So, you *are* laughing at me," he says with a domineering hint. There is a wicked gleam in his eyes.

I shake my head as I try to stop laughing, but it doesn't work. The laugh is just uncontrollable. Jaylen leans his head to the side. I know I should stop laughing, but I can't.

Jaylen pounces on me, kissing me fiercely. It takes me by surprise and stops my laughing in an instant. Although I'm sure he was just trying to stop my giggles, he's awakened a familiar need to have him inside me again. I return his kiss just as fiercely. He moans deeply and rips open the shirt I'm wearing. The sound of buttons hitting the floor echoes through the room.

Jaylen breaks away from the kiss and flings the closest chair away from the dining table across the room, picks me up, and sits me down onto the table. He drops his soaking wet sweatpants to reveal his massive and hard, throbbing manhood.

Jesus, he wasn't wearing any underwear! Knowing this turns me on even more.

I part my legs. Jaylen grabs my thighs and pulls me to the edge of the table. I lean back slightly, my hands flat on the table behind me to prop myself up. Keeping the back of my knees at the bend of his arms, he slams into me. I moan.

Jaylen pauses for a second and then slams into me again. This time he doesn't stop, and it feels incredible. My full breasts bounce to his rhythm. He grabs my left nipple and pinches it hard.

"Aaahhh."

He lets it go and puts his hand around my neck and squeezes just enough to not completely cut off my airway. "Who do you belong to?" he grunts.

"I belong to you, Daddy," I respond. He slams into me harder. "Shit," I yell.

"Give it up," Jaylen demands.

And I do, just for him. I cum and quake around him as he continues to slam into me. His rhythm prolongs my orgasm.

"My good little baby." After a few more thrusts, Jaylen quickly pulls out of me while still holding on to my neck. "On your knees and open your mouth."

I quickly drop off the table and onto my knees with my mouth open, just as he told me to. He pushes his dick into my mouth and releases his sweet cum. The mixture of my juices off his dick and his sweetness are a delicious heavenly mix.

I suck hard, trying to get every drop out of him there is for me. I swallow what's in my mouth and continue to suck him off. *He tastes so damn good.*

"Fuck, Alise!" Jaylen collapses over me onto the table.

I continue to clean him up with my mouth, licking and sucking gently. When he can't tolerate it anymore, he steps back and helps me up off the floor. He kisses me with reverence. It goes right to my heart. *I love this man.*

Jaylen takes my hand and leads me into his bedroom again. Only this time he doesn't stop there. We go into his bathroom and then into the shower. There are showerheads all around the shower wall plus a large overhead, which is more than I remember. He turns on the water and it warms up quickly. The water hitting me from all directions feels good on my already sensitive skin.

"I ordered this for you last week," Jaylen says. He's holding a bottle of my favorite lavender and jasmine scented body wash.

"You remembered," I say, surprised.

"Of course I did," Jaylen responds softly as he moves me from under the overhead showerhead.

He squeezes some onto a pouf and massages it gently on me. The scent is heavenly. Jaylen washing me is heavenly, too. I close my eyes and absorb the sensation as he continues to wash my shoulders and chest. He moves in a slow circular motion down to my stomach, leaving a soapy trail on my body, which remains because his muscular body is blocking the showerheads.

I open my eyes to see him slowly dropping to one knee so he can better wash my lower body. He isn't looking up at me. His eyes fixed on my hips, he cleans them intently. The way he washes my body, it's almost like he's worshiping me. I want to touch him, but I don't want to disturb him either.

He wraps one arm around my waist and brings my foot up to his knee. I place my hands on his shoulders to keep my balance. He washes my thighs, then my legs and my feet. I giggle as he washes in between each of my toes and a small smile plays across his face. Jaylen moves his hands up to clean my sex. I try not to get turned on by the act, but I can't help it. Before I know it, it's over too soon.

"Turn around," he says when he places my foot down. I resist the urge to pout.

I do as I'm told. Jaylen washes the back of my legs and thighs with the same reverence he did as my front. When he gets to my butt, it seems like he's there forever. I feel him rise to his feet so he can wash my back. From there, he washes my arms and hands just as detailed as he washed my legs and feet. When Jaylen is done with my hands, he places his hands on my shoulders and turns me to face him again. He puts the softest kiss on my forehead then pulls me under the overhead shower head. *Oh, this feels so good.*

"I love you."

"I love you too," he whispers with his eyes smiling back at me.

"My turn," I say as I step from under the top showerhead and grab one of the many male body wash containers on a built-in shelf. Just as he did, I squirt some body wash on a second pouf and clean him. As I wash him, I come to understand the reverential look he had while cleaning me can't be helped, because I now have the same for him. When I'm on my knees, I go to clean his dick and balls, but he stops me.

"I will clean that. You might wake him up again, and I'm not sure if either of us can handle that right now," Jaylen says with a sly smile.

I'm disappointed, but he's probably right. I continue to clean the rest of him, just as he did me.

Once we're both fresh, we step out of the shower and dry each other. Jaylen wraps me in a plush cotton white robe of his and himself in a matching black one.

"The coconut oil is in the closet," he says while pointing to a slim closet door in between the shower and bathroom door.

I grab the jar out of the closet. Coconut oil is all I put on my skin. I'm still amazed by how much of my likes Jaylen remembers. He leaves me alone in the bathroom as I moisturize. When I'm done, I grab a towel off the rack over the toilet and wrap it around my head before heading back into the bedroom.

Jaylen has laid my clothes out on the bed. He walks out of his closet, pulling a black ribbed tank over his head. He has on gray overwashed jeans that have small rips all over. The tank hugs his muscular chest. There are still some droplets of water in his arms and shoulders. *Damn, does he have to look good in everything?*

"I'm going to get started on dinner," Jaylen says as he playfully smacks my ass as he leaves the room.

I giggle and start getting dressed. Since I don't have any fresh panties here, I decide to go commando and stuff the ones I wore over into my back pocket.

I make my way into the kitchen to find Jaylen taking some marinated steaks out of a Ziploc bag and putting them onto a countertop grill. I look around the kitchen and don't see anything out for sides, so I decide to give him a hand with the couple of things I know how to cook, if he has the right stuff. Opening the fridge, I find a head of cauliflower. I grab it, plus a white onion and a bulb of garlic out of the baskets on the counter and some brown rice from the pantry.

"Do you know what you are doing with that stuff?" Jaylen asks.

"I've learned to cook a couple of things over the years," I answer.

As I prepare the garlic mashed cauliflower and rice pilaf, Jaylen sets the placemats and silverware up on the bar and pours some Merlot into glasses.

The rain and thunder continues outside. Inside Jaylen's kitchen, we are both content and sated. We both steal glances at each other whenever we can and smile when we get caught. He caresses me every time he walks past me or has to be near me, gently touching my arm here, the small of my back there, or my hips here. Life couldn't be more complete for me than it is right now.

He plates the steaks and passes them to me to add the sides. I pass them back to him and Jaylen places them on the placemats. We sit and eat, enjoying each other's silent company with the thunderstorm playing as our background music.

"How do you feel?" Jaylen asks, breaking our silence about halfway through the meal.

"The best I've felt in a long time," I smile.

"I don't mean physically; I mean emotionally… about us being back together. I know you originally wanted to take this slower than what it's gone."

"That's true. I intended to drag this out for weeks until I knew for certain you were sincere. I was too afraid you would walk away from me again when you felt that our relationship was too much. If I'm being honest, I still have that fear."

"Alise, I swear---"

"Let me finish," I say with one hand up to stop him. He nods for me to go on. "Regardless of how great or small that fear is, my love for you is so much more. I don't want to regret not giving us a chance or trying sooner. My answer to your question is still the same either way."

Jaylen regards me intently. It's almost as if he's not sure of what to say. "And let's be honest," I continue. "I'm yours. I always have been and always will be."

"And I'm yours, Alise. Forever and always." Jaylen caresses my face before we both go back to finishing dinner.

"The steak is good. What did you marinate them in?" I ask before finishing my glass of wine.

"Thanks, but you would have to move in before I tell you my cooking secrets." I spray spit wine onto the bar in front of me. "Jesus, Alise. I was joking," he says while throwing his napkin on top of the wine that went from my mouth to the countertop in the most unladylike fashion.

"A joke? Really?" I wipe my mouth while giving him a "yeah, right" look.

"Honestly, it was something I considered while you were napping. The thought of you waking up next to me and wearing my shirts on a regular basis makes me happy."

"Jaylen."

"It's too soon for you. I know. So, for now, it was just a joke."

The feeling of contentment I had just a minute ago is now gone. "Why do you do that?"

"Do what?"

"Make me go from being so happy, relaxed, and content to uneasy and uncomfortable?"

"That wasn't my intention."

"I know it wasn't, but that doesn't change how it's made me feel. We got back together not even 24 hours ago, and you are already thinking and talking about me moving in here with you and your boys? J.J. had a hard enough time with seeing me here last night. Now you want me to play mom to him and Jaleel every day? Why can't we just enjoy now for a while first? A long while!"

"Okay, okay," Jaylen says with his arms up in the air as if he's surrendering. "I'm sorry, and you're right. Moving in is an enormous step, especially with my kids living here. I just… I want to live the life we would have been if I hadn't ended it."

"Jaylen, we can't just jump right into that." I really hope he understands. "The dynamics do not need to change *right now*," I explain.

"I know we can't because of the kids."

"It's not just because of the kids. Until a week ago, we hadn't seen each other in nearly four years. I don't want to keep bringing up how we ended, but because of how we ended, we have a lot of things to work through. It would be a mistake to believe that we can just jump in where you think we could be if things hadn't ended."

"Should be," Jaylen corrects.

"Jaylen," I say exasperated. I fold my arms on top of the bar and lay my head on top. *Why can't he understand he needs to slow the hell down?*

"I will back off the subject… for now."

I loudly blow out air to show my exasperation.

"Don't get out of line, little one," Jaylen remarks as he gets up from the bar to place the dishes in the sink.

I stay exactly as I am. I don't dare look at Jaylen right now because all I can think about doing is screaming at him and that I know for sure will get me in trouble. He has gone from driving me crazy in the best way to plain driving me crazy.

I feel Jaylen's arm snake around my waist and he kisses the back of my neck. "Come watch a movie with me," he says as he pulls me up from my seat.

I follow him into the living room and curl up on the loveseat. Jaylen selects a movie from hundreds of DVDs shelved on the wall next to the fireplace and puts it into the player. Sitting down next to me, he envelops me into his muscular arms. He points the remote and skips right to the main menu.

It's *The Devil Wears Prada*, one of my favorite movies. Joc and I used to watch this every weekend. Meryl Streep can do no wrong in my book.

"I'm going to have to work on getting you into the digital world," I tell him. I don't think I have a single DVD in my home. In fact, I know I don't.

"The kids say the same thing." I smile as I feel small kisses on my hair.

After the movie, I decide it's time for me to go back to my humble abode. My time with Jaylen has been great and I don't want it to end, but I need some time for myself.

"I don't want you to go."

"I need to go home, Jaylen." Looking into his eyes, I know he wants to tell me this can be my home, too. Instead, he just sighs and I'm thankful he chooses not to bring the subject up again.

I caress his face and gently kiss him. He opens the front door. The storm has passed, and the sun is setting. The smell of fresh spring rain is in the air. Jaylen walks me to my car and opens the door when I unlock it. Standing in the car door, he pulls me close and I wrap my arms around his neck. *He smells so good.* He kisses the corners of both of my eyes, my forehead, my nose, and then my lips.

"I love you, little baby," Jaylen says.

"I love you, Daddy," I respond.

We kiss again, and I get into my car. Even though it's out of the way, I decide to take the expressway home. There's something about highway driving that clears my mind.

Once home, I change into a champagne satin cami and short set. I fix myself a glass of water and stare out onto the streets from my downtown apartment. Jaylen's desire for me to move in with him is still on my mind. I have worked hard to get where I am and I'm not sure if I want to give that up. And I don't think that I want to be an instant everyday mother to two teenagers, three if JaQuese comes to live with her father.

"We have plenty of time before that happens," I tell myself before making my way to the bedroom. I have an early day tomorrow, so I'm going to bed early.

I get under my duvet and close my eyes. This is the most content that I've been in a long time. I smile to myself as my day with Jaylen replays in my head. Then I realize something and get the most dreaded and nauseated feeling I've ever had.

"Shit!"

I jolt up into a sitting position and grab my phone off the nightstand to call Jaylen. *It's after eleven, but hopefully, he's still up. If not, then oh well. We need to talk right now.*

"My little baby," Jaylen says sleepily. I woke him up.

"I'm not on birth control."

"What?"

"I haven't been on birth control for years."

"You didn't think to say that before we had sex?"

"I wasn't planning on having sex with you today. I intended to make you wait longer."

"And once you realized we were having sex?" he asks, irritated.

"I didn't think about it. My mind was overwhelmed," I explain. I'm mentally kicking myself right now.

"Damn it, Alise."

"Don't put this all on me. You didn't ask either or put on a condom," I remind Jaylen. "Why didn't you put one on?"

"We didn't wear them before."

"I *was* on birth control then," I state.

"Exactly. I figured you still were."

"This isn't before, Jaylen. You knew I hadn't been with anyone else. Why would I need birth control?" There's an awkward silence. "Jaylen?"

Still silence. Jaylen is pissed. I don't know if it's at himself or me.

"I will come get you in the morning so we can figure it out," he finally says.

"I have appointments at work in the morning."

"Cancel them," he says like it's nothing.

"Jaylen, this is my business. I can't cancel them. They're with clients." *He is my man and my Daddy Dom, but who the hell does he think he is to tell me to cancel my business appointments? My business is MY BUSINESS.*

"Fine. I will catch up with you tomorrow."

"Jaylen, what…" The call ends. *He hung up on me. He's really pissed.* It's a shame. Today was great until now.

I lay back down, but I know I won't be able to go to sleep. I stare at the ceiling as my mind races with thoughts of a possible and very unexpected pregnancy and Jaylen not being happy about the baby at all. I already know he doesn't want more kids. He told me so years ago and his tone just now let me know his mind has not changed. I don't have any kids and never really thought about having them before. *I just got him back.*

I turn over and bury my head into a pillow.

"FUUUUUUUUUUUUUUUUUUUUCK," I scream. I try to calm myself with the possibility that I may not be pregnant. I count how many days it has been since my last cycle, 12 days. That just increased the potential of pregnancy. He released multiple loads into me today. I'm feeling so many emotions at once, but fear is the most prominent—fear of losing everything I've ever wanted before I really have it. I cry.

"What am I going to do if I'm pregnant?"

I can't do anything else but cry myself to sleep.

CHAPTER VIII

I got maybe an hour of sleep last night, spending the rest of the night tossing, turning, and pacing. I never thought about being a mother before now, outside of being a godmother to Charlie's daughter, Amber. But having that title doesn't require me to actually parent. I spoil and return.

During my pacing, I decided there's no point in stressing or worrying about it until I know for sure whether I'm pregnant. If I am, I will keep the baby. I can do a lot of things, but abortion is not one of them. Jaylen will have to deal. After coming to that decision was when I could sleep, only to wake up at 5 a.m. from the loud crash of a car accident just outside of my apartment. With my mind made up, I get started with my day.

There's nothing like keeping busy at work to avoid personal issues. In less than an hour, I placed bulk fabric orders, created design boards for two upcoming fashion shows, and created the job posting for Joc's current position replacement.

I will promote Joc to my assistant today, but he'll continue in both roles until the seamstress position is filled. I still have a couple more hours before anyone else gets here. I decide to take advantage of my focus and the quiet and work on more sketches for next season.

I'm so into sketching that I don't hear Joc come upstairs.

"How long have you been here?" he asks, startling me as he places his white with gold hardware messenger bag on his desk while never putting down the McDonald's bag. He's in a white blazer with a red and white polka dot handkerchief with a white linen shirt and white slacks that are so crispy that he must have used an entire can of starch on them, and white and red wing-tip shoes.

"What time is it?"

"Almost opening time."

"Well, nearly two hours."

"Two hours?" he asks while leaning against my door posts and raising a manicured eyebrow at me.

"There's a lot to get done with the upcoming fashion shows, new lines, appointments, and the latest incoming custom orders. I wanted to get a head start on the day," I half lie. There's a lot to do, but I don't want to get into the truth with Joc right now.

I can tell he doesn't fully believe me. He knows I usually take my work home or stay late. I hardly ever come in early. Just as Joc was about to question me some more, the sound of several footsteps on the stairs fills the air. It's Charlie, Kitty, and Kim.

"Hi, ladies," Joc and I say in unison.

They all chimed back with various versions of "hello" and "good morning."

"I'll be right back," Joc says as he pats the door post and then walks towards the lounge area on the other side of the floor.

I breathe a sigh of relief. When Joc returns, he has a fresh cup of tea for me and his work tablet. I'm thankful he's returned to work mode and not tell-me-everything friend mode.

He starts going over the appointments and tasks for the day in detail. I have only three consultation appointments for custom orders this morning and a meeting with the Flint Board of Education this afternoon about the fundraising event I put on every year. Proceeds from the fundraiser cover the salaries of teachers and counselors, as well as supply new textbooks and computers to the schools. This is the final meeting before the event a few weeks from now.

"I posted an opening for a new seamstress this morning."

"Oh?" Joc looks surprised. "Are you expecting that much of a jump in our demand?"

"Yes, and no. Yes, our demand will increase, but I'm going to be losing one of our seamstresses."

"Losing? Which one of those ungrateful heifers is leaving? Don't tell me. I already know that it's Mi Ling's mean ass."

"No one is leaving, Joc," I chuckle. "You're being promoted to my personal assistant, starting today."

"Wha… I… I…" Joc stops trying to speak and resorts to sitting there with his mouth open. In all my years of knowing Joc, I can honestly say I have never seen him speechless.

"Of course, this will mean an increase in pay for you. You fulfill most of those duties now, but in addition, you will attend meetings with me, prep the documents for meetings for me to approve, assist with any projects I require, handle both the employee and design schedules for the work floor and send those to me for approval, plus manage my calendar more extensively. Your job duties will not be limited to any of what I just stated. I also still need you to fill in as a seamstress until that position can be filled."

I pass Joc the job description I typed up earlier this morning. Still speechless, he looks over the document.

"I'm going to move my sewing station into my office after work today and move the desk in the storage room to that area for your new office. The window cubicle walls will go up around your office area, and I'll have someone come in later today or tomorrow to run the electrical through them."

"Alise… thank you," he finally says.

My desk phone suddenly rings. I take the call and hang up a minute later.

"That was Charlie. My first consultation canceled."

"I will update the calendar and get a jump start on moving your station into your office, since we now have some time," Joc says eagerly.

An hour and a half later, Joc and I have my sewing station set up in my office, and his desk and cubicle walls pulled out.

I tackle the other two consultations of the day. They were relatively easy since I've worked with both clients previously. Joc and I have lunch in my office while getting things together for my afternoon meeting. His new position elated him.

The meeting with the school board was a breeze until they asked if I would expand the funding to include some administrative costs. That's an absolute no for me. Years before I started this fundraiser, the school board took out loans to cover teachers' salaries, yet seemed to have enough money to cover theirs. Since the teachers and counselors are the ones with the kids every day, in my book, they should be paid first; not the administrators. The school board still has some debt issues. They are going to have to figure that out on their own.

Once back inside my office, I check my messages. There are four of them, and they are all from Jaylen. He also sent two texts to my cell.

> ❤ ❤ Daddy ❤ ❤: I hope you are ignoring me because you are taking care of that. Call me.
>
> ❤ ❤ Daddy ❤ ❤: CALL ME OR I WILL SHOW UP THERE!!

The last text was sent 30 minutes ago. I turn in my chair so I'm facing the back wall. No, he did not fucking refer to me not being on birth control and him loading me up with his sperm as *that.* I close my eyes and take a deep breath. Hopefully, he's not on his way here already. He isn't going to like my decision, but I don't want a faceoff with him about it.

After another deep breath, I call his number on my cell. There is an unfamiliar ring in my office. I turn around to see Jaylen standing in front of my desk with his cell in his hand.

"DAMMIT JAYLEN! YOU SCARED ME HALF TO DEATH!"

"Did you take care of that?" he asks, a little too cool for my liking.

"Well hi, Jaylen. How has your day been? I've had a rock star kind of day. Thank you for giving enough of a shit to ask." He's now pissed me off.

"Answer my question."

"What is *that,* Jaylen?" I ask crossing my arms. My voice is full of irritation.

"This is not the time to be coy with me, little baby," he quietly threatens.

I stand and place my hands on the top of the desk. "This is my place of business. You. Are. Not. My. Dominant. Here," I say through clenched teeth.

We stand there, glowering at each other for what seems to be an eternity. Jaylen breaks the silence after a few seconds.

"I don't want any more kids, Alise."

"Pregnancy is not guaranteed."

"Pregnancy isn't impossible."

I sigh, "Look Jaylen, I will not take the morning-after pill. I know that's what you want me to do, but essentially, the decision is mine. If I'm pregnant, then I'm pregnant and we'll have a child together. How you choose to handle the situation is up to you."

Jaylen looks slightly hurt by my words. "Do you think I wouldn't be there for you and the baby?"

"You just said you don't want another child. With the way you're acting right now, I don't know what you would do."

Now there is an awkward silence between us. Jaylen has his head down in his hands. "Alise, do you want a child?" he asks with his head still down.

"I never really thought about it before, but now that there's a possibility, yes. I would eventually like a child or two."

"A child or two," he repeats back to me, lifting his head up. "I already have three kids."

"Is that supposed to mean I'm not allowed to have any?" Tense silence. I have my answer. He has to leave. I can't do this right now. "I need to get back to work."

Jaylen gets up and walks out without saying a word or looking back. A couple of minutes later, Joc enters my office with a fresh cup of hot green tea. "Alise, are you okay?"

I look him in his brown eyes, and tears start rolling down my face. He closes the door and blinds and sits on my desk by my side before the first sob leaves my mouth.

"Do you want to talk about it?" he asks while passing me a tissue from the box on my desk.

"No," I answer. I love my friend, but I'm not one who shares every part of my relationship with others. I stop my tears and clean myself up.

"Did Kittie ever schedule her marketing presentation with you?" I ask to change the subject. Again, nothing like diving into work to avoid dealing with personal issues.

"Yes. She's scheduled for tomorrow."

"Depending on how well she does, she may get a promotion too."

"It's about time you hired an in-store marketer."

"I know right," I sniffle. "The company I was going through always over charges and thinks they understand my brand and products better than I do."

"And Kitty knows it better than they do. She will do a good job, I'm sure," Joc says with confidence.

"Prepare a job posting for a part-time sales position for me to look over. Don't post it until I say so. I want to see Kitty's presentation first. If it goes as well as I hope, she'll get a promotion. Another office will have to go up in here for her. Also, call the construction company I used to renovate this building. Tell them I'm interested in adding another floor with nothing but offices. I'm thinking of five rooms with an open floor in the middle for conferences. Also, check if LaTisha and

Rebecca would be open to getting some overtime just in case until we fill Kittie's position."

"Oh, we are expanding!" Joc says ecstatically. I give him a small smile. It's the best I can muster up at the moment.

"I know what you are doing," Joc says, while holding my hand. "You said you don't want to talk about it, so I'm going to leave it alone… for now. But whenever you are ready, I'm here."

"I know, thank you," I say as I squeeze his hand. I stand to hug him and tell him thank you. My desk phone rings and Joc answers it.

"Alise Rogers' office. Yes, that will be great. I will make sure someone is here. Thank you." He hangs up the phone. "That was the electrician. He can be here at 6 to do the wiring. I can stay to make sure he has everything he needs."

"You don't have to stay. Today is going to be a long day for me."

"Alise…"

"Joc, don't."

"Fine. I'm staying here with you then."

"Has the mail come yet?" I ask to change the subject yet again.

"It's on my desk. I'll get what is relevant to you shortly and get started on the tasks you just gave me."

And with that, I'm alone in my office again.

* * *

Kittie just finished her presentation and I must say I'm impressed. She did far better than what I thought she would. The girl is a marketing natural.

"How much longer do you have in school?" I ask her without giving away what I think about her presentation.

"I graduate next May," Kittie beams.

"What do your grades look like?"

"4.0."

Perfect, though. I shouldn't be surprised. When we were young, her parents insisted that any grade below a B was not good enough for them or their daughters. I was grateful my parents didn't put that kind of pressure on me. I did just fine without it. "How much would you say you make per week on average, including your commissions?"

"What?" She's nervous now, not sure of where I'm going with our conversation. I interlock my fingers, leaving my index fingers pointing up and touching the tip of my nose. I already know what she makes.

"How would you like to be the in-house marketer for Timeless Elegance… starting immediately?"

Kittie registers my question, and a broad smile forms on her face, showing all of her pretty white teeth. She tries to compose herself, so her face continues to match her professional black suit, crisp white blouse, and killer black stiletto heels, but the smile keeps coming through.

"I would like that very much, Ms. Rogers."

I start to raise my eyebrow up at her but decide against doing so. She is being professional, but I have known her since grade school. Kitty is practically my little sister. It's just weird coming from her.

"Great. Let me show you to your office. We can discuss your hours until graduation and after, as well as your new job description and some paperwork you will need to sign," I smile back at her.

We leave my office and head to the second cubicle Joc and I put up on Monday, just in time for the electrician to wire them both. Actually, Joc and I rearranged the entire setup to make room for the second office. Now all the sewing stations are against the wall closest to the stairs but facing out towards the north windows. The lounge area stayed the same, but got smaller. Joc and Kittie's offices are along the windowed walls, facing the sewing stations. Joc's office is a little smaller than what we originally planned, but he's willing to give up space for Kittie. She's like a little sister to him too, and he's more than proud of her, as everyone is.

* * *

This week's gone by fast. I'm at home binge watching *Glee* on Netflix with a chicken wrap and spinach and artichoke dip from 501 Bar and Grill across the street. The high schoolers assignment for the week is the one and only Madonna, and I'm singing and couch dancing right along with them.

My apartment buzzer interrupts my jam session. Both Joc and Charlie have the access code to my place, so I'm positive that whoever it is has the wrong apartment number. I pause my show and go to the intercom by the door.

"Who is it?" I release the button.

"It's me, Alise."

Jaylen. I hesitate. I haven't heard from him since he walked out of my office earlier this week. I haven't called him either, so he knows I'm pretty disgusted with him right now. I've been keeping busy to not think about him, whether I'm pregnant with the child he so adamantly professed he doesn't want, and that I have obviously lost him just as fast as I got him back.

"Alise, let me up."

"What do you want, Jaylen?"

"We need to talk."

"The last time we *talked*, you walked away."

"You dismissed me."

"What did you expect my reaction to be after you told me I couldn't have kids because you already have three? Do you have any idea how fucking selfish that is?" Needless to say, I'm pissed and hurt all over again.

"Alise, please. This is not the best way to talk about this."

I stare at the intercom like it's Jaylen's head with my arms crossed. If looks could kill, both he and the intercom would be toast. Reluctantly, I buzz him in and cracked my door. I head into the kitchen to fix myself a glass of wine. I'm going to need this liquid courage to get through this conversation.

Jaylen walks in and stops on the opposite side of the island just as I take my first sip. "Do you think you should have that?"

I go to say something smart but decide against it. Jaylen is kind of right—kind of only because I may not even be pregnant, a possibility I feel the need to remind him of. "There may not be a baby." I hold on to the wine glass because it's the only thing helping me to keep control of my emotions right now.

"For our sake, I hope you're not."

"*Our sake?*" I stand there and look at him like he has lost his mind. "Are you saying if I'm pregnant, that's the end of us?"

For the second time this week, he let his silence give his answer.

"After all the shit you said about leaving me four years ago being a mistake and how much you love me and would do anything to get me back. NOW you finally got me back and you're ready to run! You are a fucking liar!"

"I'm not running from anything and I'm not a liar," he says with a straight face.

"Bullshit! If you really love me, you would stick with me and support me whether I'm pregnant or not." My voice has gone up an octave.

"If *you* really love me, you wouldn't be forcing me to do something that I have told you more than once I do not want to do," he yells back at me. I throw the rest of my wine in his face.

Jaylen cleans the wine off his face with a paper towel from the dispenser on the island. Under any other circumstances, a move like that would have gotten me punished with his belt and any privileges of our Dominant/submissive relationship taken away for weeks. But he knows I'm pissed and hurt. BDSM rules do not apply at the moment.

"I'm not forcing you to do anything, you selfish bastard! If you don't want another kid, then dis-a-fucking-ppear." I slam the glass down into the sink, shattering it. I storm the opposite way around the bar to show him out. But as I try to walk past him, he grabs my arm and spins me around, putting my back against the wall.

"I don't want to disappear from you, Alise. Don't you get that? What do you think the last couple of weeks have been for?" he asks as he presses his body into mine, effectively trapping me.

"But you will let all of that go if I'm pregnant with *our* baby? How could you not want our child, *ever*? How could you not want a child with the woman you love? There's going to be a point in time where I'm going to want a baby with you." Tears start rolling down my face.

"How can I make you understand?" he whispers softly.

"How can I make *you* understand?" I whimper.

"Please stop crying," he repeats repeatedly as he kisses my tears away.

Despite our emotionally charged conversation, each of Jaylen's kisses awakens my passion for him. Notwithstanding that I don't like him much right now, I want him. I need him. Based on the hardening bulge in his pants, he wants and needs me just as much.

We kiss gently. Jaylen lifts me up and I wrap my legs around him.

"I need you to stay with me, Jaylen, no matter what happens," I beg. "I don't know what I would do if you were to leave me again."

"Shhhhhh." He kisses me again and then carries me to my bedroom.

Jaylen crawls onto my bed with me still wrapped around him and gently lays us both down. We continue to kiss while slowly removing each other's clothes. I'm so engulfed in my passion for him, I don't realize Jaylen has a condom until he tears the small package open. I look at him, puzzled.

"We're going to use these until we find out if you're pregnant or not;" he says, while holding up the gold foil package. "If you aren't, then you *are* getting on birth control as you were before."

"And if I am pregnant?" I ask, hoping there's been a quick change in his feelings about it. Instead, he kisses me while he rolls the condom over his impressive dick.

* * *

The next morning, I wake up to no Jaylen in my bed. I think back to last night and I remember falling asleep in his arms. I lay there trying to figure out why and when the hell he left. Then I become pissed off at him for leaving and at myself for letting him seduce me into bed since that was obviously all he came over for.

"I can't fucking believe him," I yell out at no one. I put a pillow over my face to continue my rant. "I'm so stupid. So. Fucking. Stupid," I say, while slamming the pillow on my face over and over again.

"You can't believe me about what and why are you so stupid?" his baritone voice says from the corner of my room.

I jump up into a sitting position and find Jaylen sitting on my chaise lounge watching me. He's naked except for his boxer briefs. One elbow is resting on the top of the chaise with that hand slowly rubbing his chin. His other hand is resting in his lap while his legs are crossed wide, forming a bent four.

"You really need to stop scaring me like that," I say, trying to calm my jumpy nerves.

"What were you just yelling about?"

"Nothing. It's not important. How long have you been up?"

"A few hours," he says. I take notice of the tone in his voice. It sounds contemplative, manipulative, and almost downright sinister. It makes me feel uneasy. I look at the clock. It's just before six thirty.

"A few hours?" He nods his head in reply. "Have you been watching me this whole time?" Again, he nods his head. My mouth goes dry, but I try to swallow anyway.

"What's on your mind?" I ask. He apparently has been thinking about something.

"You thought I left," he says while moving his hand from his chin to the side of his head, letting his head rest in it.

"I did."

"Why would you think I would leave you in the middle of the night?"

I look down at my fingers as they twist and fumble in the duvet. "You aren't exactly happy with me right now," I say, keeping my head down.

"No, I'm not happy with you right now. But if I had to take a guess, I'd say that you're not happy with me either."

I look up at him. "I'm not."

There are a few minutes of silence between us. We stare at each other to find any trace of the one giving into the other's will, but we both know that isn't going to happen so easily. Jaylen blows out some air of exasperation, puts his crossed leg down, and leans forward to place his elbows on his knees and his head rests in his upward positioned hands.

"When is your next period supposed to be here?" he asks without looking at me.

"Little less than two weeks from now."

Jaylen is silent again. After a few seconds, he gets up and walks out of the bedroom. I hear the refrigerator door open.

"Why don't you have any food? Plenty of wine and champagne, but not even a half gallon of milk, or some eggs."

"It's just me here. There is no point in cooking," I explain.

"If you would move into my place, you would have plenty of people to cook for and I wouldn't have to worry about your eating habits."

I make my way to the kitchen while Jaylen is yelling back at me. "Let's get a couple of things straight. One, I'm not moving in with you anytime soon. Two, my eating habits have me in damn good shape. Matter of fact, much better shape than when we were together before."

"True... well, at least about your shape," he chuckles.

I roll my eyes at him. He raises an eyebrow at me, and I shrink inside. "Sorry," I say.

"What made you decide to lose weight?"

"I knew how beautiful I was inside and out. I was tired of the world not seeing it. Not to mention, it's not very popular in the fashion business to be an overweight designer making bridal and couture. Where plus-sized models are being welcomed more, that hasn't been the case for designers. Even plus-sized celebrities who start their own line don't succeed and they have the connections to. My weight was going to hold me back, so I got rid of it."

Jaylen nods his head like he understands. But we both know that he knows very little about the fashion world. His wardrobe color palette consists of black and more black.

"Get dressed. We're going to the market since you don't have anything here to eat."

Less than thirty minutes later, we are walking hand-in-hand up First Street to the Farmer's Market a few blocks from my apartment.

It's a warm early June morning. The humidity is high with a gentle breeze. It makes my already big and wild 'fro more boisterous. Jaylen is wearing the black V-neck tee and stonewashed jeans he wore over yesterday, and I have on a peach tiered tank, white cotton shorts, and tan strappy sandals. In our short walk, we have chatted about the weather and the tragic state of the Angry Carrot being President.

The outside of the Farmer's Market is all brick and bright colors. People are outside at some tables enjoying smoothies and freshly cooked breakfast and snacks from some vendors inside. This is my favorite place in downtown. The inside is spacious and always full of interesting people on the weekends. Many times, I've gotten inspiration for an entire line from people watching here.

We pick up some fruits and veggies, eggs, smoked sausage, bread, strawberry jam, and apple juice. I even got a handmade natural stone earring and necklace set. Jaylen insisted on paying for everything. Because things are going so well, I decide not to fight him on it.

Back at my place, while I shower, Jaylen is scrambling eggs, toasting some bread, frying sausage, and cutting up fruit. In my hopeful state, I touch my stomach and smile to myself. *Maybe we can make this work after all.*

While I'm getting dressed, Jaylen turns on the music player, which is synced to my phone. *Smells Like Teen Spirit* by David Garrett plays. Jaylen skips to the next song. Trans-Siberian Orchestra's rock symphony version of Beethoven's *The*

Fifth roars out over the surround sound speakers. He skips forward again. This time it's *Palladio* by Escala.

"What the hell? Alise!"

"What is it?" I giggle as I make my way to him in my living room.

"How do I change this?"

"It's synced to my phone. What do you want to listen to?"

"Anything but this. When did you start listening to whatever this is?"

"This is rock orchestra, and I started listening to it a couple of years ago. It's good and goes great with a glass of wine after a long day."

"If you say so."

I giggle and shake my head at him. I change to my old school playlist, and *You and I* by Rick James play. It's more suitable for my old man. I follow Jaylen into the kitchen and sit at the bar as he places a plate and glass in front of me.

"Did I overlook it or do you not have any coffee here?" he asks.

"No coffee. Only tea, water, wine, and apple juice," I answer, lifting my glass of juice up to him.

"But you have a Keurig."

"It's not just for coffee. They make tea pods for it, too."

Now he is shaking his head at me. We eat breakfast in musical peace. I can't help but be happy at the change in Jaylen's attitude towards me.

Jaylen's phone rings while we are cleaning up the kitchen. "Yeah," he answers. "I will be there shortly."

"Everything ok?" I ask when he hangs up.

"Yeah. There's a situation at the gym that needs my attention. Someone hurt themselves on a machine. I'll call you later." Jaylen kisses my forehead and then my lips. "Love you."

"Love you, too." And like that, he is gone. After doing some cleaning, I decide I'm going to spend some much-needed time with my goddaughter, Amber. I think we'll get our nails done, have lunch, burn off a lot of energy at Chuck E. Cheese, and cap it off back at my place for dinner and an animated movie marathon. I call Charlie to set it all up.

Porsha Deun

CHAPTER IX

"When's the last time you've been on the *Princess*?" Jaylen asks me as we are catching our breath from the wild round of sex we just had.

"The riverboat? Oh, I haven't been on it in years. Why?" I respond as I turn over in my bed to face him.

"I'm taking you on it this weekend."

"You're assuming I do not already have plans."

"You are spending your weekend with me in Detroit. We can catch some old school R&B bands at Chene Park on Friday, check out the Art Institute and some of the downtown parks Saturday afternoon, dinner on the *Princess* that evening, and gambling Sunday afternoon," he states.

"There are a lot of time gaps in your itinerary, Sir," I joke.

"What will happen during those times should go without saying."

"You have this all planned out, huh?"

"Which is why you are spending your weekend with me," he says just before kissing my forehead.

"Yes, Big Daddy," I laugh.

Jaylen smacks me on the butt.

As happy as I'm to have Jaylen for an entire weekend to myself, my thoughts turn to my possible pregnancy. What if this weekend is the last one I get with him?

"What's wrong?" he asks at noticing my smile suddenly leave.

"Nothing."

"Alise."

"Let's not ruin the moment, okay?" Before he can give a rebuttal, I kiss him deeply. I kiss him like it's the last time we will ever kiss again. It's taking all of my strength to hold back my tears.

"Talk. To. Me. Alise." Jaylen demands.

"Please don't leave me," I whisper. It's been just over two weeks since he shot my club up. My period should have started by now.

Jaylen caresses my face, then pulls me close to him. He doesn't say anything but holds me tight. I need him to tell me he won't leave me if I'm pregnant.

Who am I kidding, exactly? My period is the most regular period ever. I'm never late. I know I'm pregnant. I'm scared to tell him because I just got him back. It cannot be greedy to want both. People do it all the time.

"Don't think about that," he whispers.

"How can I not think about that?"

"Stay in the here and now baby, please."

I know I should tell him. I need to tell him. I can't bring myself to do it yet. So, I do the next best thing… change the subject. "How was your day?" I fight to keep from crying.

"It was great, but I want to talk about something else."

"Oh?"

"I'm officially all yours."

"I know that... wait... you mean you won't leave or your divorce?" I can't hide the hope in my voice.

"The divorce. It was finalized this morning." Though I'm happy to no longer be sleeping with a married man, I'm disappointed that he wasn't referring to the former.

"Why didn't you tell me you had court today?" I ask, trying to not sound sullen.

"I didn't want to tell you anything until it was final."

"How did Angela seem?"

"Why are you worried about Angela?" Jaylen asks with a quizzical look.

"Divorce is hard, no matter how amicable the process is."

"She said she's okay and ready to move on, but she seemed sad."

"Do we need to worry about her?"

"Angela is not Calondra," Jaylen answers.

"The Calondra you know now was not always the Calondra you knew," I state.

"We have nothing to worry about with Angela."

"Okay," I say. I don't know much about Angela and have never met her, so I'll have to take his word for it.

"Hey, we are okay," Jaylen states firmly.

Yeah, unless my period doesn't show in the next few days. I don't dare share my thought out loud.

"It's late. Shouldn't you get home to your boys?"

"Are you kicking me out?"

"No," I laugh. "I would love for you to stay. But we both have work in the morning, and you need to get home."

"Getting home to the kids would not be an issue if you will move in."

"Can we please not have this discussion again?" I say.

"Why won't you consider it?"

"Because you won't consider being happy with our child and me," I snap as I get out the bed and put a robe on.

"Why does everything circle back to that?" Jaylen says exasperatedly.

"You're the one that's making it an issue."

"Alise, I just said we're okay. Why don't you~~~"

"Why don't I what, Jaylen? Why won't I leave it alone? Why won't I consider killing our potential child?" My emotions are getting the better of me as I raise my voice. I stand by my bedroom door with my arms crossed over my chest.

"Now you're kicking me out."

I pause and take a deep breath. "You need to get home to your kids, and I have to get ready for work tomorrow."

"We're not leaving things like this." He sits up on the side of the bed.

"What do you want from me, Jaylen?" I plea.

"I want you to listen to me. I never said I was going to leave you if you're pregnant."

"You said you did not want our child."

"Alise," he sighs. "I'm forty-one years old. If you are pregnant, I'll be damn near 60 when this kid graduates high school. 60! People have grandkids at that age."

"So, it's about your perception and ego. Got it." I'm fuming so much that I'm physically shaking.

"Are you going to twist everything I say?"

"Are you going to say something that's not fucked up?"

Jaylen rubs his bald head in frustration. He walks over to me and places his hands on the wall on either side of my head. "Will you please stop?"

Thick silence.

"Do you love me?" Jaylen asks.

"Don't you dare use my love for you to manipulate me like that!"

"That's not what I was doing, but let's be honest, here's exactly what you've been doing to me."

Silence again. Sometimes, I really hate it when he's right.

"I'll pick you up from work on Friday."

"What's the surprise?"

"This weekend, my little baby." Jaylen kisses me again and walks around the bed to put his clothes on.

"You're just going to leave me hanging?"

"You can wait a couple of days."

I don't like that he's so calm when I'm anything but. Between the sex and the emotionally draining conversation we just had, I don't have the energy to press him more as I watch him dress.

"See you in a couple of days then," I tell him as he approaches the doorway.

"See you." We kiss again, then he leaves.

I stay by my bedroom door until I hear the elevator close before walking into my bathroom and turning the shower on.

* * *

"I've met someone," Joc tells Charlie, Kitty and me as we have lunch in my office.

"Tell more," I say.

"Well, I met him on a dating app. His name is Boston, and he's gorgeous."

"Like anyone you'd date would not be gorgeous," Kitty responds.

"He works at the community college running a youth mentorship program," Joc continues.

"How did the first date go?" Charlie asks.

"We met up at the museum and things just clicked instantly. After seeing the exhibit, we stood in the parking lot for over an hour just talking. We ended up catching a movie and having dinner. He kissed me goodnight, and it was magical."

"Joc, you sound like you're already falling," I beam at him.

"Look at that smile on his face. He's definitely falling," Kitty states.

"You know I don't fall fast, but there is something about this one. I'm trying to not get my hopes up, but I can see this going somewhere."

"When do we meet him?" Charlie inquires.

"I'm bringing him to Alise's fundraiser next Saturday."

"We have to wait over a week to meet the man that has you floating!" I say.

"Why don't we have a get-together at my place this Saturday so that we do not have to wait," Charlie suggests.

"This weekend's not good for me," I state.

"Why not?" Charlie and Joc say in unison.

"Jaylen has a weekend planned in Detroit for us."

"Oh, that sounds fun," Kitty chimes in.

"Don't you think that you two are moving *too* fast?" Charlie says.

"No, I do not."

"Charlie, the love of our best friend's life is back in her life and *she's* happy," Joc reminds her.

"I honestly think she'll be happier with someone that won't leave her crying in her office," Charlie retorts.

"What?" Kitty asks.

"It was a misunderstanding," I say to Kitty. "No relationship is perfect, Charlie. We all have difficulties. And Joc's right. I'm happy, so be happy for me."

"You know I love you, right?" Charlie asks.

"Of course I do, and I love you, too. But you should be okay with me having an actual love life."

"Maybe I'm just selfish but~~~"

"You are selfish, Charlie," Joc and Kitty snap.

"Whatever. But I don't see why you need more than just the love that we have for each other."

"Charlie, how can you say that when you have a wonderful husband and a beautiful child?" Kitty asks her big sister.

"Yes, I have them, but I don't need them. You know I had Amber for Devon, and that's the only child he's getting from me. The love I *need* is right here in this room."

"Do you know how incredibly ludicrous you sound right now, Charlie? Some people would give up their right leg to have what you have," I respond.

"Don't get me wrong, Devon is a good man and good company to have when he isn't working. But I don't need him.

"I'm truly lost for words," Joc says.

"We all are," I say.

"Well, I'm heading back to work," Kitty says as she gathers up her carry out bag with an embarrassed and disgusted look on her face.

"Good idea," Joc says, as he does the same.

"What?" Charlie asks.

"Let's all just get back to work," I say, irritated.

"When are you leaving for Detroit?" Charlie asks while gathering her things.

"Friday afternoon," I say without looking at her.

"Well, what about things here Friday afternoon?"

"Joc will take care of my schedule and y'all can manage without me for a few hours."

"Oh." Charlie lingers at my desk. I see I must put my boss pants on with her right now. "Is there something you need, Charlie?"

"No."

"Good." With that, Charlie gets the hint and leaves my office. My computer pings. I have an instant message from Joc.

> Joc: CAN YOU BELIEVE HER?!?!?
> Me: Yes. But should we tell Devon? He is our friend, too.
> Joc: How do we even tell him that his wife doesn't give a damn about him or their marriage? That neither he nor Amber play a significant role in her life?
> Me: That's a good question.
> Joc: He probably already suspects it.
> Me: True.

I cannot think about this right now. I pick up the plans for the new third floor from the contractor and call him.

* * *

"Are you ready?" Jaylen asks when he walks into my office.

"Yup," I answer. This week has flown by. I hope the weekend drags out a bit. "Let me grab my things."

"You are *not* bringing work with you."

"I mean my bags for this weekend." I point to the corner where a suitcase, a duffle bag, and a weekend bag sit.

"You need all of that for a three-day trip an hour away?"

"Yes, Daddy. I do."

"I'm packing for our honeymoon," he states.

"I don't see a ring on my finger," I say with my hand out, "so I think honeymoon packing is far off."

"I have something for that smart mouth of yours," Jaylen says while grabbing his belt.

"You wouldn't have to worry about my smart mouth if something was in it," I smirk while grabbing his crotch as I walk by him.

"Get in the car," he growls and smacks my ass. He grabs my bags and is right behind me as I go down the stairs.

"Devon." I greet him when I see him standing at the front desk. "Does Charlie know you're here?"

"I'm actually here to catch Jaylen," he responds while hugging me. "Have fun on your trip. I'm so happy for you."

"Umm. Thank you… and okay." I wonder if someone informed him about the conversation with Charlie during lunch the other day.

"Kitty told me everything," he says, reading my mind. "Let's just say the talk with my wife did not go so well that night."

"Gotcha. Sorry."

"Don't worry about it." Devon removes a small bubble mailer from the inside of his suit jacket and hands it to Jaylen. "Glad I caught you," he says to my love.

"I wasn't getting on the road without it," Jaylen says. He notices me watching them inquisitively. "Let's go," he says to me and opens the door.

"Illegally parked again, I see," nodding towards his vehicle.

"Sue me."

Jaylen lets me in the car and puts the bags into the back of his SUV. He lingers back there for a bit. When he gets in the car, I notice he no longer has the package Devon gave him.

"What was that?" I ask Jaylen once he starts the car.

"A necessary part of this weekend."

"What does that mean?"

"It means you do not get to know right now," he says to me with a smile.

"I don't like surprises."

"You'll love this one."

"You seem pretty sure of yourself," I state.

"Because I am. This will be one of the best weekends of our lives."

"You have mighty high expectations."

"Rightly, so. But I'm still not telling you."

I still don't like surprises.

We pull up to a Detroit casino and hotel a bit later. The valet attendant opens my door and Jaylen gathers our bags. I follow my love into the well-lit foyer. I can hear the sounds of the slot machines at the front desk.

"How can I help you?" the young woman at the front desk says seductively to Jaylen. Her name tag says her name is Jonea.

"Checking in. Last name Williams."

"I need to see your I.D." She looks him up and down and bites her bottom lip before typing on the keyboard. Either he doesn't notice, or he is overlooking her, but she needs to stop. *He's mine.*

"May I call you Jaylen?" she asks.

"Mr. Williams," I firmly insist. This is the one time I wish I had a ring on my finger just to wave it in her face. She makes eye contact with me for the first time and there's fire spitting out of my eyes. She looks back at me like she doesn't care.

"Can you just give me the keys and let me know what room Mrs. Williams and I will stay in," Jaylen says to defuse the situation.

Mrs. Williams? I know he is trying to prevent a scene from happening, so I'm just going to go with it.

"Oh, I didn't see a ring," she responds.

"But you saw me," I snap. "That combined with the fact that you are at work and should provide quality customer service should have been enough reason for you to keep some tact about yourself."

"Did you just indirectly say that I'm tactless?"

"Be happy that I didn't call you a slut. See, it's little things like you~~~"

"The keys. Now. Please," Jaylen interrupts.

"Is there a problem?" a stout man whose name tag says Bill—Manager on it.

"Yes," I answer. "This thing you have at the front desk was more concerned with flirting with my husband than actually providing customer service."

"Like I said before, I didn't see a ring on his finger, so I didn't think y'all were married," she tries to explain.

She said that. In front of her boss. All with her chest.

The desk phone rings.

"Jonea, get the phone. I will take care of our guests," Bill says to her. Turning his focus to us, "I'm so sorry about that. Let's see here. I see you are staying in our deluxe suite for the weekend. I'm upgrading you to our premium one-bedroom suite as well as comping you for dinner and champagne from any of our restaurants tonight."

"That's unnecessary," Jaylen says.

"I insist. I do not condone that kind of treatment of my guests."

"Thank you," I say.

"Here are your room keys. Take the elevator to the 22nd floor, and your suite will be on the left."

"You couldn't just ignore her?" Jaylen asks me as we walk to the elevator.

"Would you have ignored it if it was a guy blatantly flirting with me while you were by my side?" He doesn't respond. We both know the answer to that question is no.

"I need you to focus on the positive during this getaway," he says to me once we are on the elevator.

I know what he is referencing. It's easier said than done, but I can at least make an effort. "I'll try." We stand on opposite sides of the elevator, staring at each other.

"That was kinda cute," he says with a small smile.

"What? Me claiming you?"

"Yeah. I've never seen you jealous before."

"I'm never jealous," I state as a matter of fact. "However, when it comes to you, I'm territorial, possessive, even."

"Territorial, huh?" He seems to chew on the thought for a bit. "Still, I've never seen that side of you before."

"We really didn't go out before." His smile disappears. There goes my focusing on the positive already. Let's try again. "You referred to me as your wife."

"I did."

"Is that something you still want?" The elevator door opens to our floor before Jaylen can answer.

"Come on," he says.

"Take that as a no," I whisper to myself as I follow him to the suite. He opens the door and turns to look at me.

"Stop it."

Jaylen holds the door open for me to walk through. The dark brown carpet is warm and inviting. A short hallway opens to a large living area with floor to ceiling windows that peers out to Downtown Detroit. I walk past the pale green sofa set and dark orange accent chairs to the windows to take in the view.

After a few minutes, I feel Jaylen's arms snaking around my waist. He softly kisses my shoulder. "I love you," he whispers before kissing my shoulder again.

"I love you, too. So now that we're here, can I get the surprise?"

"Tomorrow evening."

"Jaylen."

"Be patient. This surprise will be worth it."

I blow out a huff of hot air. "Why do you keep putting it off?"

"You aren't doing a good job of being positive."

I turn in his arms to face him. "Can I start over?"

"Of course." He kisses me like he never wants to stop kissing me.

"Do you want to change before dinner and the concert?" I ask when I pull away for air.

"Yes. Go. We don't have much time." He kisses me again before releasing me.

The dark brown carpet and floor to ceiling windows continue into the bedroom. The king-sized bed has pillows in different shades of blue, green, and orange. A small sitting area by the windows has the same burnt orange accent chairs as in the living room. As I get closer to the bed, I notice Jaylen has already laid out an outfit for me from my suitcase. I smile to myself as the gray romper is exactly what I was going to pull out. I grab my small duffle bag and head to the bathroom for a quick shower.

* * *

"Jesus Christ," I say in frustration after we get into our ride share car.

"What is it?"

"Charlie keeps texting me."

"What does she want?"

"Nothing really. She keeps asking me if I'm okay and if I'm sure that I want to be away for the entire weekend. I know she doesn't approve of our relationship, but this is crazy. I don't need her checking on me every ten minutes."

Me: Unless it's an emergency, please stop texting me. I'm trying to enjoy my weekend. You're getting in the way of that.

"Hopefully that puts a stop to that," I say as I give Jaylen back my phone.

"How did you like the show?"

"I enjoyed myself. I've never seen some of them live before. Thank you."

"You don't have to thank me for making you smile," he says just before planting a soft kiss on my hand. I move closer to him and kiss his lips. He fists one of his hands through my hair, returning my kiss, then pulling my head back so that he can kiss my jawline and neck.

"Aaah," I whimper.

"I love you so much," he whispers.

"Daddy," I moan. We continue kissing each other like two horny teenagers until the driver interrupts us.

"Umm, we are here," the man says.

"Oh," I say, slightly embarrassed. The driver avoids making eye contact in the rearview mirror. Jaylen and I get out of the car. "Be sure to give him a tip."

"I'm going to give you more than the tip once we get upstairs."

Giggling, I take his hand as we head to the room.

* * *

"I'm sorry, but I'm tapping out," I pant.

"What?" Jaylen responds while on top of me.

"Four times before bed last night, you woke me a couple of hours later for another round, and twice already this morning. There is a such thing as pussy abuse, you know."

"Are you serious?" he jokingly asks.

"Are *you* serious? What's gotten into you?"

"You are serious." He drops his body onto mine in disappointment.

"Yes, Jaylen. My walls hurt. I need at least an eight-hour break."

"A whole workday?"

"Can you order breakfast while I shower again? Please?"

"Sure," he says reluctantly as he climbs from on top of me. I give him a quick kiss to soothe his bruised ego and head to the shower.

"What do you want to eat?"

"Everything," I yell back.

The warm water from the shower feels so good. In contrast to the dark brown carpet in the living and bedroom areas, the stone tile shower wall is light brown and continues on the bathroom floor. The standalone shower is quite spacious, but the single shower head makes me miss Jaylen's multiple shower heads.

"Food should be here in 30 minutes."

"Thank you. So, what are we doing today?"

"Well, I was planning on making love to you until lunch, but since you tapped out on me, we have time I didn't plan for."

"You can always give me your surprise now." *I want to know what it is already!*

"Don't count on it," he says with a grin.

"After lunch?"

"Check out a couple of downtown parks, go to the art museum, then the riverboat for dinner."

"So why not play a few slot machines until lunch?" I hear him turn the sink faucet on.

"I don't play slots. We can play a few rounds of blackjack."

"I don't know how to play any of the card games."

"Great time for you to learn," he says while brushing his teeth.

Ugh. I roll by eyes. "Stop it, Alise."

I start to say I didn't do anything, but there's no point. He knows me too well. I step out of the shower with a plan in mind. "I can spend my money on the slots," I say as I wrap a towel around my body.

"You aren't spending any of your money during this getaway."

"Well, if you give me $20 to play slots, you'll have my undivided attention while teaching me blackjack, and I'll be the perfect arm candy at the table."

"You set me up for that," he says with a raised eyebrow.

"I will not agree nor disagree with your accusation," I smirk back at him.

"Fine."

"Thank you. And yes, I totally set you up for that."

Jaylen goes to reach for me, but I dart out of the bathroom before he can. "I'll get you later," he yells from the bathroom.

"You're already getting me with this freaking surprise that you won't just reveal!"

"Whatever." I hear him turn the shower on.

I open one of my bags and start putting on coconut oil. It's now when I realize how sore my entire body is. As I put on a pair of denim shorts, Jaylen's suitcase catches my eyes from across the room. I wonder if the package Devon gave him is still in it. I've never been the snooping girlfriend, but I really hate surprises.

I stare at it for a few moments, weighing the pros and cons. The pro is I won't have whatever this surprise is looming over me. The con is that if I get caught, Jaylen will probably be furious. Not to mention I'll break his trust, and I might ruin this trip that Jaylen put together. As much as I do not want to, I choose to not go through his things. It isn't worth it.

I pull on a blue tank top and dab on some lavender oil. His suitcase keeps catching my eye. I walk towards it and stop midway.

"Don't," I say to myself. I decide to find some crap show to watch in the living room to keep myself from making a terrible choice.

I grab my phone and head to the living room. There isn't much to watch, so I turn the volume down and start going through my phone. I see a text from Joc.

> Joc: I hope you are enjoying yourself. Just wanted to say I love you. Do not respond until you are back home.

I respond to a couple of emails and check the insights of some of the social media marketing campaigns that Kitty initiated. I start to send her a text on a job well done, but my phone suddenly leaves my hands.

"I told you no working," Jaylen says as he puts my phone in the back pocket of his jeans.

"I was sending a text message to Kitty. Thank you."

"Did it have something to do with work?"

"It was just a 'good job' text."

"About something work-related."

"Timeless Elegance is my baby. I can't just turn that off." Jaylen leans down, placing his hands on the armrests of the chair.

"I get that, but you need to learn how to turn it off. Allow yourself a break from business to enjoy life."

"I enjoy life."

"When's the last time you took a vacation?"

I sit there and look at him. The last time I went on vacation was the last family trip before my parents divorced. After they died, I focused on making my career dreams a reality. Well, that and Jaylen.

There's a knock on the door. A middle-aged Hispanic man pushes the food cart in. He removes the food covers and places the trays, plates, flatware, coffee, and a pitcher of orange juice on the coffee table. Jaylen tips him and, by the smile on the man's face, it's generous. The server leaves quietly.

I sit cross-legged on the floor and dig in. Jaylen sits on the opposite side of the couch.

"I'm going to make sure you slow down so you can enjoy the life you've worked so hard to have." I look at my love. "Eat up, so we can go gamble."

* * *

"Are you still sulking because you lost on the tables while I won a few thousand on the slots?" I ask Jaylen as we take a ride share service to the riverboat dock.

"I don't sulk."

"Mm-hmm. What do you call it then?"

"I was deep in thought." A phone in his pocket vibrates, but he doesn't look at it.

"About what?"

"Your surprise."

"Oh. I had forgotten about that. Shouldn't I have it by now?" The phone vibrates again.

"Soon," he says and kisses my temple.

"Aren't you going to get that? It could be the kids." Jaylen pulls the phones out of his pocket.

"It's your phone." He passes it to me. I have a missed call from my alarm company and Joc. Before I can call either back, the alarm company is calling again.

"Hello?"

"I'm calling for Alise Rogers," the female service agent states.

"This is Alise."

"There seems to have been a break in at your business. Should there be anyone there right now?"

"What? No, we are closed on Saturday evenings. The store should have locked up about three hours ago."

"What is it?" Jaylen whispers to me. I put my finger up for him to give me a moment.

"Okay. We have notified the police. Are you in the area?" the agent asks me.

"No, but I can be in the next hour or so. What happened?"

"It looks like an entry was made through a window. The police will have more facts for you once you've made contact."

My phone beeps. Joc is calling me again. "Thank you." I end that call and answer Joc's. "Are you there?"

"I'm pulling up now."

"I'm on my way back," I tell Joc and hang up my phone. "Driver, take us back to the hotel." I look at Jaylen. "Someone broke into Timeless Elegance."

"What?"

Porsha Deun

CHAPTER X

A middle-aged Black officer with a dark bronze complexion is giving me a rundown of what happened while we stand in the middle of my store. "According to your assistant, nothing seems to be missing. Someone threw these two garden bricks through the windows facing Saginaw Street."

"Have you checked the surveillance video for any leads?" I ask him.

"Based on the last imaged on them, someone disconnected the cameras outside yesterday evening."

"What? Are you saying this was planned?"

"I would not call it a coincidence," he states.

"Was it done remotely?"

"Someone smashed them against the building."

"How can that happen? They are over seven feet up the side of the building."

"Sledgehammer swung above the head, perhaps."

"What about the cameras on the surrounding buildings?"

"There aren't any cameras on this building," he says, pointing to the empty two-story building across Second Street, "and we'll check to see if any cameras in the area caught anything. But given their position, they probably won't show the act itself, though we may get a car and license plate."

"I can't believe this." I rub my head and look for Jaylen. He's near the front door having a deep conversation with Joc. Both of them look at me with concern. They either know or suspect something that I do not. They turn back to each other, and I feel that neither of them wants to be the one to tell me what's on their mind.

"Do you have any idea who would want to harm you or your business?"

What are they talking about? I don't hear the officer. I'm too focused on the two main men in my life.

"Ms. Rogers."

"Yes."

"Do you have any clues on who would want to harm you or your business?"

"Harm me?"

"This could've been done as an act of retaliation." I give him an incredulous look. "Have you received any threats?" he continues to probe.

"No. None." Then my mind goes to Calondra. Jaylen said she threatened me before. *Did she find out we were away? Why attack my business and not Jaylen's? She can't possibly be this stupid to do something that will cause her to lose her kids, is she?*

"If you think of anything else, please call this number," he says as he passes me a business card.

"Thank you," I tell him, then I make a beeline right to my guys. "You think Calondra had something to do with this?" I ask Jaylen.

"It briefly crossed my mind, but the kids said she's been with them all day. It wasn't her."

"Who else would do this?" I ask no one in particular. Jaylen and Joc give each other a look that I can't help but notice. "What?"

"I'm going to check if it's okay for me to clean this mess up," Joc excuses himself.

"Joc," I call after him. Instead of coming back, he puts his hands up near his head to say he's out of it. I turn my attention to Jaylen. "Are you going to tell me?"

"You aren't going to want to hear this," he states.

"Jaylen." We stare at each other for a few moments. "What is it?"

"Have you talked to Charlie?"

"Not yet. I need to call her, so she isn't surprised when she sees the windows boarded up Monday morning."

Jaylen closes his eyes. He looks like his next words will cause some pain. "Alise."

"What?" He opens his eyes. Now I get where he is going. "You can't possibly think Charlie had something to do with this?"

"You told her not to contact you this weekend until you got back home, unless there was an emergency. This was an emergency and now you're back home."

"Charlie wouldn't do this. She loves me. She would not hurt me this way."

"Yes, Charlie loves you," Jaylen agrees. "She also doesn't want you with me. Joc would tell you the same."

"That's what you two have been over here talking about? That my childhood friend intentionally sabotaged our weekend together by attacking my business? No!" I refuse to believe any of this. What he is saying is crazy. Charlie's my best friend.

"Alise, at least consider~~~"

"There's nothing to consider," I interrupt him. "Charlie didn't do this. It's more likely that Calondra paid someone to do this."

"How would Calondra have found out? All I told the kids was that I was going to be away this weekend and to reach me on my cell if they needed me. I never told them where I was going or with whom."

I chew over Jaylen's words. As much as I would like to point the finger at his first wife for this, it most likely wasn't her.

"Charlie. Did. Not. Do. This," I whisper to him.

"Ms. Rogers," the officer says from behind me.

"Yes?"

"We are heading out now. Someone will be in touch with any updates."

"Thank you," I say. "Please don't hesitate to contact me if you have any questions." The officers leave and Joc reappears with a broom and dustpan.

"This was not Charlie," I say to both of them. I go upstairs to check my office, even though I know Joc already did.

"I told you," I overhear Joc say to Jaylen as I head up the stairs.

* * *

"How much do I owe you for the boards to cover up the windows?" These are the first words I have spoken to Jaylen since he implied that my best friend attacked my business. That was hours ago, and we are now at my place.

"Don't worry about it," Jaylen replies from the chaise.

"How much do I owe you?" I snap at him as I remove my jewelry.

"I'm not trying to fight with you."

"Neither do I, so tell me how much I owe you. The costs of boarding up the windows is a business expense and should be accounted for properly. There's no reason for you to cover it."

"This has nothing to do with accounting for a business expense. You're mad at me for telling you Charlie is trying to sabotage us."

"Do you hear yourself? Do you know what you sound like, blaming the rocky ground our relationship has been on since you shot my club up on someone else?"

"And we are back at that."

"Yes, that. That's what this is really about. Did you really think that a weekend in Detroit would erase that?" I open a drawer and pull out a long satin nightgown.

"If the weekend would have played out as planned, yes, it would have." I turn my head and look at him like he's crazy.

"You can't be serious?" He stares at me. "Oh my god, you are! What could have possibly happened in Detroit that would have changed the fact that I may be pregnant with a child you do not want?" I start removing the gold spaghetti strap dress I put on for the riverboat. The only thing I changed before rushing back to Flint was from stilettos to flats.

"I will not have this discussion while you're worked up like this."

"So, nothing," I snap. Jaylen quickly gets up from the chaise, covers the distance between us in two steps and turns me around to face him, putting his fist in my hair to make sure I look at nothing but him.

"You do not know what you are fucking talking about," he says in a quiet but stern voice with his face close to mine. "Everything was going to change."

"But you aren't willing to tell me how."

"Not when you aren't willing to listen." I look at him like he is full of shit.

"Let me go."

"No."

"Let me go," I repeat as I try to pull away from him. Jaylen only tightens his grip on me and pulls me in for a kiss. I try to fight him off me.

"No."

"Stop fighting me, Alise." He keeps trying to kiss me.

"No! You can't fuck your way out of this, Jaylen." He lets me go, shocked at my words.

"That's not what I'm trying to do," he yells.

"You need to leave."

"Alise!"

"Leave, Jaylen," I state firmly.

"Fuck it. I'm going." He grabs his suit jacket up from the chaise and storms past me. He stops once he gets to my bedroom door. "One of these days, you are going to see that Charlie is not the friend you think she is. She doesn't want to share you with anyone that you could love or need more than her. And you are going to realize how much I love your crazy ass."

"Oh, now I'm fucking crazy!" I yell.

"In this moment, completely." With that, he walks out of my room and then out of my apartment.

* * *

I've looked at my phone more than one hundred times today. Jaylen has not contacted me since he walked out of my apartment last night. I've not reached out to him either. I cannot believe that he would suspect Charlie of vandalizing Timeless Elegance.

Speaking of Charlie, she should be here any‑‑‑

"Hey, Alise," Charlie greets as she enters my apartment.

"Hey."

She makes her way into the living room. Looking relaxed in ripped denim capris and a fitted plain white scoop neck tee, she flutters in with much more energy than I have at the moment. "Are you okay?" she asks as she sits next to me. "You don't look like you've slept."

"I'm okay and no, I didn't sleep much last night. I'm frustrated and my mind has been racing trying to think of who could have vandalized my business."

"The police are on it, right?"

"Yes, but that doesn't exactly make me feel any safer. Not saying the police cannot do their job, I'm sure they will find the person. I'll be uneasy until I know who and why."

"It was probably some kids or an addict. No need to fret. How was your getaway?"

"It was going well until we got back. We had a fight last night."

"What about?"

I'm not ready to tell anyone that I may be pregnant. I definitely don't want to tell Charlie that Jaylen was pointing his finger at her. "I don't want to talk about it."

"That bad?"

"Yeah."

"Well, let's get you some wine so you can relax and laugh."

"No wine for me. It will just make my nerves worse." This is true but also because my period still hasn't shown up.

"Let me take care of you," she says as she sits and pats the top of her thighs.

I lay my head in her lap and she begins to gently massage my scalp. This is the most relaxed I've felt since I got the phone call yesterday. I release a sigh of content.

"I love you," Charlie says softly.

"I love you, too," I smile.

"I'll always be here for you and take care of you."

"I know. That is why you're my best friend."

"You're my longest love."

"That's not true. You loved your parents and sister before you even knew me."

"Family doesn't count. And because they don't, that makes you my longest and truest love," Charlie corrects.

"I haven't heard you say that since you left for college and Devon makes part of that statement not true," I whisper as I start to drift off to sleep.

"I shouldn't have stopped telling you that. Devon counts as family, by the way."

"Why are you being colder to him than usual?"

"Someone is threatening my position," she says coolly.

"Devon wouldn't cheat on you."

"That's not what I'm worried about," are the last words I hear her say.

* * *

I wake up to the smell of food. I sit up on the couch and turn to see Charlie in the kitchen.

"Please, tell me that is your shrimp spaghetti," I say.

"Just finished it. I was just about to wake you." I stretch and walk to the stove. Charlie lifts the top of the pot, puts some on a fork, and blows it before putting it up to my lips.

"Mmmmm. I'm glad one of us knows how to cook. I would have ordered takeout today if it wasn't for you." I grab two plates out of the cabinet, and she fills them with spaghetti.

"When was the last time you had a home cooked meal?" Charlie asks.

"Jaylen made a meal for me last week." I place the plates down on the bar and go back to the fridge for some bottled water.

"He cooks!" she says with fake shock.

"Yes, he cooks. Don't sound like the thought of him cooking is so absurd." She turns and looks at me like she is gearing up to prove a point.

"I don't want to talk about him," Charlie states, apparently changing her mind.

"Good, because I don't want to fight with you. How's my goddaughter?" We both have a seat and start digging in.

"She's good. I'm looking at some early preschool programs to get her into starting this fall. She can officially tie her own shoes and has the nerve to get mad if you try to help her."

"Amber's always been a determined and independent child."

"True."

"It doesn't seem like she's three and ready for preschool yet. She's growing up fast."

"Mm-hmm."

"This is superb," I say, finishing a mouthful. "So, what is going on with you and Devon?"

"We've been fighting a lot lately. It seems as if what's important to me is not important to him."

"So much that you think he may cheat on you?"

"No. Devon is loyal to a fault," she says almost annoyingly.

"Well, what was that line about 'someone taking your place'?"

"Not in Devon's life."

I put my fork down and look at her. "Charlie, I'm confused."

"I was referring to you."

"What?"

"I don't want to be replaced in your life." Though I can tell she is sincere, I can't help but wonder what nonsense brought this on.

"Oh, my god! Jaylen is not replacing you. He's an addition to my life, and a welcomed one at that! I know you have gotten used to not having to share me in a sense with anyone other than Joc, but my romantic love life and my family life with you are not the same. How are you not comprehending that?"

Charlie pauses for a few moments before she responds. "Is that all I am? Family?" I push my plate away. This is not how today was supposed to go.

"What. Do. You. Want. From. Me?" I ask.

"I want my Alise back."

"What is that supposed to mean?"

"*My* Alise never cut me off for days because of who she was around."

"First of all, it had nothing to do with the fact that Jaylen was around. It was because you were trying to make my weekend with him miserable. Second, you weren't talking about anything."

"I didn't want you to be miserable."

"You didn't want me to enjoy my time with Jaylen, either."

"He is going to hurt you! He can't love you like you deserve to be loved. Why can't you see that?"

"Why can't you see you don't know him enough to make any of those assumptions? Also, why can't you see that I'm happy and be happy for me?"

"I think you are lying to yourself. I know my Alise. I see it differently."

"I'M NOT YOUR ALISE!" I get up and walk around to the other side of the island because I feel that a little distance would be good right now. "And you are choosing to see only what you want to see." Charlie looks at me with her eyes wide, shocked at me yelling at her. She realizes I'm serious and changes her tone.

"Alise, my concern is~~~"

"Did you throw the bricks through the windows to get me back home?" I interrupt. It pains me to ask her this, but maybe Joc and Jaylen were on to something.

"What? Do you think I would do that to you?"

"I didn't, but right now, I don't know. I didn't want to believe my best friend would be so unsupportive of me finding happiness with someone."

"I can't believe you would ask me if I did such a thing!"

"You still aren't answering the question."

"I won't answer it. That's absurd." We have another stare down. "Maybe I should go," she relents.

"Maybe you should." She picks up her plate to put it away. "Leave it. Just go."

"Okay." She walks across the room, gathers her purse and keys, and leaves out of the door without another word. I lay my head on the counter and try to figure out what is going on this weekend. First the vandalism, then the fight with Jaylen, and now the fight with Charlie.

"Was there a full moon last night or something?" I ask out loud to myself. Grabbing the plates, I dump Charlie's in the trash and change my mind as I start to dump my plate. I will not let the crazy drama stop my appetite. I take it to the couch and turn the television on to watch some crap show.

CHAPTER XI

I'm standing outside of my business with a contractor to fix my windows. "If I order the windows today, the replacements will be in by Thursday and can be installed on Friday or Saturday," the slender white man near my age tells me. He is handsome but hasn't figured out that he's too old to still be rocking the Justin Bieber swoop cut. I mean, Bieber's not even rocking that cut anymore.

"Order them today. I need the new windows in as soon as possible, preferably no later than Friday."

"I will get right on it," he says with his hand out. I shake it and he's on his way.

"Do you have a minute?" Charlie says to me as I walk back inside Timeless Elegance.

"Make it quick." I don't bother to break my stride in case this talk is not work-related.

"It's about yesterday," she says, trying to catch up with me. I stop once I get to the stairs and turn to her.

"I'm not ready to have that conversation yet. Do you have anything work related for me?"

"Oh. Um... no."

"Okay." I turn again and head up the stairs.

"Ms. Rogers," Kitty calls before I get to my office. I walk over to her cubicle.

"Kitty, please call me Alise. I know why you do it, but it just feels weird coming from someone I grew up with."

"Okay, Alise. I want to verify that these are the changes you wanted to be made to the ad for the year-end sale." She turns one of her two monitors towards me and I take a seat in her ivory round chairs.

"I like the lines here but maybe change the color. It clashes with the skin tones of the models. I will say I love that you used video from our show last year. I want to make sure we're getting our own images from now on."

"Good. I was going to ask you about that. This way, we don't have to get the rights to videos and photos from the show's photographers."

"Exactly. This font is too boxy. It needs to be something more flowing and with curves like a woman's body." Kitty clicks away, making the changes.

"Okay. What do you think now?" She plays the commercial again.

"That is great. Place the ad for it to run in December and January."

"Will do. Thanks." I walk out of her office and stop once I see Jaylen standing by my office door. Shocked would be an understatement of how I feel seeing him here, since I haven't heard from him since our fight two days ago. I walk into my office. He follows, closing the door behind him.

"You're avoiding me now?"

"Avoiding you is not possible since you haven't contacted me." I take a seat at my desk and pick up some files to pretend as if I'm not bothered by his lack of effort.

"I've been calling and texting you since yesterday afternoon." I picked up my cellphone and pass it to him.

"You must be calling the wrong number because I have received nothing from you."

"Don't try to play me like that," he says as he goes to my call log and then messages. "I know your number. It's saved in my phone."

"Well…"

"Alise, stop with the attitude."

"We fought, and you gave me the silent treatment for two days. How do you expect for me to be towards you?" I ask looking squarely at him.

"I didn't give you the silent treatment. You blocked me." He puts my phone in my face, showing his name and number on my block list.

"I don't even know how to block people on my phone."

"So, how do you explain this?"

"I wouldn't block you. You know me better than that. Did I…" my mind wonders off to the only reason that makes sense. "You've got to be fucking joking me." I toss the papers on my desk and blow out air.

"What?"

"Charlie was at my place yesterday. I fell asleep. I don't keep a pass lock on my phone. She must have done it."

"You were alone with her after what happened Saturday?"

"Jaylen, she would not physically hurt me. I asked her about the windows and she said it was crazy for me to think she would do that."

"You asked her?" he asks.

"We got into it over you and our relationship, so I asked her." I pick up my desk phone and call down to the storefront.

"You need something, Alise," Charlie answers.

"Get up here. Now." I slam the phone down and look at Jaylen. "This shit stops now."

I can hear her coming up the stairs. She pauses when she sees Jaylen and then goes to sit down.

"Don't get comfortable," I tell her.

"Oh. Okay." She fakes poise and remains standing behind the chair. "What's going on?"

"Did you speak to Jaylen when he came into the store?"

"I didn't notice him come in."

"Well, you noticed him when you came into my office." She turns to Jaylen with a fake smile plastered on her face.

"Hi."

"Wow. Hi," he responds. I inhale deeply to calm myself before I say my next words.

"You blocked Jaylen on my phone yesterday." She changes to her serious face.

"I did," she answers.

"What gave you the fucking right to block *anyone* on *my* phone?"

"I can't give you an answer without continuing the fight we had yesterday, but you know how I feel about your… relationship."

"Charlie, I'm trying to understand what I did to make you hate me so much?" Jaylen asks.

"You aren't worthy of her and I don't understand why she submits herself to you the way she does when she is stronger than that."

"Who the hell are you to determine~~~"

"Jaylen," I say to stop him. I won't get anywhere if the two of them argue. "Charlie, you have crossed the line. You, being my friend, doesn't give you the right to meddle in my love life, let alone sabotage it. You, being my friend, does not mean I belong to you."

"Alise!"

"No, Charlie," I interrupt as she starts before she can give some bullshit excuse. "My choice to submit to him needs no justifying to anyone, but since you seem to have such a hard time, here it is. I choose to let him take the lead in our relationship. I choose to submit to him because I trust him. More importantly, I choose to submit to him because I find freedom in it. I'm my most true self in my submission, flying higher than any accolade could give me and stand stronger than ever when I submit to him. I serve him because I find it beautiful. Even in my servitude, nothing happens in this relationship without me wanting it so. When I do not submit to him, I'm only fighting with myself, so I choose not to fight with myself. And I will not fight with you over it."

"That sound ridiculous," she responds.

"No, you have been beyond ridiculous since Jaylen's been back in my life. It's not only affecting our friendship but your marriage, too. I've tried to keep quiet about your feelings towards Devon and Amber, but you have been outright wrong to them. Do you know how ridiculous that is? To let the matter of who I'm dating cause so much friction not only between us but also in your marriage?"

"Your happiness and well-being are that important to me."

"As I told you last night, I'm happy. I love him. I want to be with him for the rest of my life. The fact that you aren't listening to me tells me you are just dead set on being… crazy," I say exasperatedly.

"I'm not the one being crazy."

"Did you set the alarm off to get Alise away from me?" Jaylen asks plainly. Not only does Charlie not respond, but she also doesn't even look his way.

"Charlie," I say.

"I gave you my answer on that last night," she tells me.

"It wasn't much of an answer actually," I inform her.

"Devon told you what I was planning to do, didn't he?" Jaylen asks her.

"Devon?" I ask him. Then I remember Devon showing up to give Jaylen a package just before we left for Detroit.

"I will not let that happen," Charlie responds. Suddenly, I feel out of the loop of the conversation that the three of us are having.

"What am I missing?" I ask both of them. "And Charlie, what does that mean? Are you admitting it was you who smashed the windows?"

"I'm not admitting to anything."

"What am I missing?" I ask again.

"We'll talk about that later," Jaylen says to me. "You aren't going to get in the way of it," he tells Charlie.

"Is that a threat?"

"Take it how you want it," he responds.

"Stop," I yell. "I can't have you two fighting each other."

"Are you pregnant?" Charlie asks after a few silent moments. My heart drops to the earth's core at a blazing speed.

"Why would you ask me that?" I notice Jaylen physically tense out of the corner of my eye, but I refuse to look his way.

"I haven't seen you drink wine since he's been back around. So, either you're already pregnant or he ordered you not to drink anymore. I honestly don't know which one would be more tragic."

I slam my hands on the top of my desk. "Stop trying to change the subject, Charlie. You went behind my back to keep the man I love out of my life. Those aren't the actions of a friend." *That should get us back on topic.*

"Are you saying you don't want to be friends anymore?" she asks in a panicked tone.

"I'm saying we need some distance until you figure out how to be my friend while Jaylen and I are together. We'll remain cordial at work 'til said time comes."

"Cordial?" Charlie asks, like she's confused about the meaning.

"Get back to work," I state. I'm over this conversation and her. She stands there and looks at me in disbelief for a few moments before storming out of my office. I want to cry, but I don't because I know a fight with Jaylen is coming. I take some deep breaths to rein my emotions in.

The silence is unbearable, but I don't dare break it. I wouldn't know what to say anyhow.

"Why does your best friend think you're pregnant?" He finally says something, but I can't respond. Words have escaped me while I feel his eyes burning into me. "Alise!"

His yell makes me jump. My breathing becomes heavy as I try to come up with something to tell him. I know I should have told him a week ago. I know I'm pregnant—pregnant with a child the man I love does not want.

"Start talking, Alise," he says with a step forward.

I sigh heavily. "My period hasn't shown up and I'm certain it won't." I still don't look at him. I know he's going to leave me, and I don't want the last memory of his eyes on me to be anything but loving.

"How late are you?"

"Almost a week."

"So, you could have told me before or during our trip to Detroit?"

It wasn't a question, nevertheless, I nod my reply. It's all I can muster while everything is about to go to hell. "Why didn't you tell me?"

"You know exactly why I---"

"WHY DIDN'T YOU TELL ME!"

"I wanted more time with you before you left me."

"So, you lied to me, thinking it would keep me around." This gets me to look at him.

"I never lied to you."

"A lie of omission is still a lie, Alise." My guilt lays heavy in the air, nearly sucking out all the oxygen. "How long were you going to keep this from me?" His voice strains with anger.

"I was going to tell you. I just couldn't figure out how."

"You could have just said it."

"Don't you dare make it sound so simple after you made all those grand statements about wanting to be with me to only turn around and threaten to leave me at the off chance that I may be pregnant." I know I don't have a right to be angry right now, but I am. *How dare he?*

"It's not an off chance anymore and you kept that from me. You had every opportunity to tell me, and you didn't."

"You knew there was a chance and didn't ask either." It comes out of my mouth before I realize it.

"You're making this my fault?"

"Jaylen…" I close my eyes to search my mind for the right words to say. Only there aren't any. I'm wrong no matter how I may try to spin it. "I should have told you."

"Something that important, yes, you should've."

"I'm sorry," I yell, with my arms stretched in surrender. "You're right and I'm sorry."

"You said that you'd never intentionally hurt me."

"I didn't get pregnant by myself, Jaylen."

"I'm talking about you lying to me." His eyes have gone from anger to pain and disappointment. It's like a knife in my heart.

I try to close the distance between us, but he grabs my shoulders, keeping me at arm's length. "I was going to…" he stops and drops his head like the words are too painful to say.

"Jaylen, please. I didn't mean to hurt you."

"But you meant to keep this from me." He lets go of my shoulders and walks towards my office door.

"Don't go. Don't leave it like this." I follow him.

"I need some time and space." This stops me. My feet are glued to the floor while I watch the love of my life walk out the office door. I drop to my knees and hope that his love isn't lost to me forever.

Porsha Deun

CHAPTER XII

It's been nearly a full week since we fought. I'll send a text saying, "I'm sorry," "I love you," or "Don't let this end us." He'll reply with, "I know," "I love you too," or "I just need some time," respectively.

At least he still admits he loves me, right? That has to count for something.

I've not let myself cry much over it. It was my fault and crying won't do anything to rectify the situation.

I lay on my couch looking up at the warehouse style ceiling hoping that he calls or stops by. I never thought I'd be the person to fuck up this relationship—I managed to do so in a major way.

Then there's the paranoia from the attack on my business. The police have no leads other than someone in black from head to toe on nearby surveillance cameras heading towards Timeless Elegance just before the alarm triggered and walking away directly after. Whoever it was did a damn good job of concealing their face from the cameras, so they are more than familiar with the downtown area.

Neither I, my business, nor my employees have received any threats. Maybe it was random. It's a possibility, but I can't shake the feeling that they intended it to get my attention. To what, I don't know.

I keep getting pulled from my thoughts by my neighbors, whose names I never remembered, making entirely too much noise moving out. The guy makes loud grunting noises like a muscle bound, steroid jacked lunkhead while moving items down the hallway.

I typically don't go in on Saturdays, but I'm considering going in since I can't seem to focus on the work I brought home with me yesterday. Honestly, my mind is not in the right place for anything work related. But I can't just sit here in my state of mind, and I need to make Jaylen see me. I decide to take him up on his offer and go to his gym.

I pull up to the old movie theater with William's Fitness and Recreational Center in bold black font with red trim above the glass doors. On my way in, I pass two guys as they walk out.

"Hey, baby," one of them says once they are in view of my ass. I can't stand it when a man addresses a woman he doesn't know that way. First, greet me to my face, not my ass. Second, my name is not "hey" and I'm "baby" to only one man.

I don't bother turning around to respond to them and continue towards the front of the counter in the center of the lobby. I can smell the chlorine from the pool.

"How can I help you?" a young man in a red polo shirt with khakis greets me.

"I need a day pass."

"Sure. Can I see your I.D. so I can set you up in our system?" I pull my driver's license out of my wristlet and hand it to him. While he enters my information, I look around. There is a large combined cardio and weight area to the left, basketball court behind the front desk and the pro shop to the immediate right. I didn't notice the smoothie bar by the doors when I first walked in.

"Ms. Rogers, it looks like you already have a gold membership in the system, but we just need your signature to finish your paperwork."

"I've never…" *Jaylen.* He told me he would set me up. "Where do I sign?" He turns the touchscreen monitor around for me. "Is Jaylen Williams in today?" I ask as I scribble on the screen.

"I just got here, but his office lights are off," he says while pointing up and away to a large center office that is strategically placed to oversee the lobby, workout room, and basketball court.

"Wow."

"Yeah, he can see everything but the pool and locker rooms from there, and he has cameras in the pool area. Talk about control freak," he gaffs.

"Where are your locker rooms?" I ask before he says even more. It amazes me how some people will talk so openly to a stranger. He clearly didn't pick up that I know his boss, even though I asked for him by name.

"Just past the basketball court. Here's your locker key and towel. When you're done, you can put the towel in the basket in the locker room and return your key here."

"Thank you." I make my way to the locker room, find my locker, and secure my wristlet inside of it.

As I walk back by the basketball court, a man with dark chocolate skin and a small gap approaches me.

"I don't think I've seen you here before," he says to me.

I keep walking towards the cardio machines, and unfortunately, he follows me. "You make it a point to keep track of every woman you've seen in here," I reply dryly. Hopefully, he gets the point.

"Just the pretty ones," he smiles. He didn't get the point.

"Funny."

"I didn't catch your name."

"I didn't throw it to you." I get on the elliptical, start the playlist on my phone, and untangle my earbuds.

"Why you gotta be like that? I'm just trying to get to know you." He licks his lips like it's suddenly supposed to change my mind about his advances.

"The only thing you need to know about me is that I'm neither interested nor available."

"Your man doesn't have to know. I prefer to not be committed, anyway."

"Did you intentionally dismiss the 'I'm not interested' part?"

"I'm persistent. One of my exceptional qualities." I roll my eyes. *More like annoying.*

"I'm trying to start my workout."

"And I'm trying to get your name and number."

"She's not interested," a familiar voice says from behind me. The sound of it makes my heart flutter.

"Hey, Jaylen, man. This little cutie is just playing hard to get." The man goes to turn his attention back to me, but Jaylen grabs it again.

"She's not playing. She's spoken for."

"Hi, Daddy," I say to Jaylen, to further drive home the point. It feels good to hear him openly claim me after our tiff.

"Hi, my little baby." He gives me a chaste kiss. I desperately want more, but can't show it right now.

"My bad. I didn't know she was with you." The annoying man backs up with his hands in the air.

"Yeah," Jaylen replies, then the man turns to go back to the basketball court.

"I could have handled that, you know."

"You never have to when I'm around."

"Thank you. I thought you weren't here."

"I just got here. Jared said that you asked for me."

"Just wanted to know if you were here or not."

"I have to get upstairs, but I'm glad to see you finally using your membership."

"What's that supposed to mean?"

"What?"

I stare at him to gauge whether I'm being overly sensitive or if that was supposed to be a jab. "Nothing. Forget it." I sigh. "Can we talk?"

"We are talking." His demeanor has changed. He's now guarded.

"About us, I mean."

"That's why you're here? I asked for space, Alise," he states.

"I'm in Hell. How many times do I have to apologize?"

"I'm not doing this here with you."

"Fine. Don't." I put my earbuds in and start my workout.

Jaylen shakes his head and walks away but not before trying to have the last word. "Yeah, your ass is pregnant. Emotions are everywhere."

Last word, my ass.

185

"Fuck you," I say through gritted teeth, just low enough for only him to hear. He stops in his tracks, turns around and looks at me like I have lost my mind. He starts to say something else but changes his mind and keeps going to his office.

I can't move. I watch him walk away again and even though I'm pissed off, it breaks my heart. That's exactly what I have been afraid he would do, only it was him walking away from our relationship. I take a few deep breaths to keep the tears at bay. I don't know how long I stand on the elliptical, but I get off of it when I see his office light come on through the blinds. My plan didn't work. I need to get out of here.

I move too fast and nearly fall off the damn machine trying to get off it.

"Shit," I whisper to myself. I don't bother looking up to see if anyone notices my near fumble and jog to the locker room to get my wristlet.

When I get to the front desk, I slam the key down on the counter. I don't remember his name, but the young man that checked me in is busy with another customer. I do my best to not look up, but I can see Jaylen in his office and feel his eyes on me. The other customer is too chatty for my lack of patience right now, so I leave the key on the counter and leave.

As soon as I get into my car, my phone buzzes. I don't care who it is. I no longer feel like talking. I sit in my car and stare at the building. *I can't believe he's shutting me out like this.*

"Why does he have to be such an ass? And I'm not emotional. He's just a fucking ass." My phone buzzing from another call immediately after the first one let me know it's Jaylen. I'm too emotional to talk. Since I can't work my frustrations and anxiety off at the gym without adding on to my stress and anxiety level, I decide on some retail therapy at the mall next door.

* * *

A few hours and a couple thousand dollars later, I'm back home putting my new clothes away. Having money has its benefits, but it solves very few problems. I'm still pissed and hurt. Jaylen finally stopped calling me a half hour ago.

The buzzer to my apartment goes off.

"You've got to be kidding me." I walk to the intercom. "What do you want, Jaylen?"

"It's Devon."

"Oh." I hit the release button to let him up and open the apartment door.

"Hey," he says when he comes in.

"Hey. Everything okay?" We hug.

"I should ask you that."

"Jaylen called and you are here to fix it." I say as we walk into the living room.

"I'm here to call for a couple of truces."

"So, you're here on behalf of both Jaylen and Charlie? Have a seat," I motion towards the couch. "Are we going to need wine for this conversation?"

"Do you think you should have that?" I stop in my tracks and stare at him. "He told me. The question is, why didn't you tell him?" We both have a seat.

"I take it he didn't tell you he adamantly told me he doesn't want more kids. I was just delaying the inevitable."

"Alise, come on. Jaylen loves you. He was never going to leave you."

"You don't know that."

"I do. There aren't many things in this world that I'm certain of, but his love for you is one I would never doubt." I shake my head at him.

"Then why wouldn't he say he'd stay? Every time I asked him if he would stay or leave, he'd just say, 'we'll cross that road when we get there.'"

"Because he wanted to propose to you."

"What?" Devon looks at me and it clicks. "He was going to propose in Detroit. The package… you brought him the ring before we left."

Devon nods his head.

"Oh, my god." I drop my head into my hands. *How did I not see this?* "Devon, I really fucked up."

"The good thing is that you can easily fix this with a phone call. Seeing you earlier today made him realize he needs to stop punishing you."

"Not that I don't deserve it," I say. "Wait, do you think this is too fast?"

"It only matters what you think and no one else. But you deserve to be happy."

"He wants to marry me?"

"I've already said too much by telling you. You two need to talk to each other about the rest of it."

"And Charlie?"

"I've suggested to her and Jaylen that the four of us go on a double date. I've talked to my wife, and she agreed to be civil."

"She agreed?"

"She misses you and just wants to be back in your life. It's driving her crazy, which is driving me crazy."

"Oh, so this is really about your sanity," I chuckle.

"Yes and no," he laughs. "But really, Charlie hasn't been eating or sleeping much in the last couple of weeks and she cries a lot. Amber asks her what's wrong, and she says she's lost a great love. I want my daughter to have her mother back."

"What about getting your wife back?"

"That is another discussion that'll require me to drink your wine in front of you."

"Hmmm."

"Have you taken a test yet?" my friend asks.

"No."

"You've been under a lot of stress lately. Maybe."

I shake my head. "Sorry, you're in the middle of all this."

"As long as you don't tell Jaylen I told you about the proposal, I'll accept your apology."

"Deal. Oh, I picked some clothes up for Amber at the mall today." I jog to my bedroom to grab the several bags.

"Jesus Christ, Alise. Did you buy one of everything in the mall?"

"Almost," I joke as I put the bags down in front of the ottoman.

"I'm in my sports car. I don't think I can fit all of this in there."

"Well, take what you can, and I will bring the rest to the double date."

"Okay."

"When is that, by the way?" I ask as I sit back down.

"I'll call you and let you know."

"Okay." I think over my next words carefully. "Do you understand what is going on with Charlie? Why did she act that way?"

"More than anyone else, she has always seen you and her as two halves of the same coin. She sees your relationship with Jaylen as something that is taking away the other half of her. I could drop dead and she would not cry over me the way she's been crying over you these last few weeks."

"How long have you seen this?"

He chuckles. "You realize the majority of our high school classmates thought you two were lesbians, right?" he gives as way of an answer. "Charlie and I didn't start dating until college, but I saw how close the two of you were back then. That's why I didn't ask her out until college, because I had a better chance since you weren't there."

"We were kids then. Everyone thought every female friend group was screwing each other, and any guys associated with them were screwing all the females in that clique. No one took that seriously."

"At the next high school tailgate, ask some of our classmates if they thought you and Charlie were going to be one of the first female couples to get married. Most of them would say yeah."

"I can't have her intentionally trying to end my relationship with Jaylen."

"She said she will be more respectful of your relationship if that's what it takes," Devon responds.

"She said that?" That is a shock to me.

"I left off the 'to get her back' at the end."

I shake my head. "Charlie is my oldest friend and I love her as such. But if she does anything like this again…"

"I know. I already made that clear to her."

"Don't tell her I'm pregnant. She already suspects it, but…"

"I won't. Let's see how she does with your relationship for a bit before she gets that news."

"Do you really think she'll keep her word?"

"She doesn't like you with someone, but the thought of not having you in her life is worse for her. For the sake of everyone, I hope she does."

"This has had to have an effect on your marriage." I know he wanted to save this topic for later, but there's no telling when I'll be able to drink again. Devon runs his hands through his short-coifed hair. "Devon?"

"I'm not sure I want to be married to her anymore." He looks up at me and instantly looks tired.

"I can't say I blame you," I sympathize.

"There was a time when I could say my wife loved me, but not anymore. I haven't been able to for a while, honestly. She's been indifferent towards me ever since agreeing to have a kid, but it's gotten worse since I gave you Jaylen's number that night."

"Is there any chance of saving your marriage?"

"That's really all up to her. I thought we'd reached a good turning point just before that night."

"I remember. She was glowing and looked like a woman in love again. Charlie said it was because of you." I smile at the memory of my friend that morning.

Devon huffs. "Then we fought about me being friendly with Jaylen and even more about me bringing him back into your life."

"You fought over that?" I knew Charlie had become a lot to deal with since Jaylen's been back around, but to actually argue with Devon over that? Geesh.

"Yeah. It was probably the most pissed I'd ever seen her."

"Devon, I'm sorry."

"It's not your fault."

"Jaylen thinks Charlie is obsessed with me." Devon doesn't respond immediately.

"You don't need to worry."

"I'm worrying, anyway."

"I know, but trust Jaylen and his love for you. Everything will work itself out." I sit there and let his words sink in. "I need to get out of here. And you have a phone call to make. I'll let you know about dinner."

"Okay." We stand and hug. He gathers up some bags from my shopping spree and I walk him to the door.

"You take care of yourself, my guy, and that little one," he says, pointing towards my stomach.

"Bye, Devon. And thank you."

"Anytime."

I close the door behind him and walk into my room. Picking up the phone as I sit on my bed, I try to think of what I would say to Jaylen. I don't know where to begin, but I call him anyway. I hope the words come to me when he picks up.

"Alise," he says.

"I'm sorry. I'm so, so sorry."

"I'm sorry, too. I made you feel a certain type of way about having a baby because I was only thinking of myself."

"Why didn't you tell me you felt differently?"

"I was trying to show you." We're both silent for a few moments. "I wish I could kiss you right now," he says.

"Where are you?"

"Picking JaQuese up from dance school. She just walked out."

"I'll let you go."

"Okay."

"Jaylen." I can't end the call without saying one more thing.

"Yeah?"

"I love you."

"I love you too, little baby."

God, that feels so good to hear.

"Bye," he says, then his lips smack like he's blowing me a kiss. I smile and end the call. Laying back on my bed, I rub my tummy.

"We're all going to be okay after all."

Porsha Deun

CHAPTER XIII

"Thursday it is," I tell Devon on the phone while I sit in my office. "Bye."

I lay my cell down on the desk. Jaylen and I are supposed to have our first face to face at my place this evening. I can only hope it goes well. *I need it to go well.*

My desk phone rings, breaking me from my reverie. "Your two o'clock is in consulting room one," Rebecca says.

"Thanks. I'll be right down," I say while gathering my notepad, sketch pad, a pen and a pack of sketching pencils before going downstairs. I walk into the room to find a tall, slim, light-skinned woman with dirty blonde wavy hair down her back fingering through one of the several fabric swatch-rings hanging on the wall.

"Hi, Ms. Williams. I'm Alise Rogers," I greet her as I close the door behind me. She turns and gives me a wide smile that instantly gives me the creeps. I shrug it off as bad nerves from everything that has been going on. Despite the creepy smile, she has a pretty oval face with big hazel doe shaped eyes. She looks like a model. I extend my hand for a handshake.

"Hi, Alise. I'm Angela Williams." She shakes my hand a little too firmly.

"Let's have a seat and discuss the vision for your dress." I gesture towards the small round table with four chairs in the center of the room.

"Sure." We take seats across from each other. Her eyes run up and down my body, and it makes me uncomfortable. Again, I shrug it off and stay professional.

"Now, this is for a vow renewal, correct?" I ask.

"That's correct."

"And you don't have a date yet?"

"No. My husband and I are still working things out."

"Okay, now Ms. Williams…"

"Mrs. Williams," she corrects.

"Yes, I'm sorry. Mrs. Williams, is there a theme…"

"That's Mrs. Angela Williams," she interrupts.

"Yes, that's what I have. I just misspoke."

"Mrs. Angela Williams." She sits back and crosses her arms. Now I get it. *That Angela*. I put my pen down and fold my hands on the table. "I was starting to think he didn't tell you about me."

"Jaylen has no reason to hide anything from me."

"Hmmm."

"From what I understand, that's no longer your name."

"I kept it. It was the only thing I asked for besides my house." *Why didn't Jaylen tell me that?*

"What do you want?" I ask.

"To meet you. Take a look at what he's leaving me for." We have a stare down for a few moments.

"You could have approached me anywhere. Why come to my place of business?"

"Meeting you anywhere else would have seemed a little too much like a stalker. And---"

"And making an appointment for a fake wedding isn't stalker like," I interrupt. *Another damn crazy ex-wife. Fuck.* My forwardness takes her back.

"As I was saying, I wanted one-on-one time with you. This was the only way I could see it happening."

"For what?"

"To tell you I love him."

"I love him too. The difference is *he* loves me." I don't see a reason to play nice.

"Listen~~~"

"No, you listen." I lean forward on my arms. "Jaylen is mine. He has been since the day we met, despite his time with you. He knows his heart is home with me, which is why he's no longer with you. I believe he's made it abundantly clear that he does not want you, so stop being pathetic and get the hell out of my store. Come here again and I will have you arrested for trespassing." I stand up to emphasize that this is the end of the meeting.

Her facial expression says she was not expecting this reaction from me. She grabs her purse from a chair, stands and walks towards the door.

"You're a snappy little thing. I was hoping to handle this in a civil manner, but you want to be difficult. My love for Jaylen is the only reason I gave him the divorce, but that doesn't mean I intend on anyone else having him." She turns and walks out.

I pick up the wall phone and dial Joc's extension. "Pull the image of the woman that just walked out of room one off the security camera and meet me in my office." I hang up before he can ask me questions.

I run upstairs, into my office, and take the card the police officer gave me out of my purse. Picking up my cellphone, I call the number.

"Hi. Yes, my name is Alise Rogers. My business was vandalized two Saturdays ago." Joc walks in and I point to the chair for him to sit in. "My report number is 1734811. I have someone that may be a person of interest. Her name is Angela Williams. She's my boyfriend's latest ex-wife."

Joc's eyes get big, and he points to the picture to ask if that's her. I nod my head.

"She made an appointment at my business faking a wedding renewal just so she could meet me," I inform the desk officer. "The meeting just ended. No, she didn't harm me. No, I don't need an officer unless you want the image of her today. I just need someone to look into her as a possibility for the damage done to my business. Yes, I'll hold."

"Are you going to tell Jaylen?" Joc whispers to me.

"Later."

* * *

Joc and I are closing up the shop for the day when I get the sudden feeling that I'm being watched. I ignored my instinct earlier with Angela, but I will not ignore it this time.

"Joc, walk me home," I state. I look around for any and everything that may seem out of place.

"I'm staying with you tonight. This mess is just too damn much." We walk up the street towards my apartment building.

"You don't have to do that. Jaylen is coming over."

"Well, I'm going to stay until he gets there."

"How did she know where I work?"

"There aren't many people in the city who don't know where you work, Alise." Joc tucks his hair behind his ear on one side.

"True." If there was ever a time I wish I had a low profile, it's now.

"If it wasn't Charlie or the first ex that smashed your windows, my money is on her."

"Right," I laugh. Then I get a scary thought. "Do you think it's possible for her to know where I live?" I ask as I slow down my pace and start looking around again.

"I can't say, which is why I'm not leaving you alone." Joc loops his arm into mine as a way of securing me to his side.

We hurriedly walk the few hundred feet to my apartment building. Joc lingers inside the door to watch for anyone coming as I call for the elevator. The elevator pings when the door opens and we both jump. Both of our nerves are bad.

Once inside the elevator, we look at each other. We can see the worry in each other's eyes. He puts his arms around me.

"I will get my hair wet before I let anything happen to you," he says. I laugh. This is why I love him.

"Thanks, Joc. That's very comforting since we both know you only wet your hair to wash, condition, and relax." We get off the elevator and I put my key in the door. "Really Joc, thanks." He kisses my hair and I open up the door.

"Wine and popcorn for dinner?" he asks.

"You know it."

I turn off to my bedroom and Joc heads to the upstairs bedroom to put his things there. He really treats my spare room as his bedroom. Tossing my keys onto the nightstand and purse onto the bed, I kick my heels off. I wash off my makeup in the bathroom. I really want to take a long shower to wash off the bad vibes of this day, but this will have to do for now. Back in my room, I grab my phone out of my purse and text Jaylen to let him know I've made it home.

Joining Joc in the kitchen, he hands me a glass of wine. I take a large gulp of it and remember, this may not be the best idea. I push the wine away and grab a bottle of water from the fridge before taking a seat at the bar while waiting for him to finish with the popcorn on the stove.

"You and Jaylen have grown… closer since he's been back around," I say to Joc.

"We both want the best for you, and I like you with him."

"Do you know what the surprise from the Detroit trip was supposed to be?" I want to know if Joc was in on it.

"Oh, no you don't girlfriend. You will not pump me for information."

"So, you know," I say. I take a sip of water.

"I didn't say that, now did I?"

"You didn't say you didn't know either." He pours some of the popcorn into the bowl and puts the pot back on the stove to pop the rest of the kernels. "When did you find out?" Joc turns to look at me.

"I've known for a few weeks."

"So, are you going to tell me?"

"It's not my place. Jaylen will when the time is right."

"You really aren't going to tell me? I thought I was your best friend, not Jaylen," I pout.

"Don't use the best friend card that way. It's because I'm your best friend that I'm telling you to wait for your boo."

"Fine," I huff.

"Fine," he says. He pours the rest of the popcorn into the bowl and seasons it. "Dexter," he says, picking up the bowl and pointing it towards the television. He grabs the bottle of wine with his other hand, and I grab his wine and my water. We go into the living room to cheer for our favorite murdering psychopath.

"Are we going to pretend that I didn't notice you leaving your glass of wine behind?" Joc asks without looking at me.

"I don't know what you're talking about, Joc."

"Mm-hmm."

* * *

After an episode and a half, my door buzzer goes off. I get up to answer it.

"Who is it?"

"Who else are you expecting?" Jaylen asks. I hit the release button to let him into the building and unlock my door before returning to the couch with Joc.

"Hey," Jaylen says once he makes it into the living room.

"Hey, babe," I reply.

"Hey, Jaylen. Do we have any other crazy ex's that we should know about?" Joc asks.

"Joc!" I exclaim.

"What are you talking about?" Jaylen asks.

"Angela came to see me today," I tell him. He gives me a confused look.

"Yeah, she made an appointment like she wanted a dress for a wedding just to meet Alise," Joc explains.

"Wait. What!" Jaylen exclaims.

"She gave me the creeps," I say.

"And she said that she will see Alise again soon," Joc adds. Jaylen rubs his head.

"That doesn't sound like her at all. She agreed with everything in the divorce. She said she just wants to give me what I want."

"Why didn't you tell me she's keeping your last name?"

"I didn't think it was important."

"You're joking," Joc says.

"I don't think you know the extent of her feelings for you. She said herself that she loved you enough to give you the divorce you wanted, but she doesn't intend on seeing you with anyone else," I state.

"I will talk to her."

"I think that's what she wants, your attention," I say.

"What if it was her that vandalized Timeless Elegance?" Joc asks.

"She wouldn't do that."

"Her setting out to see Alise seemed to surprise you, so you could be wrong about that," Joc responds.

"Are you okay?" Jaylen asks me.

"I'm fine. Just shaken up from everything that's going on. What if someone gets hurt in all of this? Like seriously hurt? I'm being attacked from all sides and on one end, I don't know who my attacker is. They could strike again at any moment and

I don't know how to protect myself from it. And I don't know what they want."

"Baby, relax," Jaylen says, crouching down in front of me.

"How can I?" The fears I've been pushing away for over a week are now coming to the surface.

"Will staying with me make you feel safer?" Jaylen asks.

"Jaylen, I'm not moving in with you. Uprooting my life is not the answer." *I can't believe he brought this up again.*

"If you don't move in with him, I'm going to stay here this week," Joc states.

"I'm okay with that," I say. Having someone here is more ideal than moving in with Jaylen and his boys. Besides, I haven't met the kids yet.

"What else will make you feel safe?" Jaylen asks.

"I need to know who attacked my store. I need to know if my biggest enemy is someone close to me or someone I never saw coming."

"I'll see if I can pull some strings at the police station. The chief comes to my gym," Jaylen responds.

"Don't call Angela. I honestly think today was for attention. She had to know I would tell you. I gave her name to the police."

"I understand why you did that. I just wish you would have called me first.," Jaylen says.

"You would've come rushing over. That wasn't necessary."

"What else do you need?" Jaylen asks.

"To sleep in your arms tonight."

"I'll text the boys that I won't be home until tomorrow."

"Thank you."

"I'll have my things packed and with me at work tomorrow," Joc says.

"You already have clothes in the closet upstairs."

"I need more than my clothes, girl. I need my products."

"Okay, Joc." He really is too much sometimes. I stand to give him a hug.

"Everything is going to be okay," he whispers as he holds me tightly.

"Thanks again." He goes upstairs to get his messenger bag.

"Come here," Jaylen says as he snakes his arms around me. I melt into his arms. I let his body heat warm the parts of me that have become chilled with fear. "I'll do anything to make you feel safe again, little baby."

"I know."

CHAPTER XIV

"Daddy," I whisper as I lay in his arms on my bed.

"Yes." He kisses my temple.

"I need a release." I can feel his smile. He nibbles on my neck. As good as it feels, it's not what I'm looking for.

"Not that kind of release." He doesn't say a word, but I know he gets my drift. He gets up and goes into the bathroom. I can hear him ruffling through the linen closet. He comes out and places two rubber bands and a wood bristle hairbrush on my nightstand. He then leaves the room and returns a few moments later with a fork, a plastic spatula, and a wooden spoon.

"On your back," he orders as he puts the kitchen items with the other items from the bathroom. I turn from my side and lie on my back. He bends down and starts sucking on one of my nipples while massaging my clitoris. Once they're nice and hard, he replaces his mouth with a hard pinch and twists a rubber band tightly around it. He suckles on my free nipple, starting the torture over again. With both nipples rubber banded, he gives them both a few hard thumps.

"Aaahhh," I gasp. The pain is so delicious.

He picks up the plastic spatula and flicks the edge on my nipples in turn. The feeling is like having fire and ice on my nipples at the same time. My back arches off the mattress and my hands fist the pillow above my head as he continues the delicious torture. Jaylen turns to smacking the sides and top of my breasts with it to give my nipples a bit of a reprieve.

"Is this what baby wants?" Jaylen asks.

"Yes," I respond in a low, breathy tone. He smacks me hard and quick on each of my nipples. "Yes, Daddy!"

"Good girl."

I give him a smile. Though I'm trying to not look at it, his throbbing erection tells me he is enjoying this, too.

"Want more?" he asks.

"Need more, Daddy."

He gives me solid smacks down my stomach with the plastic spatula, then he slowly rakes the fork up the inside of my leg. My entire body shivers.

"Open your legs." I spread my legs until the heel of my left foot is on the edge of the bed. The spatula smacks the top of my thighs. "Wider."

I spread wider for him. I can feel the juices that have been puddling run down my slit. He continues his path with the fork, dragging it up the inside of my thighs. I try my best to not squirm much, but the sensation is intense and everything I've been needing.

He goes back to smacks of the spatula up and down my thighs; the hits getting harder and harder with each pass. It electrified the room with carnal passion, and we both lose ourselves in it. Jaylen grabs my neck and squeezes hard while rapidly hitting my nipples with the spatula. I grip the sheets as I try to hold on to my breath. Just as I start to lose it, he lets go and bends down and kisses me intensely before I catch my breath.

"Ready," he commands when he pulls away and drops the spatula.

I quickly turn over onto my knees, push my ass high into the air while pushing rubber banded nipples into the mattress. With my body along the edge of the bed, I can feel his erection pressing into my hip. Jaylen moves towards my face.

"Open."

I welcome him into my mouth. He tangles one hand into my hair at the top of my head to keep me in place while he fucks my face. He warms my backside up with hard squeezes and smacks.

"Damn, I love your mouth," Jaylen moans. More and more of his dick goes into my mouth with each stroke until he finally hits the back of my throat. He holds himself there before pushing deeper to put the head of his dick down my throat. He thrusts short and fast for a while, allowing me to get a little air. Once Jaylen feels his orgasm building, he pulls out before erupting.

We're both panting. He picks up the wooden spoon from the nightstand and continues with giving me the release I asked for. The spoon hurts in a decadent way. I did not know that everyday kitchen items would make good impact and sensation play toys.

Forget spending money on kink toys.

Jaylen's really getting into his groove. He never hits me in the same place more than two times in a row. Since we've been back together, I've seen Dominant Jaylen a few times. Now I have sadistic Jaylen.

"Fuck," I scream when he hits me so hard that the spoon breaks. I barely heard the thuds of the pieces hitting the floor over our panting. Jaylen quickly grabs the hairbrush off the nightstand and goes back in on my ass and the back of my thighs without losing a beat.

The hairbrush is intense. Jaylen is exceptional, though I'm getting close to my limit. Tears are falling from my eyes. I'm not sure how much more of this I can take, but I want to take more. More to release the tension building up inside of me from everything going on. More for him. He clearly needs this release just as much as I do. But he hits me extremely hard and my safe word is out of my mouth before I even realize it.

"Okra!" I yell. I hate okra, which is why it's my safe word.

The hairbrush hits the floor with two loud clanks and Jaylen climbs onto the bed, pulling me into his arms along the way. I softly sob on his chest. He kisses and pets my hair.

"You did so good, little baby," he says repeatedly between kisses. "Do you feel better?"

"No."

"What can Daddy do?" I lean back and away from him.

"Off!"

"What?" he asks with a puzzled look.

"My nipples. Take the rubber bands off."

"Oh. I forgot about these." He unwraps his arms from around me and carefully removes the rubber bands. With blood rushing back to them, they're even more painful for a few seconds. "Stay here." He disappears into my bathroom again. This time, when he returns, he has a jar of coconut oil.

"You have some good bruising going on back here," he says while gently rubbing the fragrant oil on my backside.

"I figured I won't be able to sit comfortably for the next couple of days when the spoon broke."

"Your hairbrush broke, too," Jaylen states.

"You broke my brush!"

"Technically, your ass broke your brush."

"How did you break a wood bristle brush on my ass?" I ask, ignoring his correction.

"It broke at the skinny part of the handle. And it's not my fault that you have such a formidable ass."

"My ass is formidable now," I chuckle.

"Today wasn't the first time it broke an impact instrument." Jaylen climbs back into the bed and envelops me into his arms again. Memories of various paddles breaking during play comes to mind.

"Do you have any of your old toys still?"

"No. I got rid of them when J.J. moved in with me after we ended. I didn't want to risk the kids finding them and being put in the situation I put my dad in when I found his toys."

"That's why your dad taught you about BDSM?" I knew his dad introduced Jaylen to it, but I never knew why.

"He wanted me to be prepared for when and if a woman wanted it from me."

I yawn. "Are you going to teach your boys about it? Since more people are experimenting with it because of that series that doesn't properly document BDSM."

"God, I can't imagine doing that. I'd rather have the sex talk with my daughter a million times over than do that."

"Maybe you can have your dad do it."

"Sleep, Alise."

* * *

I wake up to the sensation of Jaylen devouring my pussy. With my eyes still closed, I reach down to feel his bald head in between my legs, confirming that I'm not dreaming. I turn my head to look at the alarm clock. It's one thirteen in the morning. I haven't been asleep for even two hours.

"Aaah." I grip the bed sheets as I climax.

"You taste so good." He sucks on my magic button. "You were so wet after earlier. I couldn't wait any longer to have you." He flicks his tongue quickly back and forth.

"Good. Fucking. Morning," I moan. Jaylen pushes my thighs up higher, exposing more of my treasure box to him. It's not long before his expert tongue has me with the orgasm shakes.

"Jaylen," I whisper as I come down. He climbs up my body, letting my legs go to his sides.

"Good fucking morning, indeed," he says as he slides into me. I'm grateful he doesn't stop to put a condom on. I've missed the feel of him raw.

* * *

Jaylen's head is on my chest with his arms wrapped around my waist. I groggily stretch my sore limbs and look at the alarm clock.

"Shit! Jaylen, move!" It's after nine. Why didn't the alarm on my phone go off? I pick up my phone up and realize the battery is dead. I didn't put it on the charger last night. "Jaylen, get up." I try to move from under him, but he only tightens his arms around me.

"What are you fussing about?" he says, as he looks up at me sleepily.

"I'm late for work."

"You aren't' going anywhere until you give me a kiss," he explains.

I give him a chaste kiss on his forehead. "There." I try to get out of the bed again and he pulls me back down.

"Kiss me," he demands, looking deeply into my eyes. I give him a not so chaste kiss on his lips. Just when I start to pull away, he deepens the kiss by pressing my head more into the mattress with his own and slipping his tongue into my mouth. There are still remnants of my juices on his tongue. I kiss him back passionately. He goes to maneuver himself in between my legs and I try to buck him off me.

"No. No. No."

"No what? Let me show you how amazing morning sex is," he tries but fails to con me back into bed.

"You've already done that twice this morning. Which is why I'm running late now." I try to push him off me and pull away from him, but he is too big.

"That was middle of the night sex," he says with a smile. There is a sudden loud knock on my door. Jaylen lets me go. I pull on a nearby robe and he puts on the pants he wore over yesterday.

"I thought people have to be buzzed in to get past the lobby door downstairs."

"They do. Either they have the wrong door, another apartment buzzed them in, or they walked in behind someone," I explain. The person knocks again, harder this time. I follow Jaylen to the door. He puts his hand up for me to stay back once we get to my bedroom door. I watch him nervously from two feet away and see him visibly relax after looking out the peephole. He opens the door.

"Hi, Joc," he says.

"Hi to you, too," Joc responds as he walks in. He looks me up and down. "Glad to see you are okay. You two had me worried. I was scared I was going to have to use my key to find y'all chopped up in here."

"Good morning, Joc," I chuckle. "We had a… long night. Let me shower and I'll be on my way to work."

"Mm-hmm. I'll find something for you to wear," Joc responds.

"Keep it simple, Joc," I say as I walk into my bathroom.

"Hey," Jaylen says, hot on my trail.

"You're about to go?"

"Yeah. I'll call you later. Love you." He gives me a quick kiss.

"I love you, too."

"Joc, you saved me," I yell from the bathroom once I hear the apartment door close.

"Saved you?" he yells back from the closet.

"Yes. Sex with Jaylen is great, but his sex drive wasn't going to let me make it to work today." I say while squeezing some toothpaste onto my toothbrush.

"I like what being with Jaylen is doing for you, but we can't have that. You've never been late to work before."

"I know," I say around the toothbrush. "I didn't miss any consultations, did I?"

"Thankfully, no. But you have one in thirty minutes. So, get the vital parts and let's go."

CHAPTER XV

This is awkward. Uncomfortably awkward.

None of us have said anything. The only sound coming from our table at the steakhouse is the sound of our flatware clinking on the plates of our appetizers. I can't take it anymore.

"Did Amber like her clothes?"

"She loved them," Charlie chimes. She looks at me with hopeful eyes.

"I'm glad. The rest of it in the car." I give her a small smile. I know that small talk isn't going to get us anywhere, so I put my fork down and cut to the chase. "Look, Charlie---"

"My actions were not conducive to our friendship. I recognize and regret that," she interrupts. I'm not sure if that was supposed to be an apology or what, but for now, it's good enough.

"I'm glad. You have to accept and respect the fact that Jaylen is in my life. I don't anticipate him going anywhere." I put my hand in Jaylen's hand to further drive my point. Her eyes lock on our hands. "You cannot try to sabotage our relationship again. It will end our friendship before it ends my relationship with Jaylen." Charlie looks up at me.

She nods. "I'll respect the fact that you are... dating." She said the last word like she had to force it out. I can see Jaylen shaking his head out of the corner of my eye. I look at Devon and he slightly shrugs his shoulders.

"How are we doing on drinks?" our waiter asks.

"Another cucumber water for me please," I say.

"A bottle of your best pinot and four glasses," Charlie says.

"No wine for me, Charlie," I interject.

"No?"

"All things considered, I would like to keep my full wits about me for this dinner," I explain to her. It's not completely a lie.

"Okay," she states with a smile to hide her disappointment, while her eyes scream suspicion.

"I'll have another iced tea," Jaylen says.

"We'll all stay with the same drinks we have," Devon adds.

"Okay. One cucumber water, one iced tea, and two cokes coming right up. Your main courses should come up shortly."

"Thank you," Devon says. The waitress walks off with a lot of energy. Charlie pats the table in irritation.

"This is going to take some time, Charlie," I say to her. "Trust has been broken. That takes time to rebuild. We're all trying."

"In the sake of trying, Jaylen, how's your gym doing?" she asks him. We all sit there looking a bit shocked. I nudge Jaylen under the table with my knee.

"It's doing very well." After a few seconds, I nudge him again. "Thanks for asking."

"Can I ask you something that I've been wondering for some time?" She looks Jaylen head on and straight faced.

"Go ahead," Jaylen responds.

"Why do you get off on beating on my friend?"

"And this dinner is over," Devon says.

"Charlie!" I exclaim.

"I'm curious."

"We don't have to justify what we do behind closed doors to anyone," Jaylen explains. He signals to the waiter for the bill. "And Alise has already explained this to you."

"I told you about that in confidence, Charlie. And you broke that, again." Picking up my purse, I stand, and Jaylen follows suit.

"I'm sorry. I… I… please… Alise," Charlie stutters.

"And for the record, I get off on it, too," I tell her. Jaylen and I walk towards the bar where our waitress is tapping away on the kiosk machine.

"Is everything okay?" the young woman asks, clearly concerned that we are leaving so early.

"Something came up and we have to go," I explain. Jaylen takes his card out of his wallet and hands it to her.

"Your food just came up. Would you like it to go?"

"If you can have it packed in the next minute," Jaylen says. She passes Jaylen the receipt to sign. He scribbles quickly and gives it back to her.

"Will do. Please feel free to sit at the bar until I bring you your food. Here's your receipt." He takes off to the kitchen.

Jaylen and I stand there looking into each other's eyes.

"You're disappointed?" he asks me.

Porsha Deun

"I wasn't expecting hugs and kisses, but I wasn't expecting for this to take such a terrible turn either. I miss my best friend."

"I'm sorry." Jaylen wraps his arms around me.

"It's not your fault."

"I know. I'm sorry you're going through this. What can I do?"

"Exactly what you're doing now," I say as I snuggle into his arms some more.

"Is holding you going to lead to much more like it did last? " Jaylen chuckles.

"I've only been sitting comfortably for a couple of days now," I smile.

"Is that a yes?"

"Here's your food," the waiter says, interrupting while holding the bag out to Jaylen. "Have a good night."

We turn to walk out of the restaurant, but find Charlie standing right behind us.

"Jesus, Charlie," I say, startled.

"Please, don't leave," she pleads. "This dinner is so important to me."

"Then why would you bring it up?" I ask her.

"For understanding."

"Again, what we do isn't for you or anyone else to understand," Jaylen responds. I can see Charlie's jaw tighten at Jaylen's response as she looks for me to say something. When she realizes I'm not going to, she turns her attention to him.

"Very well then," she says with a forced smile. She grabs my hand. "Can I convince you to stay?"

"No," I shake my head, "Charlie, you can't. We'll try this again another time." I squeeze her hand and take Jaylen's

216

arm. We stop when we get to the table where Devon is still sitting.

"Maybe just her and I next time, then we can work up to the four of us," I suggest to him after putting my hand on his shoulder.

"You may be right," he agrees.

"I'll catch up with you later," Jaylen says to him.

"Alright, see y'all later," Devon says. I wave to him and Charlie before leaving.

"Isn't your fundraiser thing coming up soon?" Jaylen asks me once we're settled in the car.

"Two weeks from now."

"Were you going to tell me about it?"

"I've been meaning to," I explain. "With everything going on, it just slipped my mind. You have a tux, right?"

"Three black ones," he smiles.

"Please, tell me they are not exactly the same," I joke, but not really joking.

"The lapels are different."

"Thank God," I chuckle. Jaylen eventually joins me.

"That's on a Saturday, right?"

"Yup," I answer.

"I will have my kids that weekend, but it'll be okay."

"Devon told you about the fundraiser?"

"Joc."

"Joc?"

"Yeah. He called me last week to make sure I'll be sitting next to you."

That's right. Joc was working on the seating chart last week. "Sorry, I didn't tell you. I'm not used to having to worry about a plus one for this event."

"It'll be a big night for you."

"A big night for the kids. It's not about me."

"It wouldn't be happening without you."

"I'd like to think that someone else would have thought of a way to help the city's schools."

"Hmm."

We ride in silence for the rest of the drive to my apartment, which isn't long. Jaylen puts on the hazard lights when he once again illegally parks in front of my building.

"You're going to get a ticket," I tell him when he opens my door.

"You are going to stop jinxing me."

"It's not a jinx if you are intentionally setting yourself up for it." He wraps his arms around me and hugs me tightly.

"Wish tonight would have been better for you," he says, while kissing my hair.

"Me too, but we have time." I look up at him and stretch onto my tippy toes. He meets me the rest of the way and kisses me deeply. "I love you."

"I love you too. Let's get you inside."

"You're not staying?"

"No, but I'm going to make sure you get upstairs safely. Have I ever left you out here?"

"No, you haven't," I respond.

"Come on."

* * *

The last couple of weeks have been great. Charlie and I are getting along better. We even had a successful double date last week. I cannot speak about her marriage, but as friends, I think we'll be okay.

Jaylen still hasn't proposed, and the getaway to Detroit was a month ago. A part of me wishes that Devon never told me because now I'm expecting it whenever Jaylen and I are alone.

Work's been going well too. I'm just about finished with the sketches for the new bridal season. The construction plans for the third floor are now completed, and work will start in one week. Shari, the seamstress replacement for Joc, and Lori, the sales rep replacement for Kittie are working out nicely. Shari pumps out twice as many dresses as anyone without sacrificing the quality I require.

Charlie, Joc, and I are having dinner in my living room, takeout from a local Chinese restaurant.

"So, I assume things are better with you and your boo," Joc says, smirking, with a glass of white wine in his hand.

"Things are great. I gave him the code and a key for here the other day," I respond with a wide grin.

"Really," Joc squeals. I nod my head; my happiness plays all over my place. "You've been sexed and flogged something good recently with that smile," he adds.

I laugh, mostly because it's true. Jaylen and I had a great time last night.

Charlie throws a pillow at him.

"Girl, you almost made me spill my wine!"

"You would've just licked it right on up," she chuckles.

Joc throws the pillow back at her and looks at me with his eyebrow raised as he takes another sip.

"What?"

"I haven't seen you drink any wine in a while," Joc states.

I freeze and look at my glass of club soda and pomegranate juice. I haven't talked to Joc about it, but I want to kick him for bringing this up in front of Charlie.

"You always have wine with dinner," Charlie says. I know she feels like she finally has me pinned to talk about it.

I take a deep breath. "Not always."

"YES ALWAYS," they say in unison.

"I can have something different now and then. I don't know why you two are making such a big deal about some wine," I say, trying not to lose my cool.

"Are you pregnant?" Joc asks. Just then, my door opens and the sound of two male voices laughing flows into the apartment. It's Jaylen and Devon coming over from the gym.

"Hey, Daddy," I say, jumping up to greet my man. Oh, how I'm ever thankful for this save. "Hi, Devon."

"You haven't gotten out of this," I hear Joc say under his breath. I gladly ignore him.

"Hey, my little baby," Jaylen says as he snakes his arms around my waist. He smells delicious. I have to remember to write the makers of Axe a thank-you letter. He looks just as delicious as he smells in a black ribbed tank and relaxed fit gray jeans. If everyone weren't here right now, I would present myself to him on my knees.

Charlie and her husband uncomfortably hug and kiss, and both of the new arrivals say hello to Joc. We all sit on my sofa with Jaylen and me in the middle, Charlie and Devon on my right, and Joc on my left. Suddenly Joc looks like the odd one here. I hope he doesn't feel uncomfortable.

"So, are you going to answer my question?" Joc asks looking at me.

"Nope," I snap.

"What question?" Jaylen asks.

"Joc and Charlie are nosey and paranoid about absolutely nothing. It's nothing," I answer. Joc and Charlie look at each other. I know this isn't the last I have heard on the subject from them.

I head to the kitchen to grab two plates, and Jaylen follows me. "Everything okay?" he asks.

I look at my friends laughing in the living room, then to the man I love, and I think about expanding all this love with a child of our own. "Everything's great," I smile.

Jaylen grabs two more wine glasses and another bottle of wine and follows me back to the living room.

"Are things ready to go for the fundraiser tomorrow?" Devon asks.

"Everything is all set. The kids rehearsed yesterday and will have their last rehearsal tomorrow afternoon. Local artists have donated some of their works for the silent auction. As always, there will be a live band and great food. Ticket sales wise, this is the biggest one yet. More local businesses have stepped up with donations and sponsorships. Based on the last numbers I saw, and if the silent auction does as well as I'm hoping it does, we'll be close to $500,000 raised from the event. That's nearly double what we did last year. Plus, a bigwig from Grand Rapids, whom would like to stay anonymous, is going to match whatever we raise."

"That's a million dollars," Devon says while trying not to choke.

"You didn't tell me that," Charlie says.

"I'm so proud of you," Jaylen says, wrapping his arm around my shoulders and kissing my temple.

"Alise, you have gone above and beyond this year;" Devon says.

"The community is what's making the difference. The kids' parents have stepped up from only complaining to taking part. I'm just the organizer."

"You are much more than *just* the organizer. This fundraiser is your brainchild the same as Timeless Elegance. You have brought the community together and kept hundreds of teachers employed. You deserve an award," Charlie says.

"An award? No! I'm just doing something that needed to be done," I state.

"The mayor will present her with a distinguished citizen award tomorrow," Joc says, oh so matter-of-factly.

"What," everyone, including myself, says to Joc, although mine was more of a scream.

"I received a phone call from the mayor's office last week. They want to thank and award Alise for all the work she's done in the community and for the Flint Schools. I wanted to keep it a surprise, but since we're talking about it…" Joc finishes his sentence with a roll of his hand like he's presenting something to the Queen.

"Oh, I'm still pretty fucking surprised," I say in shock.

"Congrats," Charlie squeals as she gets up to hug me. Devon and Jaylen all hug and congratulate me, too. I turn to Joc, who must have run into the kitchen for another glass because he is pouring wine into it and his glass is already full. He holds the glass out for me. This is not only celebratory but also a test. I can feel both Charlie and Jaylen watching me for different reasons. I take the glass, and everyone raises theirs.

"To Alise, a distinguished citizen of Flint, Michigan," Joc says proudly.

"To Alise," everyone says. I smile and take the smallest sip of wine. I hear a small sigh of relief come from Charlie. So much for progress.

* * *

I stand looking out my windows, watching my friends pile into their cars and drive off. Jaylen walks up from behind, wraps his arms around me, and kisses my hair. I love how perfectly I fit into his arms. I kiss his bicep in return. He pulls my hair to one side and kisses and nibbles on my neck and earlobe. The feeling it sends through my body makes me moan, and I feel his need for me growing against the small of my back.

"I'm so happy for you and us," Jaylen says just before biting my earlobe. I smile wickedly and bite my bottom lip. He lowers the shoulder straps of my dress to my hips, hooking his thumbs into my black lace panties, and pushes them down to the floor, leaving me in nothing but my black strapless bra. Stepping out of them, Jaylen tosses my clothing to the side. He stops me when I try to turn around to face him.

"Keep still," Jaylen demands.

I stare out of the window and watch the people below going about their lives, not knowing that just three stories above their heads a grand show is about to start for them to see if they would only look up. When Jaylen pushes up against me again, I can feel his complete nakedness. My body is instantly on fire.

Holding on to one hip, he pushes my shoulders forward to bend me over. To get the perfect arch in my back, he grabs my hair, lifts and turns my head to the side, and gently pushes the side of my face into the glass. He smacks my ass hard and I gasp. He eases himself into me little by little, only he's not aiming for my pussy, he's going for my ass. I knew he was going to take it, eventually.

"Your ass is so tight," he says while he works himself in slowly to make sure he doesn't hurt me. I'm biting my lip and taking deep breaths to cope with the slight discomfort I'm feeling.

"Can you at least spit on it? It needs some lubricating," I pant.

Jaylen pulls out and spits twice, once into my ass, and again on his dick. He then slowly re-enters me, but this time it feels much better. When he finally gets all his well-endowed dick into my ass, he stays still deep inside me until I give him the go ahead. Once I've adjusted to the feeling of him inside me, I nod my head. He moves in and out of me with slow, deep strokes. I moan from deep within. Keeping one hand in my hair, Jaylen reaches down with his other hand and starts rubbing slow circles on my clit.

"Mmmmm."

"You like " he asks.

"Yes, Daddy." With this, Jaylen picks up his pace with both his thrusts and fingers. The anal pleasure is intense, and combining that with Jaylen's expert fingers on my clit, my senses go into overdrive.

"You know what I want," he whispers. I moan, my breath fogging up the glass in front of me. "Give it to me," Jaylen says, pulling my hair back towards him.

"Fuck," I scream. Jaylen thrusts into me harder. My nails scrape against the window.

"NOW!" And with that final demand, I explode. My knees give out as my body quakes so hard that Jaylen has to hold me up while he finishes. After he cums, he lifts my limp body up and carries me into the bedroom.

"Oh, I'm not done with that ass of yours yet, little baby," he says with a wicked grin.

"One round that way isn't enough, huh?" Jaylen flips me over and props me up on my knees. He is going on like he didn't even hear me. With my ass in the air, Jaylen slams his still throbbing dick into my back canal. This time, he has no mercy on me. He moves in and out of me with the ferocity of a lion catching its prey. I grip the duvet and bury my face into it to quiet my pleasure screams. This only makes him go harder.

I can feel the cream from his earlier orgasm squirting out with each thrust and running down my ass and thighs. Jaylen is the only person to ever fucked my ass. It feels good for him to be back inside me this way. My body quakes and shivers from the sensation.

"Daddy, mmmmm," I moan as Jaylen continues his assault on my ass.

"What. Does. Daddy's. Baby. " Jaylen asks in between each thrust.

"I want your cum," I pant. Jaylen digs his fingertips deep into my hips as he continues to stroke in and out of me.

"You want it?"

"Yes, Daddy," I moan. Jaylen smacks my ass.

"Then come get it," he says before pulling out of me. I turn around to him as fast as I can and open my mouth. He strokes himself until he unloads, shooting his cum into my mouth and on my face. I swallow greedily. He tastes so good. His healthy diet makes his nectar almost sweet. I wipe my face with my fingers and clean them with my mouth.

Jaylen removes my bra and lifts me up to pull back the duvet. He lays me down and tucks me in.

"You're not staying?" I ask.

"It's JaQuese's weekend with me, remember? She should be at my place by now, so I can't give you aftercare like I normally would," Jaylen explains. Although I understand, I can't help but to be disappointed.

"Okay," I say, trying to mask my sadness. Jaylen kisses my forehead and runs his hand over my hair.

"Stay in bed and get some rest. I'll pick you up tomorrow at four."

"The banquet hall is just up the street, you know." The event doesn't start until six.

"You're going to walk half of a mile in an evening gown and heels?" Jaylen asks as he walks out of the room to get his clothes.

"Ummm, no. Good point," I reply. Jaylen walks back into the room moments later, zipping up his pants with his shirt hanging around his neck.

"Why can't I get out of bed?" I pout.

"Because tomorrow is going to be a long day for you, so I'm making sure you get plenty of rest. And why are you questioning me?" he asks sternly and pulls his shirt over his head.

"What if I have to get out of bed?" Because I know he has to leave, I'm suddenly in the mood to be a brat. Jaylen picks up on this and sits on the edge of the bed beside me.

"You can get out of bed to use the bathroom. But no T.V., music, or anything else that can keep you up for hours. And no work."

"What if I want something to drink?"

"Do you want something to drink?" I nod my head. He shakes his head at me and leaves the room again. This time, when he comes back, he has a bottle of water. I take a few gulps and place it on the nightstand.

"Get some rest, my little baby. I'll see you tomorrow," Jaylen whispers. He kisses me softly and caresses my face. "Goodnight."

"Goodnight Daddy. I love you."

"I love you, too."

Jaylen turns off the light and goes back into the living room. I hear him flipping light switches off and then walking out of my apartment door.

Porsha Deun

CHAPTER XVI

I'm sitting up in my bed sipping tea while flipping through the latest fashion magazine. I hear my apartment door open, and I know it's only one of three people, but one of them I won't see until later and Charlie will get ready just like I will be. That leaves Joc.

"Good morning," Joc sings as he walks into my bedroom with his hands and arms loaded with garment bags, a wheeled suitcase, a large professional makeup case, a smaller fabric makeup bag, and a Tim Horton's bag and coffee.

"Good morning, Joc."

"Why on earth are you still in bed? Please tell me you've at least showered."

"I put on a t-shirt and made myself some tea."

"You do this every year. I should have known better," Joc says with his hand on his forehead.

"And you get frantic every year for no reason. We have plenty of time to get ready."

"I don't know what I'm going to do with you, but you will not drive me crazy today. I got you an egg white breakfast sandwich. Eat, then get in the shower, please."

"Correction, YOU will not drive *me* crazy today," I say as I take the Tim Horton's bag from him. "And thank you for breakfast."

"Mm-hmm. Eat."

* * *

Joc's given me a beautiful smoky eye and a ruby red lip. He blew out my hair and created beautifully messy goddess braids that are stacked high on my head like a crown. I decide to get my Charlize Theron on and spray on some J'Dore perfume. While Joc is curling the ends of his hair, I walk from the bathroom, into my closet and stand before my black gown before removing my ivory satin robe.

My dress is a strapless mermaid gown with a sweetheart neckline, and it fits my curves perfectly. The mermaid part of the dress has ostrich feathers that start out black and gradually fades to gray at the bottom. I accessorize with diamond stud earrings and a chunky statement necklace that has three large oblong-shaped Swarovski crystals.

When I walk out of the closet, Joc is tucking his white dress shirt into his white tuxedo pants. His fire red cummerbund and bowtie are lying on my bed, and his classic white tailcoat is hanging on the bedroom door. I turn for him to zip me up.

"It's a good thing that I'm here and not Jaylen right now," he says while he zips me.

"Why is that?" I ask just before turning to look at him. He clasps my chin with his thumb and forefinger.

"Because if he had the task of zipping up your dress, it would never get done. You look fabulous."

"Thank you, Joc." He turns to the full-size mirror and starts working on his bow tie. I pick up his cummerbund and strap it on him.

"I love you," I smile.

"I love you, too."

"I don't know what I would ever do without you, Joc. This wouldn't be possible without your help. You and Charlie have been by my side, supporting me to make all of this happen. I'm so grateful for it."

"You don't ever have to find out what life would be like without us," he smiles back at me. We double air kiss, neither one of us wanting to mess up our faces. A few seconds later, Jaylen walks into my apartment.

"Alise."

"In here," I respond.

"Oh no," Joc butts in. "Jaylen, you have a seat in the living room and Alise will be out with you shortly."

"Joc!"

"Not that you need it, but the two of you don't need to be near a bed and you have a grand entrance to make for him," Joc fusses. I purse my lips at him.

"I'll be out in a couple of minutes, Jaylen. Make yourself comfortable and help yourself to anything you like."

"Not anything in here, though," Joc adds. I slap Joc on his shoulder.

"Oh. Okay," Jaylen responds, puzzled. His footsteps echo throughout my apartment as he goes into my living room. I swat Joc on his arm again.

"I will not let you be late to your own event," he fusses. "Now, where are your shoes?" I point to the Jimmy Choo box over in the corner. He helps me into my shoes, and I assist him into his jacket. He puts his arm out for me to take and escorts me into the living room, where Jaylen is looking out the window. The very same window he had me up against last night. It may just be my imagination, but I swear I can see the print from my face and hands on the tinted glass.

Jaylen is in a black dress shirt and black tuxedo pants. His jacket is hanging on the back of one of the bar chairs. Black dress shoes. Diamond cluster cufflinks. Cleanly shaven head. I can smell hints of his body spray from when he walked into the room. Even with his back turned, he's divine.

Joc clears his throat to get Jaylen's attention. He turns around and comes to a complete halt when his eyes catch mine. He stands there, taking all of me in. Only now can I see he is wearing a white tie.

"I'm going to let myself out and head over to the venue. I'll see you soon," Joc says before kissing my cheek. "Keep your clothes on and do not mess up your hair," he whispers in my ear before leaving.

Jaylen and I gaze at each other until we hear the door click. Jaylen saunters over to me, our eyes never leaving each other. He runs the back of his fingers down my cheeks and wraps his hands around the back of my neck.

"You are so beautiful," he says to me with his eyes glowing with love and pride.

"You look rather dashing yourself," I respond. Jaylen has barely touched me, yet my heart is racing. I feel a growing need for him down below. Jaylen takes me by the hand and leads me over to the couch. We sit holding hands.

"I love you so much."

"I love you too, Jaylen."

"Tonight's a big night. I'm proud of you."

His words touch the innermost layers of my heart. I smile at him. "I try."

"You do an excellent job," he beams at me and I kiss his hand. "Hopefully, tonight will be a big night for us, too," he says.

"In what way?"

"Hold on," Jaylen says as he walks over to his tuxedo jacket and gets something from the inside pocket and quickly stuffs it in his pants pocket. He sits back down beside me, looking nervous and cool at the same time.

"Remember what I told you that night at the fundraiser and again when we had lunch at La Familia?"

"You said a lot of things, Jaylen." Now I'm feeling nervous. *Is he finally about to propose?*

"Do you remember me telling you that I intend to spend the rest of my life with you?"

"Yes." *He's about to propose! He's about to propose!* "Jaylen, where are you going with? " I ask as calmly as I can.

"Marry me."

"What?" Even though I knew this was coming, I still can't believe it.

Jaylen drops to one knee and pulls out a platinum split band ring with an enormous diamond in the center and two smaller, but decent sized diamonds on either side of it. I immediately recognize the ring. It's my dream engagement ring.

"You remembered."

"I remember everything, Alise."

"Is this too soon?" I ask, my fear palpable in my voice.

"Do you love me?"

"Of course, I do. You know I do."

"Do you want to be with me?" he asks.

"I'm with you now!"

"Can you see yourself spending your life with anyone else?"

I don't have to think about this one. Jaylen has always been it for me. "No."

"Then marry me."

"Jaylen…"

"Marry me, Alise. Make me happy and marry me."

I sit there and look at him. Of course, I *want* to marry him, but I have some questions to ask him first.

"What's the rush?" I ask.

"There's no rush. I'm sorry that you feel like that, but I have known for quite some time that I want you to be my wife. I don't see any point in waiting. Why are you so scared?"

"We haven't been back together long."

"The sooner we get married, the longer we will be married. Say yes, Alise."

"Jaylen… this is just…" He leans into me, putting his forehead against mine.

"Marry me."

I blow out a deep breath of air.

"Marry me, Alise."

I can't think of a single solid reason to say no. *Fuck it.*

"Yes."

"Yes?"

"Yes, I'll marry you." We kiss feverishly, and Jaylen puts the sparkling ring on my finger. "I can't believe you remembered my dream engagement ring. Did you know this one ring inspired my debut line?"

"No, I didn't know that," he answers. "But what I know is that you just made me the happiest man in the world."

"Yeah?"

"Yes. Good. Girl. Good. Girl," Jaylen says in between chaste pecks on my lips. My heart melts every time he says it.

"The gala," I remind him before things get any further.

"You're right. Let's go, Future Mrs. Jaylen Williams."

"I could always select to keep my name, you know," I tease.

"The hell you will. Don't play with me, little baby. You are mine and your name will reflect it," he slightly threatens. His eyes say he is completely serious.

"Yes, Sir," I say coyly. I'll have to approach the subject at another time. I kiss him lightly on his lips.

"Let's go," he says, pulling away from me.

When we get outside, what I have been telling Jaylen was going to one day happen is actually happening. Once again, he's illegally parked, and an officer is writing him up a ticket. I look at him with my I-told-you-so face and shake my head.

Porsha Deun

CHAPTER XVII

The event is being held in a ballroom just a few blocks away from my apartment. The lobby is full of people waiting to go inside. Photographers are everywhere and a local news station is here reporting live. A reporter flags me down, so I make my way to her while stopping to shake hands and hug guests.

I start the interview with Jaylen standing not too far away. I love how he never takes his eyes off me and how he gives me space to do my thing without me asking him to. The reporter catches a glimpse of my engagement ring and asks me about it. I look at Jaylen and on cue; he joins me. I officially announce my engagement live on the local news station. I'm thankful that Joc is already here, and that Charlie is most likely on her way, so I still have a chance to tell them myself.

The double doors open to reveal a magical ballroom. Silver candelabras with white and blue flowers and candles adorn the tables. Joc did an awesome job coordinating the décor, as usual. The silent auction is in an upstairs meeting room. Sheer embroidered silver overlays cover white tablecloths and royal blue chair covers accented with silver sashes that tie in the back and drape down to the floor. Other than the lights on the walls and the spotlights on the dance floor, the candles provide the only light in the room. There's a small wood dance floor with a podium for the MC, speakers, and presenters at the front end of the room. There are tables on both sides of it and many more to the front.

I selected ten kids from various Flint schools to perform tonight. Of the ten kids, there are two singers, a gymnast, a ballroom dancing couple, a tap-dancing trio, a poet, and a kid that can do some amazing tricks with a basketball.

Everyone looks for their place card on the buffet tables next to the door and then find their seats. Because Joc and I finalized the seating chart earlier this week, I already know where Jaylen and I are sitting. I take advantage of this and go straight to my seat. If people want to chitchat, they are going to have to come to me. I'm saving my feet as much as possible.

My table is in front and center of the stage. Charlie and Devon, Kittie and her boyfriend Xavier, Joc and his date Boston, whom I have not met yet, are sitting with us. Joc gave me a few details about Boston when we were completing the seating chart, but not much. I'm surprised Joc even brought a date, considering he is the MC again. He refuses to let me pay someone to do it.

To the left and right of my table are the members of the school board with their respective spouses. Everyone looks happy and friendly in their black tie best, but I know most of them don't like each other. I wonder if any of them like their spouses. It makes me thankful for the strides Jaylen and I have made since getting back together. Now we're engaged. I hope he gives me enough time to plan a proper wedding.

"Don't you think you should work the room right now?"

"I know I should be, but I don't want to leave my fiancé's side," I smile at him. Jaylen kisses my temple.

"I'll always be by your side," he says while grabbing my left hand and kissing my ring finger. "Come on."

Holding hands, we make our way to the president of the school board, Flint's mayor, and a couple of city council members.

"Well, there's the woman of the hour," the mayor says. She's a tall and slender blonde with striking green eyes. Her blunt haircut frames her oval face perfectly. She looks glamourous wearing the custom pants suit I made for her. Emerald green extra wide satin pants that flow and move like a skirt. The matching satin top has a V-neck collar embellished with large yellow gemstones and small clear iridescent crystals, and accordion sleeves. It shows just enough cleavage not to be unprofessional.

"Madame Mayor," I say as we shake hands. I turn to the rest of the group and greet them as well. "This is my fiancé, Jaylen Williams."

"I didn't know you were engaged, Alise," says one councilman. He's an older man with skin as dark as coal and is sporting a soft pink tuxedo with a matching fedora hat in his hands and matching gator shoes. His nails are long and shine from the clear coat on them. He's all but verbally announcing that he used to be a pimp in his glory days.

"It just happened about an hour ago," Jaylen answers.

"Well, congratulations. Tonight's turning out to be an even bigger night for you," the light-skinned, heavy-set councilwoman says. She has bullets of sweat on her forehead. Her horrible shoulder-length wig is the color of sand, making her look very monotone, and it's sticking to her face. She has on a long shiny navy-blue dress with a matching bolero jacket with three-inch pumps her feet are screaming to break free from.

"The place is beautifully decorated," the school board president says with a tight smile. I know he isn't happy about my refusal to pay his and his cohorts' payroll with the grant money the fundraiser provides for the schools. He's short, loud, and bald like George Jefferson. Even has the little man complex like him, too. He just isn't as funny or likable. And George would have the sense to own a tux that fits, not rent one that's at least two jacket sizes too big and sleeves two inches too short.

"Thank you," I say back just as tightly.

"Alise, you always do an incredible job," the mayor interjects, sensing the tension. "Not just with the fundraiser, but with everything you do. You're the best thing that's ever happened to the Flint schools. Every student, teacher, counselor, and parent should thank you." She gives me a sinister grin that lets me know she doesn't care for the school board president, either. I give her a smile and wink, then excuse myself from the group.

I see Charlie making a beeline straight to me, and she doesn't look happy right now.

"We need to talk, alone," she says to me, but looking at Jaylen. Charlie grabs my arm to drag me away, but Jaylen grabs my waist.

"I promised Alise I wouldn't leave her side tonight, so anything you have to say to her, you can say in front of me," Jaylen says in a cool tone. She gives Jaylen an absurd look. They're both marking their territory of me.

"Charlie, whatever it is you can say in front of Jaylen," I say.

"Fine," she says through gritted teeth. "My mother called me while I was on my way here. She said you announced you're engaged to this creep."

"Look---" Jaylen starts, but I put my hand up to stop him.

"Charlie, I love you. You're my best friend, my sister. Yes, Jaylen proposed to me earlier today, and I said yes. I know you don't care for him, but I love him. I'm happy. Be happy for me."

After a beat, she takes a deep breath. I put my left hand out for her to see the ring.

"Does this have anything to do with you avoiding alcohol lately?"

"Charlie, I'm marrying Jaylen because I love him and want to spend my life with him. No other reason," I answer without actually answering her question. She looks at Jaylen, then back at me.

"Don't you think that this is all too soon? " she asks with her voice full of concern as a change of tactic.

"We love each other. We want to be with each other. I've been wanting this for a long time. There's no reason to wait."

"And there's no reason to rush," she says sharply. Now I'm irritated.

"You know, tonight's a big night for me, in more ways than one," I say while placing my hand on top of Jaylen's hand that's resting on my waist. "I hoped that my best friend would be happy for me, especially since I thought we were making some progress. I guess I was hoping for too much." I walk away, fighting tears and squeezing Jaylen's hand.

"Alise," Charlie calls after me, but I keep going.

In the middle of the sea of tables, Jaylen pulls me into him, my back to his front. He kisses my hair.

"Everything is going to be okay," he whispers. I give him a hopeful smile.

"Everything will be okay," I say, repeating Jaylen's words to reassure myself and to keep from crying. Jaylen kisses my temple and squeezes me tight.

"She's one of your best friends'll come around," Jaylen whispers.

"You don't believe that."

"No, I don't. But because I love you, I'm hoping she does."

Just then, a group of teachers and parents approach us to thank me for the event and fundraising efforts.

"Everyone, please take your seats. We'll be getting started in ten minutes," Joc says into the microphone.

"Ugh. I don't want to go back to the table with *her* right now," I complain. Charlie is seated next to me, with Jaylen on the other side of me and Devon on the other side of her.

"It'll be alright," Jaylen says.

When we get back to the table, Jaylen asks Devon for a word. I wonder where Devon was when Charlie attacked me for promising to marry the man I love. The fact that she's the only one in our little group who has such disdain for Jaylen should tell her something, you'd think. I can feel Charlie looking at me, but I choose not to look her way. I keep myself preoccupied with checking my makeup in a compact mirror.

"Alise… Alise… Are you seriously going to sit there like you don't hear me?"

I turn to her. "Are you about to apologize?"

"Apologize? You're the one about to marry someone that doesn't deserve you or loves you like you need to be loved. You should apologize to yourself."

"Fuck you, Charlie," I retort. I give her a look to let her know not to push me any further. After a moment, she speaks again.

"Alise, I know you are all in your feelings right now, but deep down you know that I'm right. You shouldn't marry him."

"And you need to stop right now, Charlie," Devon says sternly, before I can give her a piece of my mind. Devon and Jaylen are standing behind their respective woman's chair.

"Devon," Charlie gasps with surprise.

"I just heard about what you did earlier and, needless to say, I'm appalled."

"Devon, you don't understand, and it doesn't concern you," Charlie explains.

"Their relationship doesn't concern *you*. You have no business saying what is and isn't a mistake for Alise. I told you before to leave their relationship alone and I'm telling you again in front of them. If you can't be happy for the woman you call your best friend, then leave them alone."

A part of me wants to applaud Devon for how he's coming down on Charlie right now.

"Seriously, Charlie? You're just going to sit there looking at me? Fine, since you won't apologize to them and are hell bent on ruining this night for *your* best friend, move over a seat."

"Move over a seat?" Charlie questions.

"Yes, move over," Devon repeats. "You don't need to be so close to them since you don't know how to act."

"Oh, so you think I owe *him* an apology, too?"

"You realize you're the only person who has a problem with Jaylen, right?" Devon says. *Ha!* I'm so glad someone else noticed it and I'm even happier that Devon was the one to say it.

"His ex-wife doesn't like him," Charlie remarks smartly.

"Dammit, Charlie. You're not his ex-wife! Alise is not your wife. You are *my* wife. This man has done nothing to you, yet you disrespect him and his relationship with Alise at every turn. Now move over before I put you over *my* knee for being so rude and immature," Devon finishes with clench teeth.

Alise is not your wife? What the hell did Devon mean by that?

"You wouldn't dare," Charlie says.

"Charlie, don't keep testing me. If you paid as much attention to our marriage as you do their relationship, maybe we wouldn't be having the problems we have. Move. Now."

Seeing that her husband is utterly pissed off at her, Charlie moves over into what was Devon's seat.

"Alise," Jaylen says as he pulls his chair out for me to sit in. Like Charlie, I do as I'm told, but I do it out of submission and love for my man. Charlie did it because she was embarrassed and threatened.

Just as Devon and Jaylen take their seats in between Charlie and me, Joc escorts his date to the table.

"Everyone, this is my boyfriend, Boston," Joc says beaming. "Boston, these are my dear friends Alise, her boyfriend, Jaylen—"

"Fiancé," I correct, while holding up my hand.

"OMG! Congrats," Joc squeals. He gives me a big hug and pats Jaylen's arm. Now, THIS is how a genuine friend reacts to such news. Realizing he didn't finish with the introductions, Joc steps back to Boston's side. "Oh, I'm sorry. Boston, this is Charlie and her husband, Devon."

Boston flashes us with an extra bright fluorescent smile. He's tall, tan but not too tan, and muscular with blond hair as long as Joc's, and ocean blue eyes. He reminds me of Fabio, but with more of an Elvis-like facial structure.

"Nice to meet you, Boston," I say.

"Please tell me this is the man that's had you floating," Kitty says when she approaches the table with her boyfriend, Xavier.

"Boston," he introduces himself and shakes their hands.

"Joc here has been keeping you a secret for weeks now," I tease.

"We were trying to get to know each other and made it official just a couple days ago," Boston says. He looks at Joc with complete admiration. It makes me warm to him immediately. That and the fact he has the same wardrobe flare as Joc. Boston sports the same fire red bow tie, cummerbund, and shoes as Joc. Only his tailcoat and pants are black. I can see them getting married in their outfits.

"Have a seat. Five of us don't bite," Jaylen says with a chuckle. Devon and I join him with chuckles of our own. Charlie is visibly steaming. As Boston takes his seat next to Xavier, Joc leans over to me to ask what is going on.

"Later," I whisper in his ear. He nods his head. He wants to know now but gets the feeling that there isn't time for that.

"Well, I will be right back," Joc announces to the group. "I have a job to do." He gives Boston a quick peck on the lips. I'm glad my friend has found someone to care for who cares for him just as much. For his sake, I pray this will be true love for him.

"Good evening, ladies and gentlemen," Joc says enthusiastically to the crowd. "Welcome to the third annual Our Kids Are Our Future Gala." The crowd erupts with applause. "For the last three years, this gala has raised funds to pay teacher and counselor salaries, as well as provide new supplies in the classrooms. By covering those expenses with funds raised by the community, the school board can slowly, but surely, work out its ongoing debt issues while keeping teachers where they need to be, in the classroom." Another applause from the crowd and some cheers from the tables of teachers seated behind me. It makes me smile.

"This past school year," Joc continues, "we were able to upgrade every high school classroom with new computers, projectors with interactive touch board screens and tablets for the students. This has allowed instructors to present lessons in a way that students can connect with, but also with technology that's being used in the real world today. With the funds raised this year, we hope to arm the middle school classrooms and students with the same technology." And another grand applause from the room.

"As you all know, the silent auction is going on just upstairs. Check out the art donated by local artists and get your bids in anytime during dinner. Now, because I know you all are ready to eat, drink, and see some incredible talent from *our* kids, I'm going to sit down now so the servers can get the appetizers and the first round of drinks to you."

With that, Joc takes his seat next to Boston, and the servers make their rounds with appetizers and wine while other servers take dinner orders from all the guests. They have a choice of grilled filet mignon with sautéed shrimp, baked lamb chops, or roasted whole Cornish hen, served with white cheddar mashed potatoes, stuffed eggplant, and corn salad, and, of course, their choice of several wines.

While we eat, a quartet of three violins and a cello play classical music.

"Alise, what made you decide to have a fundraiser event for the schools?" Boston asks.

"Two reasons. One, I wanted to see a better school system than what I had. Don't get me wrong, I am proud of being a Flint Northern graduate because look at where I'm at today. But getting here was a little harder for me than others because I'm a product of Flint schools. They had a class in both middle and high school that taught you how to type, but it was in a DOS program, which was already ancient at that time. There were a couple of courses that required a PowerPoint presentation, but with no previous instruction on how to put one together. We weren't set up to succeed..

"The second reason was at one point, there was always something on the news about the debt problem the school board was having. Everyone had their opinions, but no one was doing anything. Loans were being taken out for teachers' salaries, yet there was money to pay administrator salaries. Teachers were being laid off and classrooms were getting larger. That's not fair to the instructors or students. There's more work for them to do, but at least the kids aren't suffering the consequences of the debt."

"That's amazing. I'm sure everyone is grateful for what you're doing and have done," Boston responds.

"All I care about is the kids being able to compete with the rest of the country academically. All of us at this table started from a disadvantage when we left the Flint schools for college." Everyone at the table nods their head in agreement. Everyone except Charlie, that is. She still has a stick up her butt.

The discussion continues until the main course is served. Xavier, Boston and I have the Cornish hen. Jaylen, Devon, Kittie, and Joc have the steak and shrimp. Charlie has the lamb chops.

"The food is excellent," Jaylen says. Everyone nods and "mm-hmm's" in agreement. Nothing else is said after that until our plates are removed from the table.

"I don't know if I have any wiggle room in this dress for dessert. I'm stuffed," I say.

"Please tell me there's some chocolate on the menu for dessert," Boston says.

"I don't put on an event without excellent wine and some chocolate," I chuckle. "And if I went crazy for some reason and didn't put it on the menu myself, Joc would take care of it."

"Yes, Joc loves his chocolate and wine," Boston says, looking at Joc adoringly. I smile, watching the two of them.

For dessert, everyone has a choice of triple chocolate mousse cake, classic tiramisu, or flambéed vanilla poached pears with apricot sauce.

Joc, Boston, Kittie, Xavier, and I all have the triple chocolate mousse cake, Jaylen and Devon have the poached pears, and Charlie has the tiramisu. Funny how she keeps being the one odd person. Jaylen and I share our desserts with each other since we couldn't decide on which one to get. After dessert, Joc returns to the mic to continue his MC duties.

"Did everyone enjoy dinner?" he asks the crowd. There's a grand applause. "Now it's time to move on to our first talent of the night, a sixteen-year-old singer from Northwestern Academy with dreams of becoming a songwriter and producer. Singing Frank Sinatra's, *My Way*, may I present Ms. Ryan Mitchell."

Joc joins us again. Ryan takes center stage wearing a long fitted white gown, and a red rose in her hair. The band plays, and she serenades the crowd. When the song ends, there's a roar of cheers. You can quickly point out who her mother is as she's the loudest person in the room. It only embarrasses her daughter, and the crowd chuckles at it.

"Up next," Joc announces to the crowd, "is some spoken word by Ronald McDermitt, an eighth grader at Holmes Middle School with aspirations of starting a non-profit to help released felons become productive members of society, and then Sonya Anderson, a sixth grader at Doyle Ryder whom will sing what she calls the theme song of her life, 'Shake It Off' by Taylor Swift. After that, we'll announce the winners of the silent auction."

* * *

The first portion of the talent show goes well, and Joc announced the winners of the silent auction. The event is on intermission right now as people make their way to restrooms and small talk with others while the wait staff refills wine and water glasses.

As I'm talking with some kids who are trying to pitch me ideas for a fashion show with designs by the kids for next year's fundraiser, I notice Charlie and Devon are having a very heated discussion in a corner. I'm too far away to hear them, but I can see Devon is turning red in the face, which is a sign he's ready to lose his cool. Devon is the peacekeeper of our group. Him losing his cool rarely happens. This is bad. Extremely bad. Charlie storms off towards the restrooms and Devon heads towards the main doors of the ballroom, which are just behind me.

We make eye contact, and he angles towards me. I give each of the kids my business card and tell them the fashion show can be its own event and they can spearhead it with my backing, but they need to write me a proposal first. They each give me a hug and walk away, brainstorming more ideas for the event.

"Devon, what's going on?" I ask when he reaches me.

"You saw that, " he responds.

"Yeah, but if I hadn't, your face would give it away."

"I always thought her possessiveness over you was just a result of the two of you being so close and because you didn't have any family around. But since Jaylen has been back in your life…," Devon trails off.

"Possessiveness? Devon, what are you talking about? What did you mean earlier by me not being Charlie's wife?" That's crazy.

"Being honest, if you were with someone else, Charlie would still be like this. No one is good enough to be close to you but her, in her mind."

"Joc's close to me. She doesn't seem to have a problem with him," I say.

"Joc is gay. He isn't a threat," Devon states frankly.

"Devon, you're making it sound like she's in love with me or something. Like, crazy in love with me and not the good crazy way."

Devon just stares at me. An uncontrollable shiver goes down my spine. *This* is what he meant by his statement before.

"Everything okay?" Jaylen asks from behind me, making me jump.

"Everything is wonderful. Glad you're here. I was just getting ready to tell Alise that I have to head up to the hospital." Devon gives me a quick hug and a kiss on the cheek. "Sorry to bail on your night, but the life of a surgeon is always on call. Congratulations on everything."

Devon and Jaylen do that man handshake and half hug combo thing before Devon congratulates us on our engagement, then heads out of the door. Jaylen walks around to my front and eyes me closely.

"What's wrong? Did something else happen with Charlie?"

"Devon and Charlie just had a fight. I'm not sure about what," I say, even though I have an idea.

"Those two fighting is not what has your mind in a tailspin. Talk to me."

"I want to, and I will. Just not right now. Please. Tonight's too important."

Jaylen nods. "Let's head back to the table. The intermission will end soon."

"How are the kids?" I ask, as an added distraction.

"They're good. Ordering pizza and watching movies."

"Good." I take in a deep breath to calm my nerves and push away the thoughts that are trying to plague my mind.

* * *

The rest of the kid's acts go off without a hiccup. It would be the perfect distraction from the thoughts Devon left in my head about Charlie. However, I keep catching glances of her out of the corner of my eyes, and each time she's glaring at me.

"And now to present a much-deserved award to the person who has brought us all together for such a worthy cause, I present to you, Mayor Hannah Turner," Joc says when he returns to the microphone only to leave it immediately after.

The Mayor takes the stage and begins her speech. I barely hear her words. Public speaking has never been my strong point and my nerves are getting the best of me. Not to mention, I'm examining any differences in Charlie's behavior when I've casually dated men before Jaylen. Devon may be on to something, but I don't have time to process it all. Charlie has been my best friend since we were kids.

She knows I'm not gay, right? That's something she should know by now. Hell, I never knew she was gay. Is she gay? What the fuck.

The round of applause brings my mind back to the here and now. Everyone is standing and looking my way. I smile and make my way to the mic. I shake the Mayor's hand and she passes the clear acrylic pyramid shaped award to me. Once the applause settles down, I take a deep breath and begin my speech.

"I don't feel I deserve this award. Taking steps to better the community… our community and our kids is something everyone *should* be doing. But since the beginning of time, man has only been about himself… about 'I' instead of about 'we.' This is very unfortunate because our kids suffer the most for it. Since I started the Our Kids are Our Future Foundation, I have operated under the mindset that the children of the city of Flint are my children too. No, I don't provide for their daily needs as their parents do, but I still have a responsibility for and to them. We all have that responsibility. For me, that responsibility is to give them what I did not have coming out of Flint schools, a fighting chance. And it's you, our sponsors, the teachers, the students, and the parents that have allowed and supported me in my efforts to giving them that fighting chance and for that, I'm forever grateful.

"As I accept this award, know that I'm receiving it for you. For if it weren't for you, all of you, none of this would be possible. As I conclude, I would like to give special thanks to two very special people in my life, one being my dearest friend Joc, who not only helps me put this all together year after year but helps me keep my head on straight. I don't know what I would do without you. The other person being my new fiancé, Jaylen. I love you and can't wait to be your wife."

I step back from the microphone and nod to the crowd, who gives me another standing ovation as I smile, wave, and make my way back to my seat. I hug and kiss Joc as he heads to the stage to finish his MC duties.

"Now, I'm dying to know what's going on with you and Charlie. Don't think you leaving her out of your acceptance speech went unnoticed," he whispers into my ear.

"Later," I whisper back.

When I get to Jaylen, he snakes one arm tightly around my waist and the other hand he puts under my chin, lifting my face to his. I rest my free hand on his chest.

"I love you, too, future wife," he says with a smile and glowing eyes. Slowly, he brings his lips down to mine and kisses me gently. It sets my entire body on fire and sends my head spinning in the best way possible.

I grab onto his lapel to not only keep my balance, but to deepen our kiss. When he finally pulls away, he looks at me with so much love in his eyes that it nearly brings me to tears.

The crowd cheers even louder at our PDA. I hear them, but I don't. For these few seconds, Jaylen and I are in our own bubble, our own world, another one of my favorite places to be besides in his arms. We give each other slight smiles, then Jaylen pulls out my chair.

Once I'm seated, I notice Charlie is outright glowering at me. It makes me a little uneasy, but I don't give it much thought since we're in a very public place and I'm sure she won't cause a scene. At this point, I don't care, and I have no sympathy for her. But I'm curious to know if her anger is due to me leaving her out of my speech or if it's jealousy. Maybe it's a combination of both.

Best friend or not, there are consequences to actions, and her actions earlier were wrong. Charlie storms away from the table and disappears into the sea of people. It doesn't go unnoticed by anyone at the table.

"Alise, you deserve this award for actually doing something when others have only talked," Joc says into the microphone. "How about another round of applause for Alise Rogers and her dedication to the community!" There is another riveting applause. I shake my head and smile bashfully at my dear friend.

"On behalf of Alise and the Flint School Board," Joc continues, "I would like to thank everyone for coming out tonight for showing their support. Based on ticket sales, sponsorships, donations, matches, and the silent auction, we've raised $1.2 million!" There are gasps and a thundering applause from the crowd. The children sitting in the back squeal and jump up from their seats in excitement. Just the sight of their surprise and joy touches my heart and brings me to tears. They're the reason I do this, and seeing their reactions right now is my verification that all the headaches I go through with the school board over where the funding goes is more than worth it.

"Now, it's time for me to conclude my Master of Ceremony duties, but the night is not over. The dance floor will open up as soon as I take a seat. Mingle, dance, and be merry," Joc finishes with enthusiasm.

Porsha Deun

CHAPTER XVIII

Jaylen and I are dancing to *It Had To Be You.* I'm careful to make sure my hair is laying on his white tie and not my face. This song is perfect for us. It had to be Jaylen I met in the taco house and fall in love with. Now, four years later, we're engaged and swaying to one of the sweetest love songs ever written at my fundraiser gala.

"May I have the next dance?" Joc asks, as the song ends.

"We need to catch up," I say to Jaylen as he looks at me for an answer.

"One song. That's as long as I can tolerate being away from my future wife on the first night of our engagement," Jaylen says to Joc with his index finger up in the air to emphasize one song. Jaylen kisses me and says, "I'll be right back."

Joc and I get into formal dancing position.

"Charlie made it very clear that she's not happy about my engagement. She was a real bitch about it. To the point that it pissed Devon off."

"She showed out in front of him? In front of everyone?"

"It was just Jaylen and me at first. Then just me. Jaylen told Devon about the first confrontation and they came back while Charlie was going in on me again. Devon even threatened to spank her for her unacceptable behavior," I say with a chuckle.

"" Joc whispers with shock.

"Yeah. It was quite comical. I would have laughed then, but I didn't feel it was appropriate. Devon and Charlie got into it during the intermission." I stare off as I think about what Devon told me an hour ago.

"What is it?" Joc asks.

"Devon thinks Charlie is in love with me. Like, crazy, possessive in love with me. That's ridiculous, right?"

Joc doesn't say anything.

"Joc, that *is* crazy, " I say, a little panicked. *I can't really be the only person who thinks the idea of Charlie being in love with me is beyond crazy! Or am I the only person who has been blind to Charlie's affections?*

"Remember that basketball player you were dating when we were in high school?"

"Chris? Yeah, but what does that---," I stop when I realize where Joc is going. Charlie wasn't approving of that relationship either. She never missed an opportunity to dig at him about something. I didn't think too much of it until now because Chris turned out to be a cheating asshat, anyway.

"Then Keith and Jackson. She's never given anyone you've dated a chance. To Charlie, they were always the enemy. My hope was marriage would calm that in her, but clearly not. I'm even more surprised that you never picked up on it."

"I thought she was just being overly protective. Joc, why didn't you say something to me about this before?" My mind is spinning as I take all of this in.

"Look at how you've been toward everyone about the idea recently. It was much better coming from the man that married her than from anyone else."

"What am I supposed to do, Joc? She's my best friend." I ask.

"She was your best friend, and you are everything she wants to be and ever wanted. I honestly think she would leave Devon for you."

"Joc, no. It can't be that bad. She wouldn't take it that far," I say, but I don't know if I'm trying to convince him or myself. Devon told me he could drop dead and Charlie wouldn't cry over him as much as she cried over the pause in our friendship.

"Charlie's not my best friend. We have had some cool moments, but if it weren't for you, she and I would not run in the same circles. We tolerate each other at best, and the only reason she hasn't gone crazy over you and I being close is because I play for the other team," Joc explains.

"Devon said the same thing."

Feeling defeated and at a complete loss, I drop my head.

"Look at me, Alise, before you get makeup on my jacket," Joc says in a serious tone. When I raise my eyes to his, he continues. "You need to prepare yourself. You're about to see a side of Charlie that you haven't seen before and what others have only glimpsed so far. I have a feeling things are going to get worse before they get better, especially since you're pregnant."

I go to deny the pregnancy, but Joc interrupts me. "Shut up. I know because I know you. I'm just mad you didn't tell me, but I get why you didn't." In all this drama with Charlie, I forgot about my unplanned pregnancy. This is all too much.

The song ends and, as promised, Jaylen is back by my side.

"Joc, do you think it would be rude for the hostess to leave the party early?" I ask him. My mind is not with the event anymore, and I need to talk to Jaylen about all of this. This isn't the place to have that conversation.

"Are you feeling alright?" Jaylen asks me with his eyes full of concern. I give him the best smile I can muster up to ease his worry and say that I'm just ready to go.

"I'll cover for you," Joc tells me. "Go."

"Thank you so much," I say as we hug goodbye.

"I know the two of you are best friends, but is it okay if I have my man back?" Boston says when he approaches us.

"You can. Jaylen and I were just leaving. It was nice to meet you, Boston. Take care of my friend," I say as I pat his arm.

"Great meeting you, too. I'll take good care of him. And not because you told me to, but because there's nothing else that I would rather do. Good night, Alise. This has been an outstanding event."

"Thank you and goodnight." I smile at the beautiful pair and give them a small wave as Jaylen escorts me out of the ballroom.

* * *

Once we're in the car, I keep going over details of Charlie's behavior when it comes to my past relationships. The signs were always there. I wrote them off as her being a protective friend. If I felt the guy she was with was a complete asshole, I would have done the same for her. Only now I see that she's been coming from an entirely different place than I would have. *She can't possibly think this is love. She's married for god's sake!*

"Alise!"

I jump at the boom of Jaylen's voice. "Yeah?"

"Did you hear me? What's wrong with you?"

"I'm sorry. What did you say?"

"I asked you what's going on and don't you dare tell me nothing. Your mind has been somewhere else ever since the intermission," Jaylen says sternly.

"Devon thinks Charlie is in love with me, and that's why she has been such a bitch about our relationship. Joc agrees with him."

"That's absurd. She is your best friend. Devon should know that. She just doesn't like me for some unknown reason. That doesn't mean she's in love with you."

"That's what I always thought, too, until Joc pointed out to me she doesn't like you because she chooses not to like you. She's done the same thing before," I explain.

"So, what are we talking about here? She wants you for herself?"

"If she can't have me, then no one can. Joc thinks things will get worse now that we're engaged and pregnant."

"Speaking of which, did you ever take a test?" he asks me.

"I don't need to. I know I'm pregnant."

"I understand you know your body, but you need to take a test. We have to be sure before we get our hopes up."

I don't have a reply to that. Suddenly, I notice the car is still moving instead of being parked outside of my building. It's

Porsha Deun

only a couple of blocks up the street, in the opposite direction. "Why aren't you taking me home?"

"Because my plan was always to take you to my place. Not to mention, you just told me not one but three people, including yourself, believe that your best friend is in love with you. She was beyond pissed when she stormed off after your speech. It may not be safe at your place."

"Oh, Jaylen, please. Charlie's not going to hurt me. And what do you mean your plan was to take me to your place? All of your kids are there."

"It's after midnight. They'll be sleep when we get in. You'll get to meet Jaleel and JaQuese in the morning. They already know you'll be there," Jaylen says frankly.

"And you didn't think to run this by me before telling your kids? Jaylen this is big. Did you ever stop to think that I may not be ready to meet your kids?"

"If you weren't ready to meet my kids, you should have thought about that before agreeing to marry me. And yes, it's a big deal and maybe I should have said something to you about it, but they already know about you thanks to J.J. They want to meet you."

Oh. My. Fucking. God. "I know I'm going to have to meet them eventually. Don't you think this is too much right now, considering the Charlie thing?"

"Charlie has nothing to do with this. I won't let her affect us in any way except for me moving you into my place as soon as possible."

"Move me in!" I scream. "Jaylen, have you lost your mind? I'm not moving in with you!"

"Charlie has access to your apartment. She could be waiting there to confront you right now, for all we know. She works for you. Charlie is entwined in so much of your life, but you need to get some distance. You may not think she will become violent, but I'm not willing to chance it. You're moving in, and that's the end of it," Jaylen states.

I sit in the passenger seat staring at him, wanting to scream, but I know he's right. Plus, I can't be mad at him for wanting to protect me. So, I say the only other thing that I can say.

"I can't exactly wear my evening gown until we get my stuff," I pout.

"I picked up some things for you earlier this week so you would have something whenever you would spend the night. You can add it to your regular wardrobe now."

"Is it all black?" I retort.

"I'm over here worrying about you and your safety and you choose right now to be a smart ass over clothes I bought as a gift to you?"

He's right.

"I'm sorry," I whisper. "I'm scared, too. About everything. And I wasn't expecting to be moving in with you so soon." My mind wonders what it will be like to live with him and his kids.

"You're taking a test tomorrow," Jaylen says, interrupting my thoughts.

"Fine." The car is silent for a few moments. "Where are you going?" He turned left when he should have kept straight.

"Walgreens." There's only one 24-hour Walgreens drug store in the entire city. Jaylen is going to make sure I take that test first thing in the morning.

"You proposed to me today."

263

Jaylen looks at me for a second with his eyebrows pushed together, not sure where I'm going.

"I know. I was there." He sounds confused.

"You were going to propose in Detroit, weren't you?"

He chuckles. "I was, but we know how that went."

"When did you get the ring?"

"The day after we had lunch."

"When did you change your mind about a baby?"

"Are we playing 50 questions?" he asks with a raised eyebrow.

"Not quite 50, but close. When did you change your mind?"

"After the first time, you kicked me out of your apartment," he answers. I think back to that night. That was weeks ago. He continues. "That was the first time I realized I could lose you for good if I kept fighting you on it."

"All that time, I thought you were going to leave me. Honestly, I still have that fear."

Jaylen lets out an exasperated sigh as he pulls into the Walgreen's parking lot. He gets out of the car and I watch him walk into the store, rubbing his head in frustration. I lose myself in thoughts of him changing his mind again while he's in the store.

I jump when Jaylen suddenly opens my car door and tosses the bag with two pregnancy tests onto the dashboard. He unbuckles my seatbelt and turns my knees so that I'm facing him. He cups my face in both of his hands and looks directly into my eyes.

"Alise, I'm not leaving you. Since I've had you back, I have never once thought of leaving you. I know I said I didn't want any more kids. After the divorce with Calondra, I swore I would never have children again. That custody battle was hell. I had to fight or pay her for every second I spent with my kids." He lets out a long breath.

"I guess I was trying to lead you to the conclusion of not wanting a kid too, and I'm sorry. I should never have done that. The rest of my life is with you, and if this life includes another child, then so be it," Jaylen explains.

"Forever?"

"Forever, my little baby."

He kisses me gently, both of our lips wet from my tears. We both repeat "I love you" to each other again and again in between each kiss.

"Are you two done yet?" a familiar, yet angry soprano voice says from the front of the car. It's Charlie. She's changed into jeans and a tank top, but still has on the makeup from the fundraiser.

"What the fuck are you doing here?" Jaylen nearly yells.

"I need to talk to you, Alise," Charlie states.

"Did you follow us here?" I ask her.

"Yes, I followed you. Like I said, we need to talk."

"You two don't have anything to say. Hell, count yourself lucky that you still have a job," Jaylen interjects.

"Your dick game isn't strong enough to make Alise fire *me*, her best friend, let alone cut me out of her life. Remember, I've been around much longer than you and I don't have any intentions of going anywhere. You, however, won't last. I'll make sure of it," Charlie says with a lethal smile that anyone else would have taken as sweet.

"You're crazy," Jaylen states. "She's marrying *me*, Charlie!"

"This is fucking insane," I whisper under my breath.

"Alise," Charlie calls. "Come talk to me, please?"

"Charlie, it's late. There isn't anything that we need to talk about right now."

"I beg to differ. There's plenty we need to talk about, starting with this ridiculous engagement."

"What the fuck did you just call our engagement?" Jaylen asks through gritted teeth.

"Alise, let me take you home so we can talk," Charlie says in a patronizingly sweet tone.

"Jaylen, get in the car," I ask him.

"Alise," he says.

"Please, get in the car. Let's go." Jaylen walks around to the driver's side of the car.

"You're coming with me so we can talk," Charlie states firmly.

"Are you in love with me?" I ask Charlie, looking her squarely in the eyes. This question catches her slightly off guard.

"Of course, I love you, Alise. We're best friends. I will always love you," she says as she recovers.

"That wasn't my question, and you know it."

"You don't belong with him."

"And who is it you think I belong with, Charlie?" I ask, irritated. She walks over to my open car door and places her hand over mine.

"You belong with someone who has been there for you. Someone who truly loves you and has built you into the person you are now and wants to build you up to be even more."

"And you think that person is you? You think you've built me?" *This heifer has officially lost her damn mind.*

"You wouldn't have been able to do any of this without me," she says calmly. I snatch my hands out of hers. Her facial expression says I've offended her by doing so.

"This is why I'm not going any damn where with you. You are very close to being certifiable, and I'm not sure how I didn't see it before. Maybe I was blind, but I'm not anymore. I built myself and my company with my hard work and two hands. I didn't need you for a damn thing. You're crazy for thinking otherwise. I loved you as my best friend and sister, but that's now done. I don't want anything to do with you. Stay the hell away from me. Now move out of the way before you get slammed in the door."

"Alise, you don't mean that. Just come with me." I push Charlie out of the way of the door and close it quickly. I let the window halfway down to say one last thing to my former friend.

"Let's be clear. You. Are. Fired. Fired from your job and fired from my life." I let the window back up, and Jaylen quickly backs out and then peels from the parking lot.

"Are you okay?" Jaylen asks me after a minute.

"There are a lot of words I could use to describe what I'm feeling right now and 'okay' isn't one of them," I answer.

Jaylen takes out his phone and makes a call. "We need to talk about your wife again," I hear Jaylen say to who I assume is Devon.

While Jaylen retells the event of the parking lot to Devon, whom apparently chose to sleep in an on-call room rather than his bed with his wife, I can't help but think about how much my life has changed in the last few months. I not only have the man I love back, but we're getting married. The person I've thought of as a best friend since we were kids wants to be my lover.

She thinks she built me.

I thought I was struggling with the thought of her being in love with me, but the fact that she gives herself credit for making me is something I just cannot get over. *She is fucking crazy. How did I not see this before? It feels like this all has come out of nowhere.*

"We're home," Jaylen says to me.

"You know this is only temporary, " I explain. Jaylen stares at me for a few moments before he gets out of the car.

"I don't think so, but we can discuss it another time. Right now, I only want to get you in our bed."

"Our bed?" He just said that we would discuss it later and then claimed the bed as 'ours.' *What the hell.*

"Later," Jaylen says with finality and grabs the Walgreen's bag from the dashboard.

I take his outstretched hand and he leads me into the house and to his bedroom. Once he closes the doors behind us, he tosses his jacket and plastic bag onto the nearby chair and tightly engulfs me in his warm embrace. It isn't until now that I realize how much I've been wanting and needing his arms around me. They're the safest place in my world and after the events of today, safety and reassurance are what I need right now.

Jaylen's hands make a slow trail down the front of my dress to my lower stomach and he rubs me there. "My little baby's having my baby," he says with admiration. "I will protect the two of you with my life".

The concern in Jaylen's voice alarms me. I turn in his arms to look at him. "What is it?"

"Do you know how frustrating it was for me when you told me to get in the car? All I could think was that I had to stay in between you and Charlie so that I could protect you and our child. And you were just too damn stubborn to grant me that one little thing. My mind went frantic when she got close to you. If she tried to do anything, I was too far away to protect you, even though I was sitting right there."

"Oh, Jaylen. I'm sorry. I saw you were reluctant to leave my side, but I honestly didn't think she would do anything to harm me. I didn't mean to put you through that. I'll try to be more considerate of you," I say while caressing his face.

"You putting me through that made me realize just how much I'm looking forward to this baby," Jaylen says.

I pull his face down to mine and kiss him like I've never kissed him before, putting all the joy I feel at this very moment at hearing him say he wants this baby. Our baby. He returns the kiss with all the love he feels for me. There's so much joy and love in our kiss—it's almost overwhelming.

While never breaking the kiss, Jaylen pulls down the zipper in the back of my dress and I loosen his tie and undo the buttons on his shirt. Once his shirt is open, I run my hands over his torso. If I could mold the perfect man's body, it would be exactly like his. His chest, arms, shoulders, and back are in shape and firm from his weight work. I have never been crazy about six-pack abs, and Jaylen's abs are flat with just enough definition to them. I lick and bite one of his nipples as he pushes my dress down. He helps me out of my dress and then steps back to admire me in my peach lace strapless bra with matching boy cut panties and killer heels.

"I'm the luckiest man in the world. You are so fucking beautiful, Alise."

Not sure of what to say, I stand there and give him a shy smile.

"Don't move," Jaylen demands.

I watch him as he removes everything but his boxer briefs, which are barely holding in his erection. *He's so damn delicious.*

Jaylen plants a gentle kiss on my forehead, then on my nose, both of my eyes, on my cheek, chin, other cheek, and then my lips. I raise my arms up to wrap around his neck to deepen our kiss, but Jaylen grabs my wrists and puts them at my sides.

"I said don't move," he reminds me.

"All I want to do is touch you," I whimper. Jaylen gives me a look that tells me not to push it if I know what's good for me. "Yes, Daddy," I say in acknowledgment.

Jaylen kisses me along my collarbone. I want to lean into him, but he told me not to move. My breathing becomes more erratic as he makes his way down the center of my chest. He skips over my bra, not touching my breasts at all. I want my nipples in his mouth. I groan in desperation.

"Shhhhhh," Jaylen urges me to quiet down. I have to remember his kids are here. I can't be as loud as usual.

He drops to his knees and kisses me all over my navel. It takes me a few moments to realize that his kisses are not meant solely for me. They are for our unborn child. *He wants this child.* Watching him declaring his love for our baby is so beautiful it makes me emotional. I don't even realize I'm crying until Jaylen asks me why.

"For a while there, I didn't think I'd ever see you embrace me having your baby," I whisper, since my tears have taken away my voice. Jaylen stands up and takes my face in both his hands. He uses both of his thumbs to wipe away my tears.

"I'm sorry for making you feel that way, little baby. I'm so, so sorry. Please forgive me."

"I forgive you."

Jaylen kisses me sweetly. His tongue finds mine for a slow dance. *I could kiss this man forever.* His hands make a slow journey down my sides and then around to my backside, where he firmly cups the underside of my ass to lift me up. He lays me down on top of the bed, only breaking our kiss when he lifts up to remove my panties and his underwear. He slowly enters me. My need for him has me ready to cum nearly instantly.

"Not yet. Wait for me," Jaylen pleads. "Wait for me."

I focus on my breathing to calm my body down. Jaylen's strokes are deep, even, and strong. In between each stroke, he tells me how much he loves me, cherishes me, adores me, and thanks me for saying yes to marry him and for carrying his child until we both orgasm nearly thirty minutes later.

* * *

I can hear the birds chirping and feel Jaylen's arms wrapped around me, my back to his front, one of his hands holding a boob. I smile to myself and nuzzle deeper into his arms. I refuse to open my eyes and move out of his embrace, although I'm not sure my bladder will allow me to do it for much longer. And then I hear other voices coming from elsewhere in the house. *Jaylen's kids are here.*

My eyes dart open and I sit up to find the time. The alarm clock on the nightstand on Jaylen's side of the bed says it's 11:10 a.m.

"What's wrong?" Jaylen asks in a groggy voice.

"Your kids are up," I say as an explanation.

"Okay, what's wrong?" Jaylen is confused.

"They are up! They can walk in and see me naked in your bed at any moment! That's not how I want to start things with them." *How does he not see this problem?*

"Alise, they're teenagers, not toddlers. They know not to just barge into my room. And like I told you last night, they already know you're here. I told them we would get in late, so they know we'll be sleeping in late."

"Oh." He sits up and kisses my forehead.

"Calm down. You don't have anything to be nervous about."

"I'm meeting your kids, Jaylen. What do you mean, I don't have anything to be nervous about?"

"I mean exactly that. You don't have anything to worry about. They already know about you and JaQuese is excited to meet you. Speaking of kids, you have a test to take."

Jaylen climbs out of bed and takes the two boxes out of the drugstore bag. He takes both tests out of their packaging and walks into the bathroom. I sit there looking at the bathroom door, wondering what he's doing.

"Come on. Bring my cell in here with you," he tells me from the bathroom.

I clamber out of bed and grab his phone from inside his tuxedo jacket. When I get inside the bathroom, Jaylen is leaning against the vanity with a small paper cup in his hand.

"You aren't planning on staying in here while I pee, are you?" I ask.

"That's exactly what I'm about to do, and I don't want to hear anything about it."

I want to tell him how inappropriate and gross it is. If I didn't have to pee so badly, I would hold it until he left the bathroom, but apparently, my bladder doesn't care that I have an audience. I take the cup from him and do my business. Jaylen puts both tests into the cup and pulls them out a few seconds later.

"One test wasn't enough?"

"In case one gives a false positive," he answers. I nod. *I didn't think about that.*

Jaylen sets the timer on his phone. I take a seat on the edge of the tub after washing my hands. We're both nervously quiet as we wait for the results until I can't take the silence anymore.

"Will you add another room or move into a bigger place?"

"I don't know. Since I've been living here again, I have considered adding another room so J.J. and Jaleel can have their own rooms. With the baby, that will be two additions. Plus, I'll need to expand the master closet for your wardrobe."

"Me living here is only temporary until we get married later." Might as well get this talk out of the way now.

"This will not be a long engagement," Jaylen says with certainty.

"How short of an engagement are you thinking?" I was hoping he would give me enough time to plan a proper wedding, but knowing Jaylen, that is a negative.

"No more than two months."

"Two months! Have you lost your mind? How do you expect me to plan a wedding in two months or less?"

"I don't mean to sound crass, but who do you have to invite besides Joc, who will stand up for you?"

Jaylen is right. Joc is all I have now, other than him. My parents are gone. I have some aunts and uncles somewhere in the world, but I don't know them and only saw them at each of my parent's funerals. They couldn't even get my name right—kept calling me Alice. I cut Charlie out of my life last night. That also means no access to my god-daughter. The thought of never seeing Amber again depresses me. I love that little girl more than life.

"Jaylen, I'll never see my god-daughter again."

Jaylen closes the small space between us and envelopes me in his arms.

"I won't let that happen. I'll talk to Devon."

"How is Devon going to make sure I can see Amber with no interference from Charlie?"

Jaylen starts to answer, but the timer on his phone interrupts.

"Moment of truth," I say nervously.

"We are together, no matter what it says," Jaylen reassures me.

We both walk over to the counter and look at the two pregnancy tests. One has a plus sign, while the other simply says "pregnant" on its digital screen. Jaylen scoops me up into his arms and kisses me.

"In less than 24 hours, you've agreed to be my wife and now we know for sure that you're having my baby. There isn't anyone one on this earth that's as blessed as I am, and I have you to thank for that."

"I'm going to be a mom," I say in shocked excitement.

"You are going to be a great mom and a wonderful wife," Jaylen corrects.

I wrap my arms tightly around Jaylen's neck and thank him for finding me again.

* * *

"You're so pretty, Ms. Alise," JaQuese says to me with a bright smile.

Jaylen's brown skinned 12-year-old daughter with latch hook braids has been my shadow since her father formally introduced me to the kids 15 minutes ago.

"Thank you, Quese," I say as we prepare sandwiches and veggies for a family lunch. Jaylen and the boys are in the backyard tossing around a football. I watch them for a few seconds at a time from the kitchen window.

"Did my daddy give you that ring?" The hope in her voice is palpable.

"Yes, he did. Last night, as a matter of fact," I chuckle.

"So, you two *are* getting " she asks with much excitement.

I laugh some more. "Yes, we're getting married."

She stops putting together the sandwiches to give me a big hug that catches me completely off guard. I drop my knife and carrots onto the cutting board and hug her back. I never thought Jaylen's kids would accept me so easily, especially considering how my first and very unexpected meeting with J.J. went. But even he seems to accept me now.

JaQuese and I carry trays with the food and drinks on them out to the furniture on the deck.

"Lunch time," JaQuese yells at the fellas.

The three come to sit at the table, the boys looking just like their father. We sit and joke around while enjoying lunch. It feels very comfortable. I guess Jaylen was right. I didn't have anything to worry about.

JaQuese spills the beans about the engagement and Jaylen promises them that this is the last time he will marry—this marriage is forever.

"I'm going to hold you to that, Dad," Jaleel says. He has the same even brown tone as his sister, but the rest of him is his dad, except for the mess of short dreadlocks on his head.

"Ms. Alise and I have another announcement," Jaylen says. I have a mouthful of turkey sandwich, so I place my hand on his bicep and squeeze it to stop him. My attempt failed.

"We'll be giving you three a new little brother or sister in about seven months or so."

Why, dear God, why did he have to announce this RIGHT now?

JaQuese squeals, Jaleel spray spits his juice, and J.J. makes a comment about his dad working fast.

"Watch your mouth," Jaylen responds.

"I didn't mean any disrespect by it. It's true, though," J.J. smiles at his dad. "But seriously, that's cool. I miss having a baby around. Being a big brother isn't cool anymore when you can't use them to pick up chicks," he teases at his younger siblings.

"You weren't old enough to use us as chick magnets," Jaleel states.

"And even if you were, you were still too ugly for anyone to give YOU the time of day, J.J.," JaQuese snaps back.

"Oh, you want to talk about ugly? Well, how about this. You're so ugly kryptonite loses its power at the sight of you."

Jaylen and I sit back and enjoy the kids roasting each other. Some of their jokes are so old that I haven't heard them since I was a kid, and that makes me feel old!

CHAPTER XIX

"Are you ready for this?" Jaylen asks me while holding my hand during the car ride.

"As ready as I'll ever be, since you're only giving me two months to plan our wedding," I say nervously. We're in his SUV going down Lindon Road to go to his parents' house for a family barbecue. I've never met his parents. I just met the kids yesterday. J.J. is following us with his siblings so he can take JaQuese back to her mother at the appointed time.

Jaylen's phone rings. He becomes noticeably irritable as he sends the caller to voicemail.

"Everything okay?"

"It's Calondra. She found out about the engagement watching the news this yesterday morning. She's called me over ten times already and texted more than that. I've been ignoring her. She still thinks you're the reason our marriage ended and also thinks I'm trying to have you replace her in the kids' life."

"That's absurd. She'll always be their mother. There isn't anything I can do to change that," I respond to the incredulous thought.

"Only if she understood that." Jaylen sighs as his phone chimes to announce a new voicemail.

"Who else is going to be at this barbecue?" I ask to change the subject, hoping to improve his mood.

"My sister," he says with almost a smile.

"You have a sister?" *How did I not know this?*

"Calm down, and yes, I have a sister."

"You never told me."

"And now you know," he says before kissing my hand.

"Older or younger?"

"Younger. Liana is my best friend and will be my best man at our wedding."

"If you two are so close, why am I just now finding out about her?" I feel like this is something I should have already known. I can't help but wonder how much more I do not know about my fiancé.

"Before," Jaylen pauses, "You know why. Now, we've only been back together for a short time."

"And yet you thought that was ample time to pop the question?" *I can't be the only person in this car who sees how backwards this is. But, of course, I am.*

"If you don't stop being a smart ass on your own, I will pull over and put a stop to it myself," Jaylen says in a tone that's meant to shut me up.

"Not with your kids following us, you won't," I retort. The kids are my saving grace from any and all punishment, and I intend to use that fully right now.

Jaylen picks up his phone to make a call.

"I have to make a stop. Go ahead to your grandparents and we'll meet you there," Jaylen says to his oldest son. *Shit.* Soon after, I see J.J. make a right onto a side street that goes into a residential area in my mirror. Jaylen keeps straight for a few miles.

"Where are you taking me?" The words are out of my mouth before I realize it and I instantly regret it. I know they will only add to my punishment. His silence confirms that.

He makes a right in the direction of the mall.

He wouldn't take me there. It's four, and the mall closes at six.

And then it dawns on me. He's going to his gym. My heart is racing. *Fuck. Why didn't I just shut up?*

Jaylen turns into the parking lot. For it to be a Sunday, there are a lot of cars here. Jaylen goes around the building and parks in the back. I stay put until he opens my door. With one hand firmly gripping my elbow, he leads me to a large metal door that he unlocks. We walk into a corridor that goes in both directions. Jaylen goes left, pulling me along.

He has a quick, determined pace. I have to keep a light jogging pace just to keep up with him. Jaylen makes a right into another corridor. I want to ask him to slow down, but I keep quiet. I'm thankful I'm wearing sandals and cotton shorts, and not a dress and heels when we go up a flight of stairs. He stops at the only door at the top of the landing, unlocks it, leads me inside, and quickly closes the door behind us. The lights come on. This is his office.

His desk is large and made of black marble. With a high back leather office chair, it looks intimidating. Or maybe I find it intimidating because I know there's a punishment coming.

Two low back curved leather chairs sit on the other side of the desk. Pictures, certificates, and trophies line the short walls on either side of the desk.

"Take off your shorts and panties and get over my desk," Jaylen orders.

I quickly do as he says. I can hear him messing with his belt and pants, and I get excited down below for a punishment fuck. Then I hear his belt slide from around his pants. *Oh god.* In the old days, Jaylen only used the belt on me when I was exceptionally bad, like when I put his car keys in Jell-O. I saw it on a show and thought it was hilarious, so I tried it on him. He didn't find it funny at all.

My heart is pounding so hard and fast that it would probably be out of my chest if it weren't for the fact I'm lying on his unforgiving desk. Jaylen places one hand in the middle of my back to keep me in place.

"I've let you get away with entirely too much since we've been back together. That ends now," Jaylen states.

"Daddy," I beg. "I'm sorry." I know it's too late. I've intentionally been pushing it since we've been back together. I would be lying if I said it wasn't to punish him for leaving me and for his initial reaction to me possibly being pregnant, but I've had to be on my own for years now. It isn't so easy to fall back in line to being someone's submissive.

Crack. Jaylen's belt makes harsh contact with my backside. I grip the other side of his desk tightly.

"You are going to watch your smart-ass mouth," Jaylen says before bringing the belt down on me again.

"Yes, Daddy," I say as a lone tear falls from my eye. Out of instinct, I pull up on the desk to get away.

"Put your hands behind your back," he orders. I do so, and Jaylen holds them down firmly with one hand. The belt bites my skin again, and I cry out.

"You will obey me," he demands through gritted teeth.

"Yes, Daddy," I cry.

"WHEN. I. TELL. YOU. TO. DO. SOMETHING. DON'T. QUESTION. OR. UNDERMIND. ME. JUST. FUCKING. DO. IT," Jaylen says in between hits.

"Yes, Daddy," I sob. Jaylen drops the belt and lifts me up into his arms. He carries me over to the small sofa, sits down, and cradles me in his arms. As much as I hate the belt, this is exactly what I have needed from Jaylen to break the walls that have kept me from fully submitting to him. This punishment is the affirmation I needed to know that this, that we are real. Finally, I can let go and be free.

Jaylen squeezes me tightly and kisses my forehead.

"You mean everything to me, Alise. I can't protect you when you're disobeying me. And if I can't protect you, then I can't protect our baby," he says in almost a whisper.

And now I understand. Jaylen expressed his fear for my wellbeing when I didn't listen to him at Walgreen's the other night, but I see that fear has not been subdued. I can't do this to him again, especially with Charlie acting crazy. Now it's my turn to comfort him. I wrap my arms around his neck and kiss his lips.

"I won't do it again. I'm sorry for adding to your fear."

We continue to sit there and hold each other in comfortable silence for a couple of minutes until Jaylen breaks the silence.

"We have to go. Go get the baby oil out of my desk so I can take care of you."

I can feel the soreness and welts on my ass as I walk. I find the baby oil and as I bring it to my lover. Suddenly, a thought hits me.

"Daddy, why do you have baby oil in your desk?"

Jaylen looks at me and grins.

* * *

"My brother and his kids have been through enough these last few years," Liana says.

Jaylen's sister and I are sitting in the formal living room of their parents' home while everyone else is in the backyard. Even though she's four years younger than Jaylen, she's a very protective sister. Her smooth skin is just as dark as her brother's with almond-shaped eyes and burgundy dreadlocks that touch her waist. She is gorgeous.

"I would never set out to hurt them. I love your brother, and by extension, I love his kids." To relieve some of the sting on my butt, I adjust in the wing-armed chair, but no matter which way I sit, it hurts. Liana is watching me closely from the matching chair that is angled beside me. A small oak sitting table is between us. The entire room has a Victorian feel to it.

"They all need a stable family. You know, consistency and reliability."

"I have every reason in the world to stay and not a single reason to leave," I respond. My unborn child is just one of those reasons. Unconsciously, I protectively rub my lower belly.

Liana flips her dreads over her shoulder and turns her body to look me squarely in the eyes.

"He loves you. I've never seen him this way about anyone, not even Calondra." Liana says her former sister-in-law's name like it leaves an unpleasant taste in her mouth.

"I take it you weren't a fan of hers or their relationship," I say.

"I never cared for her. She was needy to be controlling and manipulative. I've never cared for that in a woman. But you are not that type of woman."

I look at her, puzzled. She didn't put it as a question, and it's throwing me off.

"Oh, I've done my research on you. You're nothing like that leech," she says with a smile. "I have great intuition. My gut tells me you will be good for them. I just hope you will have the patience and inner strength to deal with his ex without catching a case," she chuckles.

I laugh too. "We'll see."

Just then, Jaylen walks in looking sexy as always. *Will the sight of him always take my breath away?*

"Li, I know Alise is the best thing since sliced bread, but I need you to stop hogging my fiancé."

"We're just having a conversation," Liana says to her brother. Then she turns to me and says, "See, never before!"

I chuckle at her statement and glow from the inside out from Jaylen's statement.

Jaylen puts his hand out for mine and I give it to him. I wince when he pulls me up from the chair.

"Just a reminder," Jaylen whispers as he kisses my temple.

The three of us walk out of the formal living room, down a short corridor that's covered in framed family photos. I stop at one that looks like a younger J.J. with a missing tooth, but from the wicker chair background, dark green turtleneck shirt and faded overall jeans, the picture is older than him.

"Is that not the ugliest shade of green?" Liana says with a grin. "And look at that gap!" I can't help but laugh at her poking fun at her big brother.

"Jaylen, I think this is the first time I've seen you in something other than black and gray," I joke.

"Oh, then you have to see some of his Easter pictures. There is one with him wearing lavender from head to toe. He looked like a girlish piece of luggage," Liana says to me.

"That I have to see," I laugh.

"Momma still has the picture of you with chicken pox all over your face somewhere around here, Li. Don't make me go find it," Jalen says.

"I destroyed that picture long ago, but she still has all of your bathtub pictures."

"You aren't too old to be put in a headlock, Li."

"And Dad will take your head off if you touch me. Checkmate," she says as she walks past the kitchen and into the great room, with Jaylen and me not too far behind.

I don't resent growing up an only child but watching the kids yesterday and Jaylen and Liana just now, I can't help but wish I had a sibling. My mother was an only child too, and all of my father's family lived elsewhere. I didn't even have a cousin to play with. The neighborhood kids were cool, but they weren't family. It wasn't until Charlie and I met in sixth grade I had someone my age to connect with and now look at us. I stop Jaylen in the living room just inside the patio door.

"I'm glad our baby will have a family to grow up with," I say to my fiancé.

"You'll never be alone again," he promises before kissing my forehead.

"Jaylen, you chose a mighty fine woman," his father, Otis, says to him when we rejoin the family on the patio. Jaylen and Liana get their dark skin from their father. He is bald on the top with salt and pepper hair on the sides and back of his head and small wire-rim glasses. He is slightly taller than Jaylen and slim.

"I couldn't agree more," Jaylen says, squeezing me in the arm that's around my shoulders.

"I hope you make this one work," Cathy, his mother, says as we sit with them. Cathy is my complexion with honey eyes and a spirit that reminds me of Patti LaBelle. I warmed to her immediately when Jaylen introduced us over an hour ago.

"Making this work is the only option I have. I can't regret marrying Calondra because I wouldn't have my kids if I hadn't, but Alise is the love of my life," Jaylen answers while kissing my hand.

"You're different with Alise. The only time I haven't seen you touching her was when Liana pulled her inside. You've never displayed that type of affection for any other woman in your life," Cathy adds.

"That is because Alise is *the* woman," Jaylen states.

"I told you," Liana says to me.

I respond with a smile. I guess she's right. They see an affectionate side of Jaylen they've not seen before. I'm seeing a family-oriented side of Jaylen I have never seen before.

"Told her what?" Jaylen asks his little sister.

"It's a sister thing. You wouldn't understand," Liana responds.

"That's alright. I'll get it out of Alise. You forget, her loyalties lie first with me."

We all continue to sit on the back patio enjoying each other's company, talking about everything from the race for Michigan's newest governor to Liana's new job with Google and when she will get around to settling down and giving her mother more grandkids. The kids are hanging out inside the gazebo a few yards away. I could spend hours like this. I imagine Jaylen and I sitting where Otis and Cathy are now, grandparents, all the kids over to visit with their children and significant others. A house full of life. Until this very moment, I never realized how badly I want it.

JaQuese comes to sit next to me and rests her head on my shoulder. I wrap an arm around her, and she adjusts. I'm amazed at how comfortable she is with me already. It touches my heart.

"Ms. Alise?"

"Yes, JaQuese."

"Can I go to work with you one day?" she asks tentatively.

"For the full day?"

"Please? I've always wanted to learn how to make my dance costumes." Her voice and face are full of hope. How could I ever say no to that?

"I'd be honored for you to come to work with me one day. We'll have to work out when it can happen with your parents, okay?"

"Thank you," she squeals as she reaches up to hug me. Her joy is infectious, and I can't help but beam back at her.

"May I ask you something else?"

"You can ask me anything, JaQuese."

"Can I live with you, my daddy, and brothers?" Her question floors me. Before I can respond, an unfamiliar female voice yells from the side of the house.

"Can you do what, JaQuese?"

A tall woman with a caramel complexion, black bob with copper highlights, and a coke bottle physique comes storming into the backyard towards the patio. It's Colandra, and she is not happy about what she just heard from her daughter.

"What. Did. You. Just. Ask. *Her?*" Colandra's voice is full of venom.

"Mom, back off!" J.J. yells as he and Jaleel jog over from the gazebo.

"You're not supposed to be anywhere near my property," Otis says.

"Calondra, you need to leave," Jaylen says, putting himself in between us.

"Are you trying to block me from my child, Jaylen?"

How long has she been here?

"Hi. My husband and I have a restraining order on my son's ex-wife, and she is currently on our property causing a disturbance. Please send an officer. She's been violent before." I look up to see Cathy on the phone.

Restraining order? Been violent before? What the hell did she do?

"You aren't supposed to be here, Mom. You know that," J.J. says.

"The way I see it, if *I'm* not welcomed somewhere, then *my* kids aren't welcomed there either," Calondra states.

"You are fucking crazy. The kids have every right to be here. You have none," Liana says.

"Swearing and bad-mouthing me in front of my kids. Li, I thought you were better than that."

"And you think your actions right now are an example of good behavior for them?" Liana asks incredulously. "And don't call me 'Li'. That's reserved for family and friends only, and you were never either to me."

Calondra stares at Liana for a moment and sucks her teeth before rolling her eyes.

"The police are on their way," Cathy says.

"Mom, leave before you get arrested again," J.J. pleads.

Again? What the fuck?

"You know *she* is the reason your father and I weren't able to work things out," she says to her kids while keeping her eyes on Jaylen.

"We didn't work because we fell out of love. I didn't want to be with you anymore," Jaylen corrects her.

"That is who you want to live with, Quese? The whore responsible for your father leaving you, your brothers, and me behind like family meant nothing to him?"

"What did you just call me?" I ask while standing up. She may be delusional, but she apparently doesn't know me. I will unscramble her eggs real quick.

"Calondra, you are going to stop disrespecting my fiancé and telling your twisted reality about why we ended in front of our kids right now," Jaylen says while putting an arm out to keep me back.

"You don't control me," Calondra says while taking a step closer to Jaylen.

"J.J., take your brother, sister, aunt, grandparents, and Alise into the house," Jaylen says.

"You're crazy if you think I'm going to leave you out here with Ms. Screw Lose," Liana says.

"Refer to me as 'crazy' one more time, Liana," Calondra threatens.

"How about I do better than refer and just tell you that you are fucking crazy and need some meds and a straitjacket?"

"Li," Jaylen growls.

"I'm staying right here, Jaylen," his sister says.

"I'm not leaving either, son," Otis' gravelly voice says.

J.J. grabs my arm to take me in the house with his siblings and grandmother, but I shake my head at him. Jaylen knows me well and orders me into the house before I can say anything. I start to object, but the soreness coming from my butt cheeks reminds me of my earlier punishment and the torment that my defiance has put him through. There's no telling what his irrational ex-wife will do, so I decide it will be safer for the baby and me inside the house.

I follow Cathy and the kids into the formal living room that Liana and I were talking in earlier. We can't see or hear what is going on in the backyard. JaQuese is crying. J.J. and Jaleel look pissed, although they're both trying to console their sister. Cathy is pacing in the front window, watching out for the police.

"Can I get you anything, Cathy?" I ask her.

"Can you help my son get full custody of his kids so that she-devil can stop using them as pawns to make all our lives miserable?"

"I would fully support Jaylen if he went that route," I respond. Cathy stares at me intently for what feels like an entire minute before nodding her head.

"She always gets crazy like that whenever I say I want to live with Daddy. I wouldn't have said anything if I knew she was listening," JaQuese sobs.

"Oh honey, this isn't your fault," Cathy says to her granddaughter as she goes to embrace her.

"But do you see why I don't want to live with her anymore," JaQuese says to everyone in the room with tears that are just barely staying in her eyes. Right then, a Flint Township police cruiser shows up. Cathy rushes outside to meet them and shows them to the back of the house.

I stay inside the house with the kids. As a distraction, I get them to tell me about what they want to be when they grow up. J.J. wants to play sports throughout college, get a degree in sports management and marketing to use in case he doesn't make it into the NFL. Jaleel wants to go into sports medicine and eventually take over his dad's business. JaQuese intends to graduate from Julliard with a degree in dance and join the American Contemporary Ballet Company, but she is also interested in fashion and design for the long run, as dancers typically don't have long careers.

I've not known the three of them long, but just listening to them talk about their dreams and the various things they are into now so they can accomplish those goals makes me so proud of them. I make a silent promise to always support their endeavors and to do whatever I can to make sure they turn those dreams into reality.

While I'm telling them about my journey through fashion school as a working adult and the importance of achieving things for yourself, Jaylen, Liana, and their parents come into the room.

"Where's Mom?" Jaleel asks. No one says anything.

"Where's Mom?" all three kids ask in unison.

"Getting into the back of the police car," Jaylen answers reluctantly.

"I don't want Mom to go to jail, but does this mean that I get to come live with you now?" JaQuese asks.

"Not permanently, but you'll be staying with me for the next few days," her father answers. "Do you have enough clothes at my house to get you through the week?"

"Yes, I've been bringing extra clothes and leaving them, so I'd have less to pack when I'd finally get to move in with you."

Everyone in the room looks at her and then at Jaylen in shock. At this very moment, my heart breaks for Jaylen's kids, especially JaQuese. I would give anything for even five more minutes with my mother, and she just wants to get away from hers.

Porsha Deun

CHAPTER XX

I'm up earlier than usual since I'm no longer within walking distance of my business. Plus, I don't have my car, which means Jaylen is going to have to drop me off after he takes Quese to dance school. Calondra will go in front of a judge this morning, so Jaylen will be downtown for a while before going to his gym. One perk of having your own business is that you never have to call off.

Jaylen and I fix breakfast together, and we all eat as a family. I essentially have a family now, with kids plus one on the way. It's a lot to get used to, but I think I'm finding my place. Jaylen has good kids, which makes it much easier. However, if JaQuese is going to move in like she hopes to, we are going to need another bathroom. The three of them spent a good portion of the morning fighting for bathroom time, and Jaylen refuses to let them into his... *our*... bathroom. Thinking of this as my home is something that's hard for me. Jaylen keeps correcting me whenever I refer to something being his.

At first, I wasn't sure what the boys were doing up since school is out. When I asked Jaylen, he informed me that J.J. works at his gym and Jaleel gets tips at a nearby barbershop by working as the cleanup boy.

While on the way to my store, I think about keeping or letting go of my apartment. I haven't told him yet, but I'm not ready to give it up. I'm leaning towards keeping it for when I need space and quiet to work outside of the office. He isn't going to be happy about it.

"Call me after court," I say to Jaylen when he pulls up outside of Timeless Elegance.

"I'll come by. Maybe we can do lunch together before I head to the rec center, depending on what time I get out."

"Okay, Daddy. I love you." I lean over and softly kiss his lips.

"I love you too, fiancé." Him saying my new title makes me smile. Jaylen gets out of the car to walk around and open my door. We kiss again, and I walk inside.

My mind goes over all the things I have to do at work this week. I need a new store manager, I have to meet with the contractor over some details for the new level, start looking over recommendation letters for a student intern for the Fashion Against Violence program, and complete the rest of the designs for the new bridal season. Just as I think about how I'm going to tell the team about Charlie's sudden departure, a familiar, yet unwanted, voice calls out to greet me.

"Good morning, Alise," Charlie says with a smile that makes my stomach turn.

"What the hell are you doing here?" I ask. I suddenly remember that during the course of me firing her two days ago I didn't get her keys. I make a mental note to have her alarm code removed from the system and remove her as an authorized officer at the bank.

"What do you mean?" I work here, remember?"

"I fired you, remember?" I snap.

"Oh, we both know you weren't serious about that. That thing you're engaged to isn't around, so there is no need for you to pretend anymore."

This bitch.

"Let's get something straight," I say while stepping towards her. "You no longer work here. You are no longer my friend. There's no longer a place for you in my life. Disrespect my man again, and you will end up in a hospital."

"Does your threat mean the pregnancy tests came back negative?"

A chill goes down my spine at her mentioning the pregnancy tests. "That's none of your god-damn business, Charlie. Now hand over your keys and get the hell out of my store."

"So, you *are* pregnant?"

"The keys, Charlie," I yell. "Give me the fucking keys and get out!" I hear shoes scuffling upstairs.

"Who are you putting on a show for? We love each other, so there will always be a place for me in your life. Besides, with you being pregnant, you're going to need me more than ever to support you once we fix that," she says while pointing to my stomach.

"Fix that? Fix that!" I've had it. I rush her and tackle her to the floor. "You delusional bitch," I yell. Charlie wasn't expecting this, so her surprise works to my advantage as she tries to get into defense mode. I get two solid punches into her face before I feel hands pulling me away. I stomp her in her groin as someone lifts me off her.

"Alise, stop! What the hell has gotten into you?" I vaguely hear Joc ask me. I look around to see Joc, Ming Li,

LaTisha, and Rebecca are all trying to keep distance between Charlie and me.

"Everyone, listen up," I huff. "Charlie is no longer an employee at Timeless Elegance. If you see her on company property, call the police. Joc, take her keys and name tag. Do not come back upstairs until she and her belongings have left the premises. Once she does, meet me in my office."

As I make my way up the stairs, I can't help but wonder how much of that my staff heard before they came down. I'm not ready for people to know I'm pregnant. I put my hand over my stomach and apologize to my baby.

"That was an irresponsible thing for Mommy to do. Please be okay." I'm not sure what number mental note I'm on now, but I add making my first prenatal appointment for as soon as possible to my to-do-list.

Once I'm in my office, I call the alarm company to have Charlie's code removed from the system, and I change the master code, just in case. The bank isn't open yet, so my next call is to Devon to tell him about his wife and to get a recommendation for an O.B..

"Jaylen told me about what happened after the fundraiser. I planned on talking to her about it, even got Kitty on board about possibly doing an intervention, but Charlie never came home, and she didn't stay at her parents. Unless she has a credit card I don't know about, she's been using cash for a hotel."

"Devon, I don't know what else to do, other than to get the police involved."

"As much as I don't want to see my wife in jail, you do what you have to do. Being arrested may be the best thing for her and everyone else involved."

"She wants to get rid of my baby," I whisper into the phone. Joc walks into my office at that exact moment. "Devon, I need to go. Text me the name and phone number of the doctor. I'll be in touch. Bye."

"You need to tell me what the hell is going on right now," Joc says with his hands on his hips.

"You're going to want to sit down for this," I tell him.

* * *

Hours have passed. My head hurts, and I cannot concentrate on work. My mind is stuck on this morning's events. I posted the new store manager position. That and scheduling my first ultrasound to confirm the pregnancy are the only things I've managed to get done today. Joc has been bouncing back and forth from the work studio and the storefront to help cover. I would help, but I just can't seem to focus my mind on anything. My office phone rings.

"Yeah," I answer.

"Jaylen's on his way up," Joc says.

"Thanks."

"Go home. Come back refreshed tomorrow."

"I'll think about it."

Jaylen walks into my office with a stone face and closes the door behind him. He stands there looking at me for what feels like an eternity without saying a word. I can't tell if he is angry or concerned, but I know he's talked to Devon. The fact that he didn't hear what happened this morning with Charlie from me has him pissed. And that it happened at all has him concerned for our baby and me. I'm kicking myself right now for not calling him. It didn't even cross my mind.

I want to say something, but I don't know what to say. Even if I did, I don't think it would be wise. I know he's trying to calm himself and find his words at the same time. But the silence and tension are killing me.

I get up and go over to him. Even though he's pissed, and rightly so, he needs comforting. We both do. He needs to know that I'm okay, and I need to know that we're okay. I wrap my arms around his waist and rest my head on his chest. He doesn't move. He doesn't respond at all. My heart breaks.

I know he's upset because I didn't call him, but I didn't think he would be this upset. He can't shut me out like this. We need each other now more than ever. I squeeze him tighter. Other than his breathing getting faster and harder, he still doesn't respond to my embrace.

A sob escapes my lips as I whisper his name.

"Why didn't you call me?" Jaylen finally asks.

"With everything going on, I didn't think about it."

"You didn't think about it!"

"Jaylen… Daddy. I'm sorry. I… was… scared," I say in between sobs. "And now… I'm… I'm scared… for us."

Jaylen sighs and his body softens. He wraps his arms around me, pulls me closer into him, and kisses my hair.

"You don't have to worry about us. We're fine."

"Are you sure? It felt like you were shutting me out again," I cry.

"No, baby. We are fine. I promise. I was upset because I had to hear about what happened from that crazy bitch's husband instead of you. You called Devon, but you didn't call me? Do you have any idea how that makes me feel?"

"I should have called you. I know," I say, looking into his eyes.

Jaylen cups my face with his large hands and looks me intently in my eyes.

"YOU. ARE. MINE. DON'T YOU UNDERSTAND THAT? MINE!"

"Yes, Daddy. Yours. Forever."

Jaylen softly kisses my forehead, the tip of my nose, and my lips. As he repeatedly kisses my lips, they go from sweet butterfly kisses to passionate and possessive kisses. I can feel all the negative energy of the last forty-eight hours wash away from both of us. Comforting and reconnecting, that's what I'd label this moment.

His tongue slips into my mouth, dominating me and taking all that I offer him willingly. I pull his shirt out of his pants, but Jaylen reluctantly stops me. Confusion and rejection were all over my face.

"I want to take you all over this office, but first, we need to get you and the baby checked out."

"I have an appointment scheduled for next week with an O.B. that Devon recommended," I explain.

"Devon called in a favor to that doctor. Your appointment's been moved up to 2 p.m. today."

"The office didn't call me to…," I say as my cell phone interrupts me.

"That would be them now," Jaylen chuckles.

I take the call and confirm my new appointment. Shortly after, Joc calls on the office phone.

"Joc, you're on speaker," I answer.

"Good, because your man is the one I want, anyway. Jaylen, please tell me you're taking her home. She doesn't need to be here today."

"Yeah, I'm taking her home," Jaylen says.

"Thank you," he responds with relief. "Alise, even though I know you probably won't do it, stay home tomorrow, too. We can manage for a couple of days without you. If we need you for something, I'll call."

"I will think about it," I say.

"She'll be home tomorrow, Joc," Jaylen corrects. I give him an exasperated look. *Great. The two men I love are teaming up against me. Or for me?*

"Thank you, Jaylen," Joc replies

"Thank you for being her loyal friend," Jaylen says. There is silence for a moment.

"Alise has been a genuine friend to me. I'll always have her back."

"And I yours," I say with love. I can hear the emotion in Joc's voice getting ready to boil over. He takes a couple of deep breaths.

"Do you need me to pick up anything from your apartment?" Joc asks with a more even tone.

"No. I have enough for the week at Jaylen's. He was prepared," I say jokingly. Joc chuckles with me. Jaylen stands there with a "really?" look on his face.

"I'll call you later. I don't want to see you in here until later this week. Love you."

"Love you too, Joc."

"Take care of her, Jaylen," Joc demands.

"That's my number one priority," Jaylen answers. Joc hangs up.

* * *

"I'm going to insert the probe into your vagina to see the baby. Just take a deep breath and relax," Dr. Turner says. Dr. Turner is short and round with a slight southern drawl and a bright smile. She seems nice. I hold Jaylen's hands as I take a deep breath and try to relax. There's nothing about being in stirrups with your legs spread that's comfortable, which is why I don't go to a gynecologist regularly. I don't like to be that vulnerable in front of anyone, except Jaylen, of course.

The doctor hits a few buttons on the machine.

"The baby is… hold on…" she says before trailing off and clicking some more.

"What do you mean 'hold on,'" both Jaylen and I say in unison.

"Calm down, calm down. They are alright. I just spoke a little too early."

"What do you mean, you spoke too early?" Jaylen asks.

"Did you say 'they'?" I ask.

"Twins," Dr. Turner says, answering my question, "and they are doing well. I'd say that you are about eight or nine weeks along and you would be due sometime around mid-February."

A few moments pass with silence in the exam room. Dr. Turner chuckles. "Are the two of you still breathing?" she asks.

"Twins," I whisper.

"Yes, twins," she confirms.

Again, silence. I can't get my mind around it, and I would imagine Jaylen is feeling the same way since he hasn't said a single word.

"I want to schedule your next appointment for a month from now. I can get a better estimate of your due date and ensure that both of the babies are still there."

"Still there?" I ask in a whisper. I can't seem to manage more than a whisper, it seems.

"More people are conceived with a twin than you think. Sometimes one twin disappears or is absorbed by the other twin during the first trimester," Dr. Turner explains.

"So, I could lose one?"

"That's always a possibility with multiple fetuses, but I would say that is a low risk at this point, since you're only a few weeks out from your second trimester."

I nod my head to let her know I understand, but the thought of losing one of them terrifies me already.

"Try not to worry about it. I'll write you a prescription for prenatal pills and give you some pamphlets to read over. The sooner you start the prenatal pills, the better the chances are for your twins."

"Okay," I respond.

"Is your fiancé going to be okay?"

"I think so," I say as I look up at him. He hasn't let go of my hand, but still hasn't said anything. He hasn't even moved. First, I was worried about the possibility of losing one of our babies, and now I'm worried about Jaylen's feelings towards having not one, but two babies on the way. He accepted having another child and twins, maybe more than what he bargained for.

"You can get dressed now. The prescription and pamphlets will be waiting for you at the front desk," the doctor says as she moves the ultrasound machine back to its proper spot against the wall.

As the physician leaves the room, I start getting up from the table. Before my feet hit the floor, Jaylen engulfs me in his arms and kisses me reverentially. I squeal in surprise.

"You are so damn amazing," he says as he lifts me up and swings me around.

"I didn't do this all by myself, you know," I giggle.

"No, but this couldn't happen with anyone but you." Jaylen puts me on my feet. "I love you."

"I love you, too."

"Now get dressed. We have to get your meds and work out some plans."

"Plans?"

"Yes, wedding plans, the house renovation, and how we're going to tell the kids about the twins tonight," Jaylen explains.

"You want to tell them today?" I ask. *He can't be serious.*

"Yes, tonight. Preferably at dinner," he answers. *Of course, he's serious.*

"Don't you think we should wait? You know… in case we lose one?"

"Stop that right now," Jaylen demands. "You will not lose either of them."

"You can't control that," I reply.

"Stop it, now," he says sternly. I don't say anything else, but I'm sure he can see the fear in my eyes. I touch my stomach as if it's supposed to will them both to stay put. Jaylen wraps his arms around me again. "You are going to have two healthy babies. You're not going to lose one. Neither of them will disappear. One will not absorb the other. You. Will. Have. Both. Of. Them. So, don't fret."

"Thank you," I say.

"Anytime, my little baby. That's what Daddy is for. Now get dressed," he says with a quick swat on my ass.

* * *

We're back in his SUV headed to his, no, *our* home, listening to jazz and holding hands when he says the craziest thing that I have ever heard him say.

"I think we should have the wedding a month from now instead of two months. We can have my parents keep the kids for the two weeks after for our honeymoon."

"Wait, what?"

"The wedding… a month from now," he repeats.

"Why the rushier rush?" I ask.

"Rushier? Did you just make up a word?"

"Did you just make up a new wedding date?"

"With everything going on with Calondra and Charlie right now, I don't see a reason for us to wait two months. Plus, with you having twins, you'll be showing sooner than most. Do you want to walk down the aisle showing?"

Sometimes, I really don't like it when he is right.

"I understand your logic, but I don't see how I can get it done in a month," I say, exasperated. I can't believe he is cutting my time like this.

"You are overthinking it again. Just keep it simple and small. I'm sure Joc wouldn't mind helping you if you need it."

"What if I want you to help me instead of Joc?" *I need him to give me more time.*

"Do you want an all-black wedding?" Jaylen asks sarcastically. He knows I'm trying to push back his proposed wedding date by having him involved in the planning process. And, of course, he knows how to shut the idea down.

"No," I pout.

"Alise, I'm fine with going to the courthouse to marry you, but I'm trying to keep open the option of a wedding because you've never had one before, while I have. I don't want to take that from you. But you have one month, or we're going to the courthouse."

FUUUUUUUUUUUUUUUCK!!!!!!

"Fine. Is there anything you object to for the ceremony?" I concede.

"Yes, don't put me in any shades of pink or orange." We both laugh.

* * *

Jaylen, the kids, and I are at the dining table enjoying freshly grilled turkey burgers and fries when Jaylen makes our announcement.

"Alise and I have some good news to share with you." The kids get quiet. "As you already know, we're engaged. The wedding will be one month from now."

JaQuese squeals are so loud that everyone puts their hands over their ears.

"Oh, I can't wait. You are going to be the prettiest bride ever, Ms. Alise. Can I be in the wedding? Can I help with the decorations? Can I help you design your dress?"

"You don't even know if she's designing her dress, Quese," Jaleel retorts.

"That's what she does, duh," JaQuese smarts back.

"Umm… I'd love to have your help, JaQuese. There's a lot to do in a very, very small amount of time," I answer. "We can get started this week and you can come to Timeless Elegance with me later this week?"

"YES," she squeals, just as loud as she did before.

"Okay, just calm down. There's more," their father says. "Instead of one new sibling, you will get two."

Crickets.

"I'm confused," Jaleel says.

"Twins?" J.J. asks me. I nod.

"Twins," he says again.

"Yes."

"Wow."

"It may seem fast," Jaylen answers. "But you must remember that Alise and I have known and loved each other for a long time. No, the pregnancy wasn't a part of the initial plan, but it's happening, and we're happy about it. It would be great if you three were happy about it, too."

"I finally get to be a big sister, so I'm excited," JaQuese says before getting up to hug me and then her father. "Can I help pick out the names?"

"Let's wait for that," Jaylen chuckles.

"I'm happy for you both. I just don't want to get used to all of this for it to only be gone a short time later," J.J. says.

"Me too," says Jaleel.

"This isn't as it was with Angela. We shouldn't have gotten married. Alise and I love each other, and I'm not going to let her go again," Jaylen explains.

"And I don't plan on going anywhere," I add.

The boys both give me a smile, Jaleel's smile being bigger than J.J.'s. These poor kids have been through so much. I only hope I can somehow help them.

"Well, since they're twins, I hope they are both boys," Jaleel says. J.J. agrees with him by giving him a high five.

"I hope they're both girls or one boy and one girl. But not both boys. We have enough boys in this family, and I want a little sister," JaQuese says.

"We hope that they both will be healthy," I say, glowingly.

"And healthy they will be," Jaylen says.

"I don't mean to hamper the mood, but how did things go in court today with mom?" Jaleel asks.

In all the drama of this morning and the excitement of the afternoon, I completely forgot about the court hearing today. I feel shitty for not asking about it. Jaylen never brought it up either.

"The judge sentenced her to 14 days in county jail. It could have been less if it wasn't for her outbursts while I was telling the judge what happened. I called her sister to let her know what was going on. She isn't going to bail your mother out this time. When she does get out, she's not to contact me or your grandparents," Jaylen explains.

"But we are all living with you now," Jaleel says.

Jaylen nods. "Y'all have cell phones. If she wants to contact you, she can that way. I scheduled an emergency hearing with the friend of the court in a couple of days."

"Are you going for permanent custody?" J.J. asks.

"Yes," his father answers.

"Good. And don't you bail her out either," J.J. states.

"You want your mother to sit in jail?" I ask.

"No, I don't *want* her to sit in jail, but she needs to," J.J. responds. "Consequences and repercussions, Ms. Alise."

"Does this mean I get to live with you, too, Daddy?" JaQuese asks. The hope in her voice nearly brings me to tears.

"As long as things go well in court, yes."

"I'll ask God to make it so in my prayers tonight," she says.

I sit back and think about when my parents got divorced. As much as I loved my father and missed him being there with my mother and me every single day, I couldn't imagine not being with my mom. The things these kids must have seen to make them not want to be with their mother. For the second time tonight, my sympathy for them and all that they are continuing to go through swells.

CHAPTER XXI

A few days later, I return to work. I took an extra day to get a jump start on wedding plans before getting JaQuese involved. She's so excited about the wedding, the possibility of her dad getting full custody of her, and the twins that sometimes I think we need to give her something just to mellow her out for a few hours. It's all she talks about now. But it's given me a look at how great of a big sister she will be. She and J.J. insist on reading a story to the twins every night before going to bed. She's even started calling me "Momma Lise." There is a soft knock on my office door that takes me out of my reverie.

"Come in."

"Hi, Alise," Kitty says.

"Hi, Kitty. Have a seat." I don't believe I have a meeting with her today. I can only assume she's here to talk about her big sister. "How do you like your office?"

"It's fine. Great, really," she says with a smile that seems to be forced. The poor girl is worried.

"You don't have to worry about your job, Kitty," I explain. "It's yours as long as you want it. I don't hold anything that's going on with Charlie against you."

"That is good to know," Kitty sighs. "But I'm more worried about you... and my sister."

"Physically, I'm fine. Mentally and emotionally, I'm still trying to get my head wrapped around this."

"And you're pregnant?"

"With twins," I say with a smile as I touch my stomach.

"I'm happy for you, Alise. I've seen you with Amber. You will be a great mom. You've been a great god-mother to her."

"I'll always be her god-mother, no matter what happens," I tell her.

"That's good to know. Consistency will be good for Amber."

"Charlie still hasn't come home?"

Devon shook his head. "She's turned her phone off and emptied her personal account. No one has seen or heard from her. No one knows where she is. Devon is scared that she'll kidnap Amber," Kitty explains.

"I doubt she does that, but with Charlie being so unpredictable right now, I'd say his fear is justified."

Kitty nods her head in agreement.

"I don't know what's going through my sister's head, but I want to thank you for not pressing charges against her for what she did on Monday."

"She needs mental help, not jail. Even with all that's happened, I want to think that my friend is still somewhere in there and she just needs help. But I can't say I won't get the police involved if she comes after me again."

"And you should, if it happens again. I pray it doesn't for the safety of you and your babies, but unfortunately I think her coming after you again is the only way she'll reveal herself and the only chance we may have at catching her to get her the help she needs."

"I'm afraid you're right," I respond.

Kitty reaches her hand across my desk, and I grab it quickly. Looking into her eyes, I can see the pain she feels for her sister. I also see the little girl with pigtails that used to follow her sister and me around. Things were so much simpler back then. Now, I don't know what to think or do.

"Well, I'm going to get back to work now," Kitty says with a smile and a last squeeze of my hand.

"Me, too. Let me know if you need anything," I beam back at her. As Kitty walks out, I catch her wiping tears from her eyes. I rest my head in my hands and take a couple of deep breaths to calm my emotions. Between feeling sorry for the kids, dealing with this Charlie mess, planning a wedding, and being scared for my twins, I haven't thought about what Amber is going through. I make a mental note to spend some time with her soon. She needs one of her mothers around.

Once I have my emotions reigned in, I pick up the proposal the kids from the night of the gala foundation gala sent to me about their fashion show. They have some superb ideas and designs. They even contacted some venues and have a sponsorship from a local grocery store chain, pending my backing, of course. I must remember to ask them who helped them with the proposal. I'm surprised by the level of professionalism in it. This is exactly what I need to lift my spirits. I get busy contacting the first of the three proposed venue spots.

By the end of the day, I've set up appointments for my fashion kids and I to check out venues and tastings with vendors, sent them an email giving them all the details, found someone to marry Jaylen and I, a venue for the ceremony and reception, set up interviews for the student intern position, reviewed the resumes for the store manager position, and a meeting with my contractor about possibly doing the work to expand my new home.

There are some things I need from my apartment, so I call Jaylen to tell him to meet me there instead of the office, but I end up getting his voicemail. I don't bother leaving a message. I just let Joc know where I'm headed as I leave. Jaylen will be here soon. I may have time to get back before he arrives.

I take my time walking to my apartment. It feels like forever since I've made this two-block walk. The sun feels good on my skin. These short walks are one of the things I'll miss the most about living in my apartment. And the quiet. But I guess the quiet will end soon with twins on the way.

As soon as I open the door to my apartment, I stop. Something's wrong. Someone is here. There's a smell of food cooking. *Who the fuck is in my apartment?*

Before I take another step, I spread my keys between my fingers and make a fist. Whoever this is, they're about to get fucked up. I step in slowly and quietly, stopping off in my bedroom first. It's clear and nothing seems to be out of place. I curse myself for not having at least a baseball bat. I slowly head towards the great room where I find Charlie sitting at the bar with two champagne glasses. She's expecting me.

"Hi, Alise," she sings. "You finally came home, and alone, I see."

"Is this where you've been staying since the fundraiser gala?" I ask. No wonder no one could find her. No one thought to check my place.

"I made dinner for us every night in hopes you'd come home. I even have your favorite champagne." She holds out a glass for me with a grin that makes me sick to my stomach.

"What are you doing here, Charlie?" I ask sternly, ignoring the glass she has outstretched to me.

"Have some champagne. You seem to be wound up. It'll help you relax."

"What. The. Fuck. Are. You. Doing. In. My. Home," I yell. Charlie steps towards me and I step back.

"It's your favorite champagne, Alise," Charlie says with a tight smile.

"I don't want the fucking champagne. Answer my question." She wants to end my pregnancy, so I know I cannot take anything from her. I have to keep the distance between us to keep the twins safe and keep her talking in hopes Jaylen and Joc notice it's taking me too long to get back.

"This is the only place I thought we could talk in private and we need to talk," Charlie finally answers.

"About what," I snap.

"Well, our future, of course."

I take the glass she hands me, even though I don't intend to drink it. I know I have to play her game somewhat if I'm going to get out of here safely. I just have to figure out how far I can take this without taking a sip of this champagne.

"What's in the champagne, Charlie?"

She gives me a surprised look. "Why would you think I put something in it?" she tries to say innocently.

"Because you know I'm pregnant and can't drink this," I answer.

"Oh, a few sips won't hurt *you*," she plays.

Her emphasis on "you" makes me feel even more uneasy. I need her to turn her back to me.

"What's for dinner?" I ask as I take a seat at the bar close to her half empty glass.

"Bolognese. I need to put the finishing touches on it now."

"One of my favorites."

She smiles at me and caresses my cheek. It takes everything in me to not flinch away or throw this champagne in her face with an immediate backhanded slap to follow. I give her a small smile in return, and she heads over to the stove.

"How have things been at Timeless Elegance?" she asks.

"They've been good," I respond. *This will be my only chance. I have to keep her talking and hope she keeps her back turned long enough.*

I grab her glass and lean over the bar. While keeping my eyes on her, I slowly pour her champagne into the sink. I breathe a sigh of relief once I make it back into my seat.

"After all this blows over in a few months, I was thinking we would go away for a little while. You can do most of your stuff remotely and Joc can step in to do everything else," she says.

Halfway there. "You think so? For how long exactly?"

I pour half of my drink into her glass. Accidentally, I spill some on the bar, so I decide to pour a little on myself after I move her glass back to its proper spot. "I'm such a klutz," I gasp.

Charlie turns around to see me wiping at my blouse.

"Oh, Alise. Here, let me help you." She comes around the bar, towel in hand. I reach for the towel.

"I can get it," I say, but Charlie moves the towel away.

"Let me." She blots at the wet stain on my blouse. As I look at her, I can tell she's very much enjoying this. Suddenly, the old gospel hymn *Jesus is on the Main Line: Tell Him What You Want* starts playing in my head. I really want to beat the hell out of this crazy bitch right now, but I don't think Jesus works that way.

"To answer your question, two or three months," she says.

"Charlie, I can't leave Joc to run my business for three months." *Now I just have to get her to drink it.*

"Sure you can. It will all work out." She gives me a swift kiss on the lips and I have to fight even harder with myself to keep from hitting her.

"You haven't had any champagne with me," I say. I can't stand her being so close to me.

Charlie steps back to pick up her glass. She holds it up for a toast.

"What are we toasting?" I ask.

"Our beautiful future. I knew you would eventually come around."

We clink glasses. She guzzles down her drink while I sit mine down on the bar. *Thank God.*

With her last swallow, she realizes I switched the drinks.

"How did you…" Charlie falls to her knees.

"You see, Charlie, we do not have a future. My future is with Jaylen. Your future is in a padded cell." She grabs my legs, like it will keep her from falling into the drug induced abyss she's headed towards. I kick her away and she falls over onto her back.

315

Charlie turns her head towards me and barely lifts her arm off the wood floor, reaching for me. I walk over and look down at the woman I once considered a sister. "You are fucking crazy, Charlie."

And with that, Charlie falls out cold.

I sit on the floor across from her. Even though she seems to be in a drug induced sleep, I still keep my distance. I pull my cellphone out of my back pocket to make two phone calls. The first to Jaylen. I get his voicemail again. The second call is to emergency.

Because the police station is only a few blocks up the street and this is downtown Flint, the response time was just a few brief minutes. Jaylen and Joc show up just after the police and EMT do.

* * *

Jaylen and I are sitting on the couch in the living room. He has his arms wrapped tightly around me. Joc is pacing back and forth in front of the television.

"Who is running the store?" I ask Joc.

"Damn the store, Alise," Joc and Jaylen say in unison.

"Joc, sit down," I say to him.

"I can't sit down right now. My nerves are too bad. If she weren't already knocked out, I'd be over there stomping the hell out of her."

"Joc, please?" I beg.

"Yes, please have a seat, Sir," a detective says.

Joc sits down on the other side of me and holds my hand.

"Ms. Rogers, I'm Detective Jones. Can you tell me what happened here?"

The detective has on an ill-fitting light gray suit with a royal blue tie that has a coffee stain on it. His ivory skin has a severe case of rosacea and an even worse toupee. I would say he's in his late forties to early fifties.

"I came to my apartment to get some clothes and other things to take back to my fiancé's," I begin.

"You haven't been staying in your home," the detective interrupts.

"Her home is with me now," Jaylen answers protectively. I squeeze his hand to let him know I'm okay and the detective is only doing his job.

"I moved in with Jaylen this past Saturday after an incident with Charlie at Walgreen's after the gala."

"This is the one you put on for the schools," the detective asks. I nod. The detective scribbles in his notepad. "What happened at Walgreen's?"

"Detective, look at this," an officer interrupts just as I recount last weekend's events. He is one of three officers searching my apartment.

The cop is coming from the room upstairs with an evidence bag full of small brown bottles. The detective gets up and meets him in the kitchen. They have a brief discussion before Det. Jones returns to the living room.

"Ms. Rogers, did you ingest anything while you were here?"

"No. Why?"

"Were you injected with anything?" he asks.

"No! What is going on?"

He pauses as we all watch the EMTs take Charlie out on a gurney. Seeing her right now, I feel nothing but anger. I turn my attention back to the detective.

"Det. Jones, what was in those vials?"

"There's been a dangerous liquid form of LSD going around the city lately. Those bottles look similar to the ones we've confiscated in some drug raids."

"LSD? Where would Charlie get that from?" I ask to no one in particular.

"How did she end up like that?" the detective asks me.

"For you to get the full story, I need to go back to the night of the fundraiser," I state.

I tell the detective everything that happened from Saturday up to this afternoon. I notice he can't quite believe I never knew of Charlie's romantic feelings towards me until recently. He said some bottles they found were empty and a test would have to be run on all of them to be sure they are LSD. Charlie will face charges of trespassing and assault with the intent to do bodily harm. If she's cleared from the hospital, she'll go to the county jail until her arraignment.

After an hour of questioning, the detective and his band of officers leave my apartment. I feel so tired and numb. This afternoon… this whole week… has been nothing short of draining. I attempt to pack up some of my things to take to Jaylen's, but he doesn't allow it.

"Stay here on the couch and rest. I don't want you hurting yourself or the twins," he says.

"Putting a few things into a suitcase will not hurt the babies or me," I explain.

"Sit, Alise," Jaylen demands.

I don't fight. I'm too tired to, and I know his desire to keep me safe is on overdrive right now. I can only imagine how it makes him feel for Charlie to get so close to harming me and our unborn kids twice in one week, let alone at all. He's upset about me coming here on my own, though he hasn't said it yet. In hindsight, I know I should have called the police when I realized someone was here.

When will I learn? I can't keep doing this to myself or Jaylen.

Joc grabs some of the storage tubs I keep in the upstairs bedroom and brings them to my room. He and Jaylen are in there packing things away while I'm left sitting on the couch to contemplate life. I realize I could have lost not only my babies today, but I could have lost my mind, if not my life. I watched enough soaps with my mother when I was young to know that LSD poisoning is not something that leaves you in your right mind.

I essentially have a family now, a growing family, and I could have lost it all today due in part to my recklessness. I risked entirely too much today, and for what? Some material crap I could have just repurchased?

It's at this very moment that I decide I don't want to wait any longer.

I go to my bedroom to find Jaylen. He is dumping my chest of drawers into a tub. I can hear Joc in my bathroom.

"Do you think your parents will be okay with having our wedding in their backyard two weekends from now?" I ask him.

"What?" he asks.

"Two weekends from now. Our wedding. Your parent's place. We can keep it to us, the kids, your parents, your sister, Joc, Devon, Amber, and Kitty. Order some catered food and---"

"From La Familia?"

"You want La Familia to cater the food at our wedding?" I ask jokingly.

"Yeah. It's where we met. Tacos, nachos, rice, and beans sound good to me," Jaylen says with a smile.

"Done," I reply. I don't need to think about it. Jaylen tosses the drawer onto the floor, making a loud thud.

"Are you serious?" he asks as he steps towards me.

"Yes. What I did today was stupid. It made me realize I could have lost everything and because of that, I don't want to wait.

Jaylen wraps one arm around my waist, and he fists his other hand in my hair, angling my head upwards towards him. He looks deeply into my eyes. He doesn't have to say a word. I can see all the love he has for me. I can also see the stress and worry he's been dealing with since Saturday.

This man loves me so much. He's willing to do anything for me and right now he doesn't feel like he has done much of anything. That's partly my fault. I become overwhelmed with emotions of my love for him and sympathy for what I have put him through.

"I'm sorry," I say as a tear runs down the side of my face.

"Shut up," Jaylen says while slowly bringing his face closer to mine. He stops just before his nose touches mine. "Yes, I'm mad at you for taking such a risk today and for coming here without telling me after I told you your apartment was no longer safe. I'm not stupid. I know you've been considering keeping this place. I'm telling you now, that's not going to happen. As much as I'm mad at you, I'm a million times more grateful that you're okay. I can't lose you, Alise. Promise me you will not put yourself in harm's way like this again."

"I promise."

"You promise what?" Jaylen asks.

"I promise not to put myself in danger again."

"Thank you." And with that, Jaylen kisses me like he hasn't kissed me in a thousand years. He's holding me so close to him, like he's trying to weld our bodies together. I can feel his need for me, both in his kiss and in his growing erection. I feel my need for him pooling in between my legs.

Before I know it, Jaylen has ripped open my blouse and nearly has my bra off. Dropping to my knees, I undo his pants and his big throbbing dick is in my mouth before I get his pants and boxer briefs past his knees. I alternate back and forth between sucking him greedily and gently. Both are driving him crazy. I want him. I want him to erupt in my mouth now, and I know just how to get him there. While massaging his balls with my other hand, I use one hand to work him back and forth along with my mouth.

I look up towards him, and his facial expression tells me he's getting close. I remove my focus from his dick to the soft patch of skin just under his balls. Jaylen moans loudly and his grip on my hair gets tighter. I flick my tongue quickly, making it dance on that sweet spot, and then move up to his balls to suck on them.

I take pride in the way I make Jaylen react when I pleasure him with my mouth. A shiver goes through his body, showing just how close to the edge he is. He can feel it too, so he pulls me away from him. Never letting go of my hair, Jaylen stands me up, walks me over to the bed, and pushes me onto it. He knows I love it when he manhandles me.

Jaylen works on my pants while I stroke his manhood with my foot. Once he gets the buttons undone, I lift my hips to help him pull them down. He spreads my legs wide, looks down at me in pure awe before burying his face in between my legs. He eats me like a starved man at an all you can eat buffet. I writhe and buck on the bed while moaning incoherently. Jaylen knows how to get me there quickly, just as I with him. I pinch my nipples and curl my toes in pleasure. Just as I'm about to cum, Jaylen climbs on top of me and slides his dick deep into me.

"Oh god," Jaylen moans. He moves slowly at first, like he's trying to keep from blasting off too quickly. Once he pushes his orgasm back, he starts a little faster, but much stronger. His entire upper body covers mine, making it impossible for me to move. I wrap my arms around his back and get lost in us. Jaylen's strokes are powerful, fueled by both his love and anger towards me.

"Jaylen, I love you," I moan.

"I love you, too, Mrs. Williams," Jaylen responds. I dig my nails into his back, ready to cum. "Don't cum yet, baby. Please. Wait for Daddy." Jaylen pleads.

"Daddy," I beg.

"Be a good girl and wait for me. I need to do this with you."

I do my best to hold my impending orgasm at bay. The pure perfection of Jaylen's strokes is hitting all my spots, and it's making it hard to hold on. I moan loudly to let him know I can't wait much longer.

"Now. Cum now," Jaylen demands.

We cum together like two speeding trains that hit each other head on and crash into a million pieces. We kiss, at first reverentially and then fervently. I can feel Jaylen grow hard again inside of me. He moves just as strongly as he was before. And I have no complaints.

"I want to swallow you this time," I say.

"Another time. I have to be inside of you."

I understand. It would require him to pull out of me, and he feels too good right now to do that. Jaylen slams into me hard, repeatedly, and bites my neck.

"Promise me," he growls.

"Promise what?"

"To be mine. Forever. To stay safe. To never leave me." Jaylen's words catch me off guard. "Promise!"

"I promise to be yours always and forever. I'll never leave you. I'll stay safe."

Jaylen drives into me deeply. His moans seem to have a touch of pain to them. Like they're coming from a dark place he prefers to keep hidden. I've never seen him this emotional before. Naturally, it only peaks my emotions more. I now realize he wasn't referring to me leaving him in the sense of walking away from our relationship. He's been scared for my life.

"I'm here and I'm okay. I'm okay," I repeatedly whisper into his ear. He seems to be so driven by his pain and fear that I don't think he hears me. I'm not 100% sure because I can't see his face, but I think he's crying. I hold him as tightly as I can to comfort him.

"Daddy, I'm fine," I say.

He growls in response. Even though it's not his usual primal growl, it still turns me on. I orgasm again. He does the same a few moments later. Jaylen lies on top of me, holding me and kissing my temple.

"Talk to me," I quietly demand. He rolls over onto his side and takes a deep breath.

"Joc had just told me you came here when we heard the sirens. We stepped outside and saw the police and ambulance outside of your building. I knew something terrible had happened to you. I was scared I lost all three of you," he says while rubbing my stomach.

"We're all fine," I tell him as I caress his face. "I called you twice. I got your voicemail both times."

"I didn't hear it ring." Jaylen gets up and starts checking his pants pockets for his phone. "If it's not in the car, I must have accidentally left my phone in the office."

"Is it safe for me to come out of the bathroom now?" Joc yells.

"Oh, shit. Joc, I'm sorry," I yell back in shock. "I forgot he was in there," I whisper to Jaylen.

"Me too," he chuckles.

"Give us a minute to put our clothes back on," I giggle.

"Yeah, ha ha. This is hysterical," Joc says, annoyingly.

CHAPTER XXII

By the time Jaylen and Joc pack up most of my things, all three of the local news stations are in front of my building.

"Rebecca called me while you were in heat. She's been filtering calls from the news stations for nearly an hour," Joc tells me as we stare out of one of the tinted floor to ceiling windows.

"Good," I say.

"She's interested in the store manager position. I think she'll be good at it."

With all that's been going on, I didn't even stop to think to see if one of our own wanted the position before posting it to the public. I can only imagine the number of people that will start applying with all of this drama going public now.

"Take the posting down immediately. See if… if…" The name of the girl that filled Kitty's sales position slips my mind.

"Lori," Joc assists.

"Yes, Lori. Thanks. See if she can go from part-time to full-time. If not, post a full-time sales position. If she takes it, repost the part-time position we used after Kitty's promotion. Also, check to see how much OT LaTisha is willing to pick up. Rebecca will be the new store manager starting Monday. Schedule some time for me to meet with her tomorrow."

"You're not going to work tomorrow," Joc states.

"No, she is not," Jaylen agrees from behind us.

"I need to work. I can't just sit around wondering and waiting," I explain.

"You won't be sitting around wondering and waiting," Jaylen says.

"You have a wedding to plan, remember?" says Joc.

"That won't be a lot of work," I defend.

"You're not going in, Alise," Jaylen says in a stern tone.

I concede unwillingly. I don't have a chance of winning this fight with Joc and Jaylen on the same side.

"Has anyone called Devon?" I ask. The three of us just stand there and look at each other.

"He was probably already at the hospital when they brought Charlie in," Joc says.

My intercom buzzes. Jaylen walks over to answer it.

"Who is it?" he says.

"Devon." Jaylen lets him up. The three of us look around, wondering what he is doing here instead of being with his wife.

"What are you doing here?" I ask him before he gets completely in the door.

"Are you okay?" he asks me. Devon marches right to me and holds me out at arm's length, giving me a look over.

"I'm fine. You don't seem so well, though." Devon looks like he has been crying and yelling. His skin is flushed red with anger and worry. His usually bright eyes are rimmed with exhaustion and redness.

"I'm not doing this shit with her anymore," he explains. "I'm filing for divorce and full custody of Amber."

"Devon, calm down," I say.

"She could have killed you, Alise. She could have killed you and your unborn child."

He's right. Instinctively, I touch my belly. *I will do everything I can to keep you safe, little ones.*

"I'm sorry," Devon says as he pulls me into a tight hug.

"It's not your fault, Devon. It's not anyone's fault," I try to explain. I wish I knew how to comfort him right now. I'm so shaken, I don't know how to calm myself. A few days ago, we were all here in my living room having a good time. It seems like such a distant memory with everything that has happened since.

"Things were so different last Friday," Joc says, speaking my thoughts. Everyone is quiet and reflective for a few moments while we all take a seat on the couch.

"Have you talked to Charlie's parents?" I ask Devon.

"I called them while I was on my way here," he answers. "They should be with her now."

"Where's Amber?" I know Charlie's parents babysit her during the weekdays.

"With Kitty. I called her first. She was in class. I told her to meet them at the hospital so Amber wouldn't have to sit up there and see her mother like that. Kitty got there right before I left. She's as lost about this as I am, but I can't be there. I just can't be there."

Devon sits there with his elbows on his knees and hands massaging his temples. My heart breaks for him and my goddaughter. I feel like my heart should also break for the woman that was my best friend, but it isn't. She's going to need support when she wakes up... *if she wakes up...* and her support circle is much smaller now.

It's then that I realize Devon is still in his hospital standard issued blue scrubs. Stubble shadows his face. For the first time in the years I've known him, he looks like shit. The man hasn't had a chance to breathe.

"Devon, when is the last time you slept?" I ask him.

"It's been a few days," he responds.

"Devon," Joc sighs.

"And ate?" I continue.

"Not much since the fundraiser."

"If you are going to be any kind of support for your daughter, you have to take care of yourself first," Jaylen pipes in.

"I know." I get up and head towards the kitchen, but Devon stops me along the way. "Don't do that Alise. Honestly, I can't even think about food right now."

His eyes are weary. He seems like such a weakened version of the strong man I grew to love as a brother. I'm suddenly hit with the wave of emotions I've been holding back since I walked into my apartment. Now it's my turn to charge towards him and give him a tight hug.

I can't fight back my tears. Neither can Devon. Joc joins us in our hug. Although he and Charlie never considered each other best friends, his heart is breaking, too. Jaylen completes the group hug.

"And it's children, not child," I correct Devon's earlier statement while still buried under the guys.

"What?" Devon asks.

"We're having twins."

"And you didn't tell me," Joc shrieks, officially breaking up the group hug.

"There's been so much going on. But now I'm telling both of you."

"She can never find out," Devon says, looking me straight in the eyes. By "she," I know he means Charlie.

"I know," I say while rubbing my stomach.

* * *

"I'm thinking pizza for dinner," I say to Jaylen as he, Joc, Devon, J.J., and Jaleel unload the cars of my things into the basement. JaQuese is helping me organize everything. I didn't realize how much stuff I had until we determined that my and Jaylen's SUVs weren't going to be enough. A moving company will move my furniture here this weekend. Until the renovations are done, we will store it all down here, and I'll have to make a home office space down here somehow. Eventually, the basement will be another family sitting area with my living room furniture and JaQuese will get my bedroom furniture, Jaleel will get what is currently in JaQuese's room, and J.J. will get what he is now sharing with Jaleel. I will donate my mattresses.

"Pizza sounds good," Jaleel chimes in.

"Pizza it is then," his father says.

"I'll place the order. Joc and Devon, are you two staying for dinner?" I ask.

"I have to get to Amber," Devon says.

"And I have a date with Boston, but I can cancel it if you need me," Joc replies.

"No, Joc. That isn't necessary." Apparently, I'm not the only person who has to get used to me having a family now.

"This is the last of it," Devon says while dropping a tub on the floor.

"Okay. Thank you for everything, Devon," I say, while giving him a hug. "Kiss Amber for me. This mess with Charlie doesn't change anything. She'll always be my goddaughter. I will always be there for both of you."

"She has a whole god-family now," Jaylen states. "That's if you're okay with it."

"Of course. Thank you, Jaylen," Devon says almost breathlessly. He is taken by surprise by Jaylen's words just as much as everyone else is.

"We're all here for both of you," Jaylen adds.

"Thanks, Jaylen and Alise. I will keep you updated on everything." He does the manly-man handshake and half hug thing with all the guys but gets pulled into a full embrace when he gets to Joc.

I'm grateful the drama hasn't divided us.

Joc says his goodbyes, too, and I'm left organizing everything with my instant family.

* * *

After dinner, the kids are off doing their own things. Jaylen and I are still at the dinner table discussing renovations. Our two options are to either expand up or back. Expanding back would be the easiest and what we settle on. During the conversation, we realize we use the same contractor.

"I already have a meeting scheduled with the contractor on Wednesday. He is going to be here at three, if you can make it," I state.

"I can be here for that."

"We need to show the kids a picture of Charlie, you know, just in case she wakes up," I say to my fiancé.

"I agree. We'll wait until we hear from Devon. There's no reason to alarm them if she doesn't know that one plus one equals two when she wakes up."

"You need to call your parents to see if they are okay with the wedding being at their place. Once you confirm that, I can see if the officiant will be available and call La Familia for the food. I'll put Joc and JaQuese together to work out the other details."

"My parents will be good with it, but I will call them. That reminds me, we didn't even tell the kids," Jaylen says. "Family meeting right now!" he yells.

The kids all make their way into the dining room. So much of their lives has changed in the last week. I don't know how many more surprises they can take.

"We set the wedding date. It's two weeks from now and will be at your grandparents' house," Jaylen states plainly.

As usual, JaQuese squeals. Her brothers say congrats and ask if they have to do anything.

"You two are going to be my best men," Jaylen says.

"Oh, wow, Dad," J.J. states. He seems to be both shocked and honored. I'm shocked as well, since Jaylen told me before he was going to ask his sister to be his best man.

"Have you two picked out rings yet?" Jaleel asks.

Jaylen and I look at each other, realizing we've missed a step.

"You two will help your dad pick out a ring for me, as well as clothes," I say to the boys. "JaQuese and Joc will help me pick out a ring for your dad and create my dress."

"What about decorations?" JaQuese asks.

"Well, it will be in the gazebo if it doesn't rain. If it does rain, the formal living room will work. Either way, not much is needed for decorations. Plus, this will be casual." I answer.

"But we still need bouquets, cake, and food," JaQuese goes on.

"The food will be La Familia," her dad interjects.

"The taco house!" JaQuese clearly thinks this is the craziest thing she's ever heard of.

"This will be the best wedding ever," J.J. says while rubbing his stomach.

"This is what we want, JaQuese," I tell her.

"Okay, Momma Lise." She sounds disappointed. I'm sure she was hoping for a grander affair. "Well, what about colors?"

"Your father doesn't want pink or orange," I smile.

"We don't want black," all three of the kids say together. Jaylen raises an eyebrow at them and I burst out laughing. It's nice to know I'm not alone in wanting to get him into some color.

"How about gray and pale yellow?" I ask the group. I like how the wedding planning has turned into a family affair.

"Do we have to wear yellow?" J.J. asks.

"No. All the guys in gray," I say after taking a few moments to think about it. "The ladies will be in yellow with gray accents. I'll be in gray with yellow accents."

"First La Familia and how you are not wearing white," JaQuese exclaims.

"It will be beautiful. Calm down. What you should worry about is designing your dress," I tell her. "Here's your shot to show me what you got."

"Really?" she squeals.

"Yes. Get started. I will need it by tomorrow if we are going to pull this off in such a short time. You're going with me to work tomorrow."

"We'll start looking online for something to wear," Jaleel says.

"No jeans or khakis," their father tells them.

And with that, the kids disburse. I sit there looking at Jaylen in amazement.

"I thought you were going to ask Liana to be your best man?"

"I was, but I thought having the boys in that role would mean a lot to them and hopefully let them know that we're still a family unit. They've said before they don't want something that's here today and gone tomorrow. Hopefully, this and you getting them involved with the planning will serve as a silent promise that this is forever."

"Forever, Daddy?" I ask him.

"Forever. Never to be lost again."

Porsha Deun

Or so Jaylen thought…

To be continued in Love Lost Forever

Available now.

Porsha Deun

Epilogue

Jaylen

Porsha is giving me a chance to speak for the first time in the three books of this series. Well, that's not completely truthful. She tried to get me to say something for the end of Love Lost Revenge and the first edition of this book, but I couldn't find the words for what she was asking me to do. Of course, Porsha got impatient with me and moved on with finishing and publishing the last book in this series.

Now I'm ready to talk.

I love Alise. There are no words for me to explain the depths of my love for her. I know I come off as an asshole sometimes. Some of those times that is my intention, but nonetheless, it doesn't change what Alise means to me.

I can't get into too many details without giving away major points in the following two books that detail my and Alise's love story, which is fine with me. I don't enjoy talking much, no way, and looking back on some of them, I don't want to relive them. Not even for the author who put our story on pages.

There is one… event… I'm willing to talk about.

As cool as I tried to be, I was nervous when I showed up at the fundraiser looking for Alise that beautiful May evening. I stood in the door watching her for minutes. My heart was racing. I kept wiping my palms on my pants.

The love of my life was standing a few feet from me, and I was frozen in place. I almost chickened out and left, but then she spotted me. I could feel it. Our connection was still there. She was stuck where she stood, just as I was moments before.

Hurt and anger were in her eyes, but so was love and lust. That was enough to make the small bit of hope I had after Devon told me Alise still had a thing for me to turn from a flicker to a flame.

I was getting my woman back, come hell or high water. I was getting Alise back.

Speaking of Devon, I really need to treat that man to a tomahawk steak dinner or something. Having Alise back in my life is possible because of him.

Back to my little baby.

God, I love that woman. She was still as beautiful as I remembered. I, however, was not happy to see Charlie, which given all that's happened with her even to the end of this book, I'm sure you can understand why. And after this book… let's just say I wish that drug overdose had killed her.

Back to my Alise.

She came back into my life, became a mother to my three older kids, and gave me more. I knew my life was not complete without her, but she has shown me I was still only seeing a small part of the puzzle that was my life. To say she has given me everything is an understatement.

I know my actions in this book made some of y'all not like me much. I will get on your nerves even more throughout the rest of the Love Lost Series. Honestly, I'm not interested in being anyone's book boyfriend. I have all the fanfare I could ever need with Alise and my family.

But I love Alise.

That's all I wanted to hop in to say.

I love Alise.

Thank you for reading.

Jaylen.

Porsha Deun

Thank you for reading my book! I feel honored, truly.

Did you enjoy Love Lost? Be sure to leave a review on Amazon, Goodreads, Bookbub, or my Facebook Page!

You can preview and purchase the rest of my books on my website, as well as with your favorite online book retailer! Be sure to sign up for my mailing list while you are on my website. My Love Bugs get cover reveals at least a month before the public, as well as surprises and giveaways. www.porshadeun.com.

Love Lost Series
Love Lost
Love Lost Forever
Love Lost Revenge

Addict Series
Addict – A Fatal Attraction Story
Addict 2.0 – Andre's Story
Addict 3.0 – DeAngelo's Story
Addict 4.0 – DeMario's Story

Standalones
Intoxic

Flash Fiction Collection
Eyes of the BeholdHer

Children's Book
Princesses Can Do Anything!

Printed in the USA
CPSIA information can be obtained
at www.ICGtesting.com
JSHW020033151123
51896JS00009B/12